WE'RE NOT US WITHOUT YOU

CHRISTINE KEIGHERY

Published in 2025 by Ultimo Press,
an imprint of Hardie Grant Publishing

Ultimo Press
Gadigal Country
7, 45 Jones Street
Ultimo, NSW 2007
ultimopress.com.au

   ultimopress

All rights reserved. No part of this publication may be reproduced, stored in a retrieval system or transmitted in any form by any means, electronic, mechanical, photocopying, recording or otherwise, without the prior written permission of the publishers and copyright holders.

The moral rights of the author have been asserted.

Copyright © Christine Keighery 2025

 A catalogue record for this work is available from the National Library of Australia

We're Not Us Without You
ISBN 978 1 76115 351 8 (paperback)

Cover design Christabella Designs
Cover images Background by chasehunterphotos / Shutterstock; campfire by Cosma Andrei / Stocksy
Text design Kirby Jones
Typesetting Kirby Jones 11.5/18.5 pt Sabon LT Std
Editors Dianne Blacklock and Adolfo Aranjuez
Proofreader Pamela Dunne

10 9 8 7 6 5 4 3 2 1

Printed in China by RR Donnelley.

 The paper this book is printed on is from FSC® certified forests and other sources. FSC® promotes environmentally responsible, socially beneficial and economically viable management of the world's forests.

Ultimo Press acknowledges the Traditional Owners of the Country on which we work, the Gadigal People of the Eora Nation and the Wurundjeri People of the Kulin Nation, and recognises their continuing connection to the land, waters and culture. We pay our respects to their Elders past and present.

For Gab Williams.
Rooms are darker without you.

PROLOGUE

Midnight seemed an appropriate time for the four teenagers to meet in the park, primed for talk of impending, forced separation.

'I hate Papa. I hate all those arseholes on the school board,' Lani said, passing a bottle of Hibiki whisky around the group. She noted that Maya – even in this most important of moments – didn't take a slug, or even a sip, before she handed it to Tinker.

'Our conch,' he said, holding the bottle aloft. Their laughter was forced, thinning out into the blackness even as it began. 'Stig, you can't go.'

'I can't stay either.'

To the other three, Stig seemed a ghost of himself. His usual animated ways had been erased, bit by bit, over the last weeks and they wanted him back full throttle. Their plan would work. It had to.

'My father can barely look at me,' Stig said quietly. 'Everyone at school thinks I'm disgusting.'

'We know you're not. You've been maligned and mis-represented,' Maya said. 'We can't give up—'

'You've tried,' Stig interrupted. 'All of you have.'

'Fat lot of good that did,' Lani said, grabbing the bottle. 'Cheers to the heroic school counsellor.'

'At least she was kind,' Stig said, and the knowledge of corresponding unkindness, of the utter nastiness he'd endured, silenced them all.

'So, it's really happening,' Tinker said finally, and his plaintive tone was so far from his regular one that it seemed this situation was killing him the most. 'When?'

Stig got up from the bench, theatrically saluting them as though it was his last chance to express himself. 'Tomorrow, the moment I turn seventeen and nine months, they'll begin making an honest man out of me.'

Tinker stood too, pressing his forehead to Stig's. 'We're not us without you.'

The four of them huddled together.

'We won't give up,' Maya said, the steeliest of them all. 'We'll clear your name and then you'll come back.'

From his backpack, Tinker produced his trusty pocketknife and walked over to the oak tree. The others followed. In the light of his torch, they studied the love-heart carvings on its giant trunk.

Lani went first, LG. Then Maya, MD. Tinker, TH. And finally, Stig, SJ.

Theirs was the first love heart with four sets of initials. The only one.

Stig held out his hand and the others piled their own on top.

'Promise we will be friends forever?' he said, and one by one they made that vow aloud.

Stig chose not to say goodbye, feigning a spring in his step as he wandered off, but they all understood it was because he would break down if he tried. When he'd disappeared into the darkness, Lani took another swig of her father's whisky and opened her bag to reveal two more bottles. 'Shall we do it?'

It was unanimous. The three of them were committed.

They couldn't have known that, by sun-up, their own lives would be changed forever.

CHAPTER ONE
Twenty Years Later

'So, it's just us and thirty-seven of your other best friends,' Maya teased.

Lani looked down the guest table. Most were donning the ridiculous hats she'd left at the entry.

Standing on either side of her, Maya was wearing a maroon drop-waisted number that made her look like an extra from *The Handmaid's Tale,* and Tinker's version of smart casual was his customary white T-shirt and Levi's.

Both Maya and Tinker were holding their hats rather than wearing them. Lani would have liked to chasten them, but she let it slide. She had bigger fish to fry.

'Some of them are Papa's cronies,' she said.

'And since he's paying ...' Tinker said.

Lani bumped his shoulder and he staggered back exaggeratedly, like he'd been doing since they were kids.

'Watch out,' she warned, 'or I'll instruct the hordes to eat you alive. There are already whispers that a man shouldn't be included in a hen's party. Though, as usual, I can see the over-fifties checking you out. It seems your reputation precedes you.'

Tinker feigned shock, but there was no point denying the succession of older women over the years. Lani couldn't remember all of their names, but their job titles resonated. CEO. Owner of a chain of restaurants. Lawyer. Et cetera. The common element was that they made his decisions and charted his course according to their desires. The correlation between what happened to them as teens and Tinker's life choices might seem nebulous to an outside observer, but Lani could draw a direct line. She, Maya and Tinker all had their own manifestations of arrested development.

'Hey, you guys want another drink?' Tinker asked. 'It's on me.'

Maya rolled her eyes. 'Generous,' she said, 'since it's an open bar.'

'That's the best time to shout,' Tinker said with a chuckle. 'How about you go for the hard stuff, Maya? Really let loose. Raspberry lemonade? I think they even have sarsaparilla.'

Lani grabbed Maya's drink and took a sip. 'Jesus, mate – lemon, lime and bitters?' she said, already wishing she hadn't taken the Lord's name in vain. Despite all that had happened, Maya had doubled down on her faith while she and Tinker had abandoned it entirely. They'd tried for a while, but singing hymns and reciting prayers in the church used by St Audrey's and St Fabian's combined had done nothing to alleviate the guilt. They'd become experts at lip-syncing. There'd been years of it.

'I'll have a glass of wine with dinner,' Maya said. 'And I promise I'll have a good time. It's just that I'm a bit stressed about Luke switching schools.'

Being stressed about parenting was Maya's natural state. Lani knew Luke had scored a dance scholarship at a boys-only Catholic school, but that should have been good news. It wasn't as though history was bound to repeat.

'Tonight, we leave our worries behind,' Tinker said, coming back from the bar with two negronis and a soda. 'In support of our gorgeous Lani, who's getting hitched.'

At the far end of the table, a woman pointed to him and waved. Then she whispered something to another woman, whose phallic hat prevented Lani from recognising, and they laughed.

Tinker's sudden discomfort suggested he'd slept with one of them. Or both.

'Has Gino decided to give you away?' he asked.

Lani plastered a smile on her face. 'Unfortunately, Papa draws the line at walking his lesbian daughter down the secular aisle.'

'How about I nab that role as well as being your bridesman,' Tinker said, not missing a beat.

Maya reached out and grabbed Lani's hand. 'I'm delighted to be your matron of honour and Sophia is *totes* excited she gets to be junior bridesmaid. It's going to be a beautiful wedding – regardless of who gives you away.'

Lani's eyes welled. What she needed to tell them had been weighing on her mind for almost two weeks. She had to trust that they would – at least eventually – align themselves with her perspective. Because friendship was a religion of its own. At least, that's how she and Tinker had justified becoming godparents to Maya's twins, Sophia and Luke, respectively.

And that's the rationale she'd use to argue her case tonight while they were beholden to keep things nice. Straight after she'd had a sip, or two, of that fresh negroni.

•

As soon as Lani dragged Maya and Tinker into the private room next to the restaurant, Maya's hackles were up. It was that familiar, determined look on her face, like she was about to try to manipulate them into doing something against their will.

'I've asked Stig to my wedding.'

For a moment, Maya was winded, unable to speak.

'You absolutely cannot do that, Lani,' she said finally. 'You know it—'

'Hear me out,' Lani interrupted. 'I ran into him at the wholefoods store a couple of weeks ago. He looked really good! Clearly, he hasn't been using for ages. He reckons he's joined some kind of ... community, in the country, and he finally feels like he belongs somewhere. He was so warm and lovely. We went for a coffee and reminisced and I realised I really want him to be there on my special day.'

'Well,' Maya said, crossing her arms, 'thanks for not sharing that with us immediately.' She sighed deeply. 'Look, I'm glad to hear he's doing better and that he's found his *community*, whatever that means. But having Stig there – it would be opening Pandora's box, you know that. It's not too late, Lani. The official invitation can get lost in the mail.'

'I've thought about it a lot,' Lani countered. 'Weddings provide the opportunity to let bygones be bygones. Stig was so thrilled to hear that I'm marrying Bridget. I mean, after all the shit he suffered, times have changed. I want him there to celebrate. Stig was instrumental in shaping the story of my life – our lives.'

'That chapter's closed,' Maya insisted, trying to keep the ice out of her tone. 'For very good reasons,' she added.

'We never stopped caring for Stig,' Tinker said softly.

Maya felt the ice inside her melting a little. They all carried the guilt and shame, but both she and Lani understood Tinker's burden was the heaviest.

'I loved him too,' she said. 'But his experiences – his life experiences – will have made him a different person. And apart from Lani running into him by accident, we're not even on his radar anymore.'

'I heard from him when Dad had a stroke,' Tinker objected in his sweet way. 'And didn't he contact you when you had the twins?'

'Yes,' Maya conceded. 'Fourteen years ago, through Messenger, but it was congratulations with a backhander. I'll never forget he added a facepalm emoji when I posted about you guys being Luke's and Sophia's godparents. Clearly he hates anything to do with religion.'

'Friendship is also a kind of religion – our religion,' Lani said. She allowed a pregnant pause to let that settle and Maya knew she would have rehearsed the line, most probably in front of a mirror. 'Remember the vow we made the night before Stig was supposed to leave for the army? Don't we owe it to him to play our part?'

Of course Maya remembered. She could see that Tinker did as well. But circumstances changed that night. Some promises shouldn't be kept.

'We were just kids,' she said. 'We tried to help Stig and we failed abysmally.'

'We sure did,' Lani said. 'But that school counsellor we put him on to, what's-her-name, was useless.'

'Not totally,' Tinker said. 'At least she assured him there's nothing wrong with being gay.'

'She was creepy though,' Lani said. 'I remember her sitting in her bomb of a car outside our house for hours one day.'

Maya rolled her eyes. She adored Lani, of course, but the Galletas were all so dramatic, each one thinking the universe revolved around them. There were umpteen reasons why the counsellor might have been parked in their street.

'Listen,' she said, 'we're going in circles. The point is that's all over. Now, we need to let sleeping dogs lie. Surely both of you can see the risk of dredging up things best left buried?'

'Stig doesn't even know we were there the night Joe Carruthers died, so as long as none of us let on about that, where's the risk?' Lani replied.

There was a perfunctory knock at the door and Lani's mother strode in. 'It's rude to cluster in your little threesome while your guests are waiting,' she said. Then she did a double take. 'For goodness sake, what's wrong, Maya? It looks like you've seen a ghost.'

CHAPTER TWO

'I am the pure child that I was,' Stig chanted along with the others. 'I seek enlightenment. I look up to the sky.'

Tonight, at Soul Haven, the stars were out in full force. For a moment he was mesmerised, lost in their divine beauty. He felt touched by every single one among the infinity.

'I am cherished,' he resumed. 'I deserve to be cherished.'

Cleansing tears coursed down his cheeks. He willed more and they arrived. Acharya saw him, saw the essence of him. She was so tall and lithe that she seemed to float through the space between them. Her short auburn hair glowed in the flickering light from the bonfire. Her emerald-green eyes shone with knowledge. She cupped his head with her healing hands.

'I am powerful. The universe is within me.'

'Oh, yes it is, Stig,' she whispered in his ear. 'I see it in you, all there, poised for further awakenings.'

It was a special blessing. He held it close and let it expand in his chest.

Stig hadn't seen the woman next to him in previous sessions. She had face tattoos of creatures that looked alive. When she fell to the ground in pure gratitude, Acharya went to her, hands hovering above her chest. Which was right. Other people needed her too, but that didn't stop his feeling of loss, even if temporary.

Someone wailed. It was Thomas, the ex-accountant. He'd joined them only recently, committing the proceeds from the sale of his house to their communal betterment.

'That's wonderful, Thomas,' Acharya said, her voice amplified by the roving mic. 'Let it out. Release your suffering. For you are renewed.'

Others joined in, the communion of cries echoing into the night sky, curling around magnificent gum trees. An owl Stig couldn't see hooted in unison. He raised his hands in celebration. Healing was a process that was never quite finished, but Acharya understood that. She understood everything in a way Stig had never experienced. Until her, he'd lacked stability and inner strength, as though he was always kicking in midair. His parents had cared for the bumps and bruises of his childhood but run away from the emotional aspects of life. He'd tried to talk with them so many times, even as a teenager. They didn't want to know when he was questioning his sexuality. They were even deeper in denial when the rumours spread out of control, drowning out the sounds of his night-crying with the TV volume up.

Cajoling him into joining the army had been a desperate act, contrary to everything he was by nature. But he was going to suck it up. Until finding out about Joe's death pushed him over the edge, and he ran away instead.

How deluded he'd been through the fog of drugs, guilt and self-loathing, still ridiculously attached to the conviction that the Catholic faith his parents and school thrust upon him would eventually provide answers. He stayed in that zombie state for years before Acharya rescued him.

The session was coming to a close. Some of the participants had set up tents for the night. If anyone should request a bed, Stig would share his cottage, but so far no one had, which was a relief. He'd only ever been comfortable sharing his living space with one person. Despite the squalid conditions of the squat in Kings Cross, Marcus's presence had made it their home.

'We praise and thank and love you, Acharya,' came the final chant.

She raised her hands, palms up. As she walked to the main house, the resident goats, Sadie and Gertrude, trailed on either side as though pulled by her energy.

Opening the door to his cottage, Stig felt elated. Because, finally, he belonged.

•

Even after being almost two years sober, it still amused Stig to put on the kettle at the end of an evening rather than hunting for the next hit. He sat in his armchair and sipped chamomile tea.

He wasn't going to open the embossed gold envelope he'd found when he emptied the letterbox yesterday. He knew he was supposed to deliver all mail to Acharya. Yes, it was addressed to him, but she was in charge of filtering what went through. And it was for his own good. *Every moment wasted looking back prevents us from moving forward.* But wasn't it serendipitous that, on one of the rare occasions he had gone to Melbourne to run errands, he bumped into Lani Galleta?

She was even more stunning as a grown woman than she'd been as a kid. How he'd adored her. How many times had they shared her giant bed, trading secrets about crushes deep into the night? She'd been the only one he could do that with freely. The only friend who'd not only tolerated his sexuality but understood it.

Thinking of her was a link to the others. Straight-talking, sweet Tinker, his only true male buddy. That boy of few words, who'd said, 'We're not us without you.'

Was that true? Or did his best friends manage to retain what they'd had as four? It seemed so, since Lani had mentioned both Tinker and Maya were in her bridal party.

And darling Maya. In many ways during those turbulent teen years, Stig had loved her most of all. Her black-and-white stance seemed so consistent. Drugs were bad. God was all-powerful, all-seeing. True friends remained loyal, no matter what. Yes, she'd been unbending, but that's what he'd found most admirable in a world where nothing he thought or felt seemed to fit.

He didn't blame them for losing touch. There had been attempts, but he'd at least had enough dignity not to respond. He hadn't wanted them to witness his reduced state.

There'd been so much pain and suffering in his life, so much heartache. His last year at St Fabian's had been the beginning of the end, but now he'd found a new beginning. He couldn't risk what he had.

Perhaps it wasn't a risk though. Maybe he was meant to go to Lani's wedding?

The envelope was so *gold*. It stood out – almost beckoned. In honour of friendships past, he would open it.

Gino and Yvette Galleta
request the pleasure of your company at the
wedding of their daughter
Lani Louisa
to
Bridget Anne Sykes
Saturday 25 February 2023
from half-past six
At the Galleta residence: 684 Albany Road, Toorak

Gino Galleta. That man had been pivotal in the decision to send him away. Would there be a chance to confront him, finally? Did he even want to?

Stig would do the only thing that made sense. He would consult Acharya.

CHAPTER THREE

Maya found a car park in Albert Street, East Melbourne. She loved her local parish, but the church didn't have the same magic as St Patrick's. The Gothic architecture with all the spires made her feel small, in a good way. Like the significance of her thoughts and actions were just a tiny speck in the world order.

She walked through the giant bronzed doors, dipped her fingers in holy water and made the sign of the cross, remembering the many instances she'd done so as a child.

There was so much history here. She paused to study the stained-glass windows. St Brigid had always been her favourite. And there she was, as ever, instructing the people with kindness and compassion. Maya made a mental note to bring Luke and Sophia here soon. Of course she'd do it on Luke's behalf, but he could personally pray that the transition from his high school, where he had good friends and fit in despite his quirks, would be smooth.

Faith was a beacon in a dark world.

There was a green light beside the confessional. Maya took a deep breath and entered.

'Bless me, Father, for I have sinned.' Her grandmother had given her a tile with the Act of Contrition prayer printed on it. She used to hold it while rehearsing what she would say. *I've been rude to my parents* and *I took the Lord's name in vain* had been frequent but genuine admissions, before everything changed.

'It's been six months since my last confession, and these are my sins.'

Behind the screen, just as she'd hoped, was Father Patel. While other priests opted for fire and brimstone, his sermons were entertaining and stimulating. Her baby brother had declared that his voice 'danced'. His humour was the drawcard for her dad. On the contrary, her mum thought he lacked the solemnity God deserved from his servants.

As a conduit to God, Father Patel would have heard thousands of secrets. Perhaps most sins were venial, but some must have been mortal. The sacramental seal was inviolable, yet she'd never had the courage to tell. So she'd skirted around her biggest sin, and Father Patel had managed to give guidance when her teen soul was the heaviest and her nightly prayers lasted for hours. Maya brought up the Notes app on her iPhone.

'I've been petty and jealous,' she said now, 'in ways that don't become me. At my age, I should have the wisdom to accept my two best friends are so close.' Even as she said it, Maya couldn't help but measure Lani's and Tinker's adoration for each other against their affection for her. It had seemed more even when there were a foursome with shifting allegiances on a stable base. Or that's how she remembered it. Maya shook herself out of that thought. Was she a 'glass half-empty' woman, like her mother?

'It's human to feel jealous,' Father Patel said. 'We are a work in progress, created in God's image and yet imperfect. And on the subject of age – age and wisdom are separate entities. The latter, I'm afraid, we have to work at. Though the former seems to be thrust upon us with the deliberation of a freight train.'

He was old now, but his chuckle was youthful.

'Is there anything else weighing upon your soul?'

Maya breathed deeply. 'There was a time, many years ago …' she began. Father Patel waited patiently for her to continue. 'I did something very wrong, and it caused great suffering.'

Through the screen, Maya could see Father Patel nodding.

'I can't tell you what it was. I've promised. But it plagues me.'

'So, there's never been a reckoning?'

Maya squeezed her eyes shut. 'No, but I fear it may be imminent.'

Father Patel sighed. 'Well, it's never too late to make restitution. If you can't talk to me, you can confide in our Heavenly Father. For your penance, as well as a Hail Mary and an Act of Faith, you should seize the opportunity to show kindness to a stranger.'

There were two bank-card readers in the exit foyer with signs suggesting amounts for donations. Maya remembered her mother's raised eyebrows as her father contributed a couple of notes rather than the recommended ten per cent of his income to the collection plate, him then sheepishly and reluctantly adding more. She tapped her phone and gave ten dollars.

As she left the church, there was a young man dawdling outside, as though weighing up whether to enter. He was small and wiry. His brown hair was knotty, the strap on his left thong had come loose from its socket and the holes in his jeans were definitely not designer. Someone had circulated a photo they'd taken in Kings Cross a few years after Stig ran away. He'd looked similar.

Maya held the door open. 'Peace be with you,' she said gently, and it was good to see the young man, however tentatively, walk through.

Then she nipped back in and donated an extra twenty dollars.

•

The traffic on Hoddle Street was bumper to bumper and there were ticking sounds coming from the engine in Tinker's ute. He'd have to do an oil change as soon as possible. Hopefully that'd fix it, because replacing the valves would be pricey.

He arrived at Fiona's warehouse apartment in Fitzroy half an hour after he was supposed to.

'Hello, you.' Fiona tapped her wrist. 'Tick tock,' she said, but at least she was smiling.

'Sorry,' Tinker said. 'Car problems and traffic. Look at you, you're a knockout.'

'That I am,' she agreed, doing a twirl in her sexy dressing-gown. 'Would you like a drink, Tim? I know you like to be called Tinker, but, darling, it's a bit naff for a grown man.'

He shrugged. Given he'd always been obsessed with cars and electronics, he felt the nickname was a good fit. But perhaps Fiona had a point.

'I'm having my first martini a little early,' she continued. 'It's a celebration because I won the golf tournament.'

'Of course you did,' he said, putting his arms around her waist. She leaned into him for a moment before going into the kitchen to make a drink.

Tinker looked around. There was heaps of art in Fiona's lounge room. The abstract kind where you really didn't get what was going on. Or more to the point, he didn't. The video thingamabob on the wall kept changing. A vagina here, a kettle, a greyhound, squiggles, lines and a flower. What the fuck did it mean? His own version of art on the walls were Grand Prix posters stuck up with Blu Tack.

'That installation's called *Valentine's Day*,' Fiona said, returning with the martini. 'Which is apt because I fell madly in love with it. Doesn't it totally suck you into its vortex?'

'I guess,' Tinker lied, 'but not as much as you do.'

Fiona put down her drink and kissed him deeply. Tinker tried to get lost in the moment, but his mind was going haywire. Maybe that moving screen had triggered something in him – images from the video that had sent things south for Stig kept coming back to him.

Nobody knew who took it, but it was sometime during rehearsals for *The Wiz*. The Tin Man and Cowardly Lion costumes were laid out on a bench in the change rooms. Joe Carruthers, dressed only in a towel, was running water in the communal shower. The video showed Stig approaching from behind, naked. He ripped the towel from Joe's torso and pressed up against him. Then there was Joe's right hook to Stig's eye.

God, and it looked as though Joe was disgusted. But images sometimes lied. At least they didn't tell the whole story.

'Shall we take this upstairs?' Fiona suggested.

Her sheets were silky smooth and there were scented candles on her bedside tables. As she lay down, her dressing-gown fell open. Tinker took off his T-shirt and Levi's.

When Stig told Tinker their relationship had been going on for months, he'd believed his friend right away. Yes, his gaydar must have been off because he hadn't picked up that Stig wasn't straight. But he'd been such a gentle guy, and the idea that he'd force himself on anyone was crazy.

That's not how other students saw it.

Tinker moved his hand between Fiona's legs and she moaned. 'Yes,' she whispered in his ear, 'that feels so good.'

Joe Carruthers had been a jock, the best footy player at St Fabian's. When the video was passed around, he'd let everyone think it was what it looked like.

Even then, Tinker got why. Joe had a macho image and he sure as hell wouldn't have wanted the treatment Stig was getting. It wasn't long before Joe's mates jumped on the bandwagon with their own accusations. It had all spiralled out of control. Tinker had heard so many rumours that any truth had been erased. It nearly killed him to see Stig suffering. Tinker even got into a fistfight to defend him. The result had been a beating and getting locked in a cleaner's storeroom. He'd had to jump out the window. When he fell heavily to the ground, twisting his ankle, the jocks were waiting for him, whooping and hollering like it was the funniest sight they'd ever seen.

When Lani suggested they go to Joe and try to get him to tell the truth, he and Maya were keen. But they were stupid, impetuous teenagers who couldn't see what harm could come of their actions.

Maybe, deep down, Tinker was still that kid.

Fiona went down on him.

'Am I doing something wrong, Tim?'

'No, you're doing everything right,' he assured her, but his dick was limp. He tried to focus on the sex, but the memories kept coming.

They all had Joe Carruthers' death on their consciences, but he was the one who'd done the worst thing.

Maybe Maya was right. Maybe they should let sleeping dogs lie.

'I'm sorry, Fiona,' he said, making a move to switch it up and go down on her so she'd get to orgasm, but she pulled away.

'It's not you, it's me.' As soon as he said it, he wished he hadn't. Tinker could see she'd taken it the opposite way. It was how she tied the belt of her dressing-gown, tucking her breasts away. He'd made her feel like shit.

'It's fine, truly,' she lied. 'It happens.'

It didn't happen to Tinker. Not unless he was drunk.

He tried for a light tone. 'So, tell me about your dinner tonight.'

'It's a work thing,' Fiona said, opening her closet. 'You know the drill. A table full of investment bankers discussing the stock market.'

Tinker had zero idea what a bunch of investment bankers might talk about. He wasn't exactly a career guy. His most recent job had been at Midas Motors, and he'd quite liked it. Until his boss took him aside and told him that although he was a great mechanic, he couldn't work around Tinker's unreliability.

In Fiona's bedroom, the silence that followed was painful. Tinker couldn't think of a single thing to say to break it.

'Well, I'd better get ready,' she said eventually.

Tinker got up and pulled on his jeans. 'Shoot me a text when you want to see me again,' he said over his shoulder.

She nodded, but he doubted that would happen. He'd fucked up – again.

He let himself out.

CHAPTER FOUR

Stig opened the door of his cottage. Mornings in Creswick were his favourite, and this one was exceptional. There was a cool breeze, but the sun was out, the bushland surrounding him bathed in light. Giant gum trees and wattles were dotted around the vast space. A mob of kangaroos dozed on the hill above the dam and two kookaburras laughed their way into the day.

Thomas, the ex-accountant, was doing yoga on the grass outside his fibro shack. Through the window of her campervan, Marnie waved. There were three tents already set up, and several other people were in the process of hammering pegs into the ground and erecting canopies.

As Stig got closer to the main house, he felt the nerves kick in. Which was silly. Acharya would give him the advice he needed.

The scent of sage coming from her living room was stronger than usual. More unusually, someone was crying. Stig stopped in the hallway to listen.

'They call me Povo Patty behind my back,' a wavering voice said in between the sobs.

'Yet you're the one with the true riches. You may not have material things, but there's a god in your heart, a spirit in your soul. We just need to awaken them.'

Acharya's tone was soothing and melodic. She caught Stig's eye and nodded to indicate he could enter.

'Patty, this is Stig,' she said. 'He's my right-hand man. You can trust him completely. Whatever you want to tell me, however confidential, you can say in front of him.' Acharya turned to Stig. 'Patty is one of my clients from Cosmic Counselling,' she told him. 'She's come for extra guidance.'

Stig gave the girl what he hoped was a comforting smile. It was hard to tell her age but he guessed somewhere between sixteen and eighteen. She was hunched over in her chair. Her front teeth were gappy. Her hair was stringy, hanging down over her eyes as though she was hiding from herself. Her sweatshirt and trackpants were oversized. Originally, they might have been white but now they were greyish and stained. She didn't pay him any attention as he sat in the armchair at the window.

Acharya preferred to work from her office in Ballarat but she made exceptions for those in deep distress, and Patty's was clear. Her devotion to the downtrodden was over and above. He was sure she wouldn't be charging this poor girl.

'They're having a party and I'm practically the only one who's not invited,' Patty resumed. 'Mum says bugger them bitches and not to care, but I do. I do care.'

'Your mother's right, Patty,' Acharya said. 'And it sounds like she's on your team, which is something. When I didn't fit in, my mother told me it was my own fault.'

'But you're not poor,' the girl said, looking around at the vast, rambling living room that overlooked the grounds. 'So, why didn't you fit in?'

Acharya's smile had a rueful quality. 'I just never could. It seemed like I was always chasing belonging. The moment I convinced my parents my skirts needed to be short, the others decided long was more stylish. By the time I got into popular music, it was unpopular. All of it, really.'

'Same,' the girl said miserably. 'I never get nothing right.'

'You see, Patty,' Acharya said, 'this property is a physical inheritance from my beloved aunt who passed away. The spiritual, I've had to invent for myself. And being an outcast kickstarted that process for me, as it can for you, if you allow it.'

Stig remembered his own introduction to the spiritual life, at the tail end of withdrawals. Acharya had been his psychedelic guide, caring for him during the rough patches of a life-altering psilocybin trip when the first of his breakthroughs happened. He'd experienced the dissolution of ego, the connection with nature, the utter joy and love, through her. Afterwards, he knew he'd never touch synthetic drugs again. He didn't need to. Even if it meant not seeing Marcus anymore.

'Patty, you must reclaim your power.'

'I never had none of that.'

'Well, you're about to.' Acharya got up from her chair and hovered her healing hands above the girl's head. 'How does that feel?'

'Nice, I suppose. Like someone cares. Like you care.'

'That's because I do,' Acharya said. 'As does Stig,' she added, pointing. 'We've been where you are. We were lost, but now we're found. Repeat after me: I am cherished.'

'I am cherished,' the girl squeaked.

'I am powerful.'

'I am powerful.'

'I have self-love.'

'I have ...' Patty's voice trailed off.

'Affirmations will make these things true,' Acharya urged.

Patty looked like she was steeling herself. 'I have self-love,' she said finally.

'Excellent. Now, what are the names of the two girls who've been cruel to you?'

'Melinda and Alice.'

'And did you bring something of theirs, like I asked?'

Patty reached into her tattered schoolbag and took out a prefect badge. Next came a locket. 'Alice has a pic of her and her dweeb boyfriend in there. Don't look at it or you might puke.'

Without a word, Acharya left the room and Stig was alone with Patty.

'Where's she gone?' Patty asked.

'No idea,' Stig replied with a shrug. 'Acharya's ways are sometimes hard to follow, but my advice is to go with whatever she sees fit.'

When Acharya returned minutes later, it was to an awkward silence. A black lace veil covered her face. Stig had never seen the dolls she carried. They were made of beige felt and had no features – no hair or eyes – just a blank canvas.

'This can be Melinda,' Acharya said, handing one to Patty.

For the first time since Stig had arrived this morning, Patty looked animated.

'OMG, are these voodoo dolls?' she asked. 'I seen them in movies.'

Stig squirmed in his seat. Of course he saw that Acharya was trying to give Patty a sense of power and control. The dolls were just a symbol. But no one knew better than him that Acharya's methods were potent. And, in Stig's experience, some people – like Joe Carruthers – went along with things because of weakness rather than maliciousness.

'First, we cleanse the poppets' energy,' Acharya said, picking sage from the altar she'd set up especially for Patty, lighting it and waving it over the dolls.

'Can I stick the badge into her?' Patty asked eagerly. 'She's so up herself about being a prefect.'

'Yes,' Acharya replied. 'And as you do so, ask your ancestors to come to your aid – to bring justice to your situation.'

It was a little disconcerting to see Patty pressing the badge down on the doll's chest, but Stig needed to trust Acharya's process. The way she'd rescued him from certain doom had been unconventional too. That she was able to tailor her treatments to particular clients was amazing. Acharya was amazing. She was a fearless and unapologetic advocate for the disenfranchised and vulnerable.

'Now, for Alice.'

Patty grinned as she wrapped the locket around the second doll's neck.

'So, what's going to happen to them? Melinda and Alice, I mean.'

Acharya smiled. 'Spirit ways are complex. We'll have to see.'

'I can't wait. Can I take the poppets home with me?'

'You may,' Acharya replied. 'But remember, the generator of their power is here, with me. You'll need to bring them back regularly to recharge.'

Without warning, Patty threw her arms around Acharya. 'You're like ... *hope*,' she said.

Stig nodded as Patty beamed at him, showing her that she was now one of the lucky ones. Because she too had stumbled into the light.

•

'You seem agitated,' Acharya said, pouring chai after Patty had left to get the bus back into town.

Stig tried to stop his foot tapping, but it felt impossible. 'I've been asked to a wedding in Melbourne, next Saturday,' he said.

Acharya's expression darkened. 'Whose? Someone from before?'

'Yes. It's my old schoolfriend Lani Galleta,' Stig said. For a fleeting moment, he could see her recognising the name, and the bucketful of memories it brought up.

'And you want to go?'

'I do,' Stig said carefully, 'with your permission.' He sighed. 'I mean, I had a close friendship with Lani, but it was fractured after I went to Sydney. I think that it could be part of my healing. You know, a kind of catharsis. I have other friends who will be there too, and I'd like them to see how I've ... evolved. I hate the idea that they all still think of me as a loser junkie.'

Acharya's face softened. No one knew more than she did about the state he'd got himself into, the state she'd pulled him out of. She looked at the high beams of the ceiling. 'We don't leave Soul Haven on a whim,' she reminded him. 'Only for duty. And yet, I feel a truth coming.'

She put her hands over her eyes and Stig knew to be quiet as she consulted her oracles.

'I'm getting ... unfinished business,' she crooned. 'I'm seeing danger in going back to the past, the need to be fleet of foot when returning. Ah, but also, a chance to rectify past wrongs.'

Stig gulped. Was it his own wrongs she was referring to?

'Not your wrongs,' she said, as though reading his mind. 'They have secrets, your friends.'

'What kind of secrets?' he asked, but Acharya was far away with the oracles.

'This wedding may be a pilgrimage of sorts. It may be an opportunity to spread the good word about our Soul Haven. Will you do that, Stig, if I give you this exemption?'

'Yes,' Stig said. 'Yes, Acharya, I will, if you think I'm worthy.'

Acharya cupped his face with her hands and Stig felt her wonderful energy coursing through him. 'You are worthy,' she assured him, 'though others may not be. You must bring them here and I will decide.'

Stig kneeled at her feet and she stroked his hair. 'Come back, come home to me whole and not splintered,' she whispered. 'You're my right hand, my four-leaf clover. Through saving you, I came to believe in myself.' She paused. 'You plan to stay with your mother.'

'Yes,' Stig replied, though it wasn't really a question. 'But this – you – will always be my home and my true family.' And, perhaps it was a vanity, but the need to be her most important person felt more primal, more essential, than breathing.

Acharya gently lifted his head, giving Stig the cue that chai time was over. She went to the supply cabinet and brought back some ampoules.

'Take these,' she said. 'They will help you remember your learnings of wisdom and self-love. You've done the work, evolved, and now you're someone other than who you used to be. A universe of stars will light your way.

'And Stig,' she said as he got up to leave, 'it's time to give you your real name.'

CHAPTER FIVE

'The crankshaft on my GMX Drift isn't spinning properly, Tinker,' Luke said, standing in Maya's front yard. 'It gets stuck about three-quarters of the way around, then I have to back-pedal to release it.'

Tinker smiled. Luke always used the full term for the go-kart Tinker had fixed up for his godson.

'I think I can see why, buddy. One of the screws isn't secure in its thread.' He reached into his toolbox and got to work. 'How are you feeling about the race?' he asked. 'Is it okay if I come and watch?'

'Sure,' Luke said. 'I have friends in it too, Nick and Paulo. Paulo's actually coming to St Christopher's with me, but on a sports scholarship, not a dance one. He's faster, but I'm kind of praying the adrenaline kicks in so I can thrash him for a change. Is that wrong?'

Tinker stopped working. 'No way,' he said. 'I imagine beating your mum at all kinds of stuff – Monopoly, pool, darts ... even Mouse Trap would do. It's never happened in real life, but a bloke can dream.'

Luke's voice still hadn't broken. His laugh was high and warbly. 'Mum's Type A,' he whispered. 'She beats everyone at everything, so you shouldn't feel bad.'

'Too right,' Tinker said. 'Coming second to some people – your mum, for example – is as good as it gets.'

'I beat Mum at loads of stuff,' Sophia said, suddenly looming over them.

'No, you don't. Name one,' Luke demanded.

Sophia put her hands on her hips. 'Tennis,' she said.

'As if. Mum whops you.'

'Doubles,' Sophia added.

'You mean when you and Dad are against me and Mum? Sophia, that doesn't count. Dad's the one who gets most of his shots in.'

'But doubles is a team sport. Both players get the credit. Don't they, Tinker?'

Tinker put the screwdriver back in the box and closed the lid. He wasn't keen on triggering the wrath of Sophia and he definitely didn't want to disappoint Luke, so it felt like a bit of a save when his phone rang. He walked to his ute and put the toolbox in the tray.

'He's RSVP'd,' Lani said with a nervous chuckle when Tinker answered the phone. 'Stig's coming to my wedding.'

•

The kids were still squabbling when Tinker walked into the kitchen where Maya was sitting with her laptop.

'Did you find out what the problem was?' she asked without looking up.

'Yeah, it's fixed.'

'Thanks,' Maya said. 'Well, we'd better get a move on and start packing the go-kart onto the trailer.' Finally, she looked up. 'What is it, Tinker?'

•

'Get out there and try your hardest. Regardless of what happens on the circuit, you're all winners. Luke, Paulo, Nick, best of luck.'

Tinker stood by, trying not to roll his eyes at Connor's half-arsed motivational talk. As the others went to look at the go-karts, Tinker took Luke aside.

'Remember, buddy, don't turn in too early and cut the corner. Do it a bit after you cross the green line. Aim for the corner apex at, say, about a sixty-five-degree angle. Got it?'

Luke nodded, serious as Sophia bounded up to them.

'I'm starving,' she announced.

As Connor and Maya approached, Tinker could see how agitated she was about Stig coming to Lani's wedding. And, most likely, about the race. As much as he loved her, Maya was bloody hard to be around when she wasn't in control. He'd have to put some work into smoothing things between Lani and her, because this could boil over.

'Race four starts in five minutes,' came a voice over the speaker. 'Category: fifteen and under.'

'That's you, right, Luke?' Tinker asked. Luke nodded.

'Best of luck,' Connor said.

'You've got this,' Maya added.

Luke waved and went to the starting gate.

Three, two, one. The starting gun rang out. Luke got off really well. Tinker was glad he'd painted the carriage bright yellow since it was easy to watch his progress. But Sophia seemed suddenly miserable. Standing beside her mother, she looked like Maya's mini-me.

'What's wrong?' Tinker asked, nudging her. 'Look, Luke's coming first.'

Sophia shook her head. 'Now he is. But he's getting the wobbles.' He could have sworn she brushed away a tear, but her jaw was set hard.

Tinker focused on the race. Luke had taken the last corner too slowly. Tinker should have explained better. Now Luke was fifth, sixth.

He came in last.

'Stupid go-kart race,' Sophia said.

•

Lani leaned back against the bedhead, watching as Tinker pulled the suit pants over his boxers. The three of them – well, the four of them, before everything went south – had spent copious hours at Lani's place before Gino and Yvette decided to upgrade. This house had seen laughter and tears. Good times and some very, very bad ones.

'Okay, hit me with it,' Lani said. 'How did Maya react?'

Tinker grimaced. He had to choose his words. There was no point rocking the boat with the whole lot of Maya's rant.

'You really want to know?' he replied. 'Then shove over.' He blew out a sigh. 'She thinks you're being selfish, and you haven't thought about how Stig coming to the wedding would impact us.'

'But we've been through that,' Lani said. 'As long as we avoid mentioning we were with Joe the night he died, it will be fine. Besides, it's *my* wedding! I'm not being selfish, I'm being magnanimous. You know, generous. I'm bringing us all back together again, just like we promised.'

In the ensuing silence, Tinker could practically see Stig's small, wiry body leaping out from Lani's giant walk-in robe and bursting into a hilarious version of 'I'm a Mean Ole Lion'. He'd been a star in their Year 11 production of *The Wiz*.

Lani had been Dorothy, of course. Tinker had been one of many munchkins. Maya had been cast as Evillene and, shit, she really let that character seep into her.

'Hmm, those pants are too short for you. You can't be my bridesman and giver-away in ankle-freezers.'

Tinker tried to smile but couldn't quite manage it.

She pulled him in for a hug. 'Maya will get over it. It'll be the best thing – for all of us. You get that, don't you?'

'Yeah,' he said. 'I'm keen to see Stig.' It didn't seem enough, but they were the only words Tinker could find.

'Good,' Lani said. 'Now get me your phone. I'm going to put in Stig's details.'

CHAPTER SIX

Maya hadn't had hair and make-up professionally done since her own wedding. The curls wouldn't last – they never did, given her hair was so fine – but for the moment, she almost felt pretty.

'You'll need some stronger hairspray for me,' she warned.

'No, this one will work perfectly,' the hairdresser assured her.

'You look like a supermodel, Mum,' Sophia joined in. 'We *all* do.'

Maya felt a swelling of pride. She wished at times that Luke had some of Sophia's chutzpah. Her daughter had come first in every regard. She'd burst into the world with a piercing scream. When Luke followed fifteen minutes later, his reaction had been more of a mewl. Sophia had always been tougher, stronger, less malleable and more resilient than her twin. Her daughter would never be anyone's bunny.

Lani's mother, Yvette, pursed her mouth as she spoke. 'Something old,' she said, thrusting a diamond necklace at Lani, who really did look like a supermodel even though she hadn't had a skerrick of make-up applied yet. The curls in her thick blonde hair would stay put until she decided otherwise.

'Something new,' Yvette continued as Lani sat in front of one of several mirrors. If the house Lani had grown up in – the one that was literally given to her by her parents – was extraordinary, Gino and Yvette's was next level. Being an executive producer clearly paid well and certainly brought kudos, but it was Yvette who'd inherited most of their wealth from her grandfather's zipper company. They probably raked in more in a week than Connor did in a year. And they were not shy about showing it.

'I want to live like this one day,' Sophia declared, dancing around the enormous powder room in the gorgeous pink and orange junior bridesmaid dress Lani had bought for her.

Yvette raised her eyebrows, as though she thought that was a pipedream. 'Something new,' she repeated, handing Lani a lace garter belt.

'You're the most beautiful bride I've ever seen,' Sophia said, sitting next to Lani in the oversized chair. 'Though I haven't actually seen any in real life. Not this close up anyway.'

Lani laughed as the make-up artist laid the first strokes of foundation on her chiselled cheekbones.

'Don't you think Lani might need more space?' Yvette asked pointedly.

'Not as much as she needs her goddaughter close by on her special day,' Sophia's response came in a heartbeat.

'It's okay,' the make-up artist said. 'I can work around her.' She turned her attention to Sophia. 'Would you like a bit of foundation too?' she asked. 'I could easily cover up that birthmark?'

'Yes,' Yvette said.

'No,' Sophia objected, clapping a hand over the almost heart-shaped patch on her forehead above her left eye. 'My birthmark makes me unique.'

Maya smiled. She and Connor had obviously done something right. Although they'd initially been inclined to risk a tricky operation to remove it, Sophia had always shown the way to embrace her difference.

Yvette rolled her eyes. 'Something borrowed,' she said, making a show of having to navigate around Sophia.

'Oh Mama,' Lani said, holding up a miniature horseshoe, 'isn't this Aunt Elise's lucky charm?'

'Yes,' Yvette answered. 'It's a meaningless, superstitious talisman, but she insisted you have it for the day. She said you will reap blessings from it, though that seems not to have worked so well for her, given her many failings.'

'Well, I think it's sweet of Elise,' Lani countered.

Yvette shrugged. 'Something blue,' she continued, pinning a sapphire brooch on the ribbon of Lani's bouquet. 'Chop chop,' she said to the room in general. 'There's only an hour before the photo shoot. Oh, hello, Tinker, don't you look handsome.'

Maya couldn't remember a single compliment ever coming her way from Yvette, or Stig's, for that matter, but there'd always been plenty of positive feedback for Tinker. It was true though. He looked like a Hemsworth in his stone-coloured suit and burnt-orange tie. Sophia got out of Lani's chair and made a beeline for him.

'We're going to be in the photos, Tinker,' she said. 'And Lani reckons there'll be *paparazzi* here from *The Women's Weekly*.

If we make it into a mag, I'm totally going to show off at school. The peasants will be so jealous.'

The thought hadn't occurred to Maya. She could already imagine it. Everyone else would look amazing. Then there'd be her, one lone frump.

Tinker ran his hands through his hair and the hairdresser immediately went to smooth it down. 'Stig texted,' he said falteringly. 'He's at his mum's.'

Maya's stomach lurched. For a moment, she felt as though she might throw up on the expensive designer dress Lani had paid for. If Tinker had received a text from Stig, that meant they'd been in contact and she was the only one behind the eight ball.

But Lani just beamed, as if the murky past could be washed away with this glorious reunion. If she could be more gorgeous, the make-up made it so.

'Great,' she said. 'I've seated him next to Barry and Lil at the reception, so he should be in his element.'

Maya doubted that. Stig hadn't had an element for nearly twenty years – not since everything had imploded. From what Maya had gathered, he'd been a drifter for over ten of them. But she had no choice now. She'd have to suck this up.

'By the way,' Tinker said, and on his face even a grimace looked pretty good. 'We're supposed to introduce him as ...' He looked at his phone.

'Sadiki.'

CHAPTER SEVEN

The house Stig had grown up in was frozen in time. True, his mother's collection of Apostle teaspoons hanging from a stand in the kitchen had been added to. He'd sent some over the years. He'd found the St John with his cup of sorrow at an op shop in Kings Cross, the same day he'd so proudly bought Marcus an eternity ring. Marcus had been overjoyed to receive it and they'd laughed about the odd combination of joy and sorrow that seemed to infest their lives together.

He couldn't remember where he'd found the Judas Iscariot holding a bag of money, but he did recall the moment he'd put it into a padded bag at a Sydney post office. He'd still been racked with guilt then, and the act had felt somehow sacred amid the chaos of his life. Judas, the betrayer. No sainthood for him.

The view into their lounge room showed his father's pride and joy – a framed soccer jersey signed by Gunnar Nordahl. It had been a rare splurge, and it elicited the same reverence his mother had for her spoons.

As a child, Stig had wished some of that reverence on to himself. One time, he'd put a trophy he'd won for 'Most Improved Tap Dancer' on the mantelpiece underneath the jersey. Hours later, without explanation, it was gone. A neighbour had found it in her skip and returned it. He'd thrown it into the bottom of the cupboard in his room and cried silently into a pillow.

His father was gone now. How long had it been? Like everything else, his parents had been stoic about the Alzheimer's diagnosis. Father hadn't requested him to come home, insisting he'd rather be remembered as he'd been before the disease. Stig didn't know a time he'd like to remember his father for. He didn't know a time *he'd* like to be remembered for. His response had been to up his drug intake. To voluntarily drown in a sea of sin, shame and heroin.

His mother carried a tray into the lounge. Stig chose an armchair that didn't face the soccer jersey. He made sure the stud of his shirt pocket was securely done up. The ampoules were safe. It might be helpful to microdose right now. It'd be easy to do it without his mother noticing, but it would have to be without the accompanying ceremony, so he decided to wait.

'Lani was such a pretty girl,' his mother said as she poured the tea. 'It's a wonder she wasn't snapped up before now. Who's the lucky groom?'

'*Her* name is Bridget,' Stig said. His mother knew Lani was gay, but she seemed genuinely to have forgotten – or erased – the information.

'Your father had a great deal of respect for Gino Galleta,' she detoured. 'He was such a help when …'

She'd always done this, touched on a subject then flittered away. Gino Galleta had certainly not been a help. His sole motivation for influencing his parents to send Stig away had been to maintain the reputation of St Fabian's. And his mother refused to acknowledge how that turned out, burying herself in denial. Stig had been a sacrificial lamb. There should have been a teaspoon made in his honour.

'It couldn't be in a Catholic church,' his mother said, and it took Stig a moment to realise she was talking about the wedding. 'That must be a great disappointment for Gino and Yvette.'

'It isn't,' Stig said. 'It's on the grounds of their house. With a celebrant rather than a priest because, as you know, the Church still doesn't sanction gay marriage.'

'Well, of course it doesn't, dear, because that wouldn't be right.'

'Mother,' he said, 'the Catholic Church does many things that aren't right. And I'm gay too. You know that.'

'It's not a sin to have homosexual thoughts,' she parroted. 'Only to act on them.'

His mother didn't want to know if he'd acted on his thoughts. There was so much she didn't want to know. There hadn't been anyone since he joined Soul Haven. In Sydney though, there'd been more encounters than he could tally up. Times for money and times for lust. And, of course, one time for love.

They'd taken risks together, he and Marcus. So many risks. And his memories of that period were tainted by the junk. But this one, he seemed to recall vividly.

They never had a pimp. The deal was, they'd look out for each other. The client Stig had found that night for a rendezvous in a park toilet block had become aggressive. He hadn't been able to articulate what he wanted, and Stig hadn't been able to glean it. So instead, the middle-aged balding man, who'd stunk of beer and cigarettes, had rammed Stig's head against the wall and told him not to turn around.

Stig didn't know how long it had been. The door was flimsy, the lock not functioning.

'Arthur?' came Marcus's voice. The man let go of Stig.

'Who wants to know?' he mumbled.

'My guess is your wife, Catherine,' Marcus said as he threw the man's pants his way. He looked through the phone he must've swiped from Arthur's pocket.

'Oh look, it's under Catherine Honey,' he said. 'Isn't that just so sweet? The last text, from a minute ago, asks where you are. Given that you're ... otherwise engaged, how about I answer it?'

Arthur had paid double the negotiated fee.

Afterwards, they'd got high and held each other tenderly until morning.

Yes, Stig had acted on his thoughts. But all these experiences were to be unceremoniously cancelled in the house of his youth.

'I could cut your hair if you like. It's rather too long,' his mother said, conjuring up the bowl cuts of Stig's youth. 'And what are you wearing to the wedding? Because I kept your father's good suit. Let me get it for you to try on.'

Before he could respond, she was heading towards her bedroom. It must've been in a prime position in the wardrobe because she was back with it in seconds, holding it aloft.

Stig could see his father in his one good suit. He could visualise his crew cut and the way he looked out with those stern blue eyes. One day, when he was eight years old, his father had reached into his pocket, pulled out a packet of soccer cards and given them to him.

'Thank you, Father!' he'd said. 'So, are these ones I can trade with the other kids?'

'Yes, of course,' had been the response.

He'd been so happy the next day when Veronica agreed to trade the whole packet of sports cards with the swap cards she'd collected. Kittens were so very sweet. The pictures had helped to teach him the breeds. Ragdolls. Persians. Siamese. Burmese. Abyssinian. Russian Blue. Bengal. Egyptian Mau.

'Imagine, a cat without hair? Isn't that mind-blowing?' he'd asked his father as he showed him the Sphynx. He hadn't seen the slap across the face coming until he felt the sting.

'Try it on,' his mother suggested, bringing him back to the present.

Stig shook his head. *Sadiki* shook his head.

'No haircut, Mother. And I have my own suit.'

CHAPTER EIGHT

Lani walked down the aisle on the grounds of her parents' house. Bordering the path were rows of peach and orange dahlias they'd flown in from Darwin that complemented the bridal party's colour palette. The sun dipped its head politely in the twilight above the matching arch. She was arm in arm with Tinker – didn't think she'd be able to take a single step forward if he wasn't there to support her. She wondered whether Papa felt a pang of regret at not being the one to give her away, but most likely he wouldn't. Her father had always stood firm in his opinions.

Before her, Sophia scattered cream and orange rose petals. In the front row, on Lani's guests' side, Papa rose and everyone followed suit. Mama, dressed up to the nines in Balenciaga, wiped what Lani suspected was a non-existent tear.

Raymond the celebrant looked uber cool in his retro rust suit. He was the one thing Bridget had insisted upon. Well, that and the imperative that no god, Christian or otherwise, should be mentioned.

Her fiancée, soon to be wife, looked amazing, standing tall and proud in an off-white suit with yellow pinstripes and a matching tie. Lani had a sudden urge to throw herself into

Bridget's arms, then hold hands and run away together. Instead, she took her place while the wedding party arranged themselves.

Bridget's best woman was her mum, Dawn. The glistening in her eyes was unmistakably real.

'Welcome, friends and family,' Raymond began, the booming voice at odds with his slight frame. 'We are gathered here today to celebrate the union of Lani Louisa Galleta and Bridget Anne Sykes. We are all here to …'

Lani looked out at the sea of their 136 guests. On Bridget's side, there were people she didn't know and it made her shiver. There must be a lot she didn't know about the woman she was about to marry.

There were definitely things Bridget didn't know about her.

'We are delighted to share the joy of Lani and Bridget as they choose to spend their lives together,' Raymond continued.

Lani looked at her mother and Yvette blew her a kiss that landed on Lani's cheek like a rare butterfly.

'Do you, Lani Galleta, take Bridget Sykes to be your lawfully wedded wife? To have and to hold from this day forth?'

'That I do, wholeheartedly.' Lani sounded like a voice-over professional. Maybe a career was finally looming.

'Tinker, do you have the ring?'

Tinker feigned searching his pockets and everyone laughed. It was a gift the way he could shift a mood from serious and reverential to playful and fun. She nudged him and he staggered backward, pretending to find the ring behind his ear.

As Raymond turned to address Bridget, Lani spotted Stig. He was in the back row on an aisle seat. His hair, as she'd realised the day they had coffee, was thinning and tied back in a ponytail. The suit he wore was ill-fitting, as though it had been borrowed. But he was here. Tinker had seen him too. Lani could feel adoration and guilt emanating from him in equal measure.

The moment Maya saw him she did a double take, as though it came as a surprise that he'd turned up.

'As a sign of your union,' Raymond said, as Sophia puckered up in anticipation, 'you may now kiss.'

•

'Nice to catch up with you, finally,' Fiona said.

Tinker offered her an apology that was kneejerk. Yes, the wedding party photo shoot had taken a long time, but that wasn't down to him. Fiona had been generally shitty with him lately. She'd given him second, third, fourth chances and his lack of performance in bed was wearing thin. She had a glass of bubbly and the vibe in the reception marquee was generally friendly. It was a worry that she hadn't seen fit to mingle. And now he had little choice but to desert her again, because walking across the floor towards him was his old mate.

'Why don't you find your seat and we'll catch up a bit later?'

Fiona rolled her eyes. 'You'll be way up the front, I suppose?'

It was so confusing. She didn't seem to enjoy his company but still required it.

'Yep, we'll be right up there,' Sophia answered for him, pointing at the stage, 'because that's where the bridal party's going to be sitting. As you can probably tell, I'm in it. I guess the brides are the main thing but being a junior bridesmaid's pretty spesh too. And in case you were wondering,' she said, doing a spin, 'I'm wearing Comme des Garçons.'

Fiona didn't even crack a smile.

'Sorry,' Tinker said (how many chances was she likely to give him?) and began walking to meet Stig halfway. He really could've done without it, but Sophia shadowed him. Stig looked older than he should. His grin, though, was the same one Tinker remembered. His blue eyes had the same twinkle.

'Mate,' he said, and he couldn't help it, the bear hug came naturally. And, yes, Stig was still small and wiry, but his return hug was strong.

'What's wrong, Tinker?' Sophia asked, pulling at his sleeve.

Tinker smiled through misty eyes. 'Stig, this is Sophia,' he said. 'Maya and Connor's bundle of mischief.'

Sophia rewarded him with a whack on his arm. 'Bundle of mischief,' she scoffed. 'Tinker, you're making it sound like I'm a baby when I'm actually fourteen.'

'Lovely to finally meet you,' Stig said, shaking her hand.

'I know who you are,' Sophia declared, refusing to release the handshake. 'You used to be Mum's friend but she reckons you went off the rails.'

Tinker grimaced, his heart thumping, but Stig's laugh broke through the tension. The *before* laugh – throaty and contagious, and sometimes, in their teens, broken up by uncontrollable hiccups.

'You're just like your mother, Sophia,' he said finally.

Sophia looked like she was weighing up whether it was a compliment and Stig must've seen it too. 'That's a good thing,' he said. 'She's ballsy, your mum.'

'I'm not so sure about that,' Sophia said loudly. 'I'm much more ballsy. I—'

Sophia didn't get to finish because Tinker clapped a hand over her mouth. He got a sharp little bite for his efforts.

'So, Stig,' Sophia said, hardly missing a beat, 'when you went off the rails, where did you go?'

'All sorts of places,' Stig replied. 'But the journey hasn't only been physical.'

'What does that mean?'

Stig tilted his head. 'It means I've been searching in a spiritual sense as well,' he said. 'And that's taken me many different places and landed me in the one I was destined to find. I've been lucky enough to release baggage from the past and find belonging in a true and loving community.'

'Didn't you find that in the Church?' Sophia asked. 'Mum and Dad have, and me and Luke.'

'If that works for you, then it's all well and good. But, Sophia, it isn't for everyone. It certainly wasn't for me.'

'Hmm, I get it,' Sophia said with a shrug. 'It's not for Lani or Tinker either, but I think they're missing out.' She turned to Tinker. 'What's your community?' she asked.

The only response Tinker could give was a shrug.

'Thought so,' she said, and even though it was a little awkward, or perhaps because it was awkward, it made both men smile broadly.

'The way I live now is different, but I love it,' Stig continued. 'Which brings me to this ...' He switched his attention from Sophia to Tinker and back again. 'Do you think you could call me Sadiki?'

Sophia screwed up her nose and Tinker found himself apologising again. With all the wedding stuff, he'd forgotten Stig's request.

'Why?' Sophia asked. 'That's a bit weird, because your real name is Stig, right?'

'It used to be,' he said, 'but I've evolved so it's been decided that my name should too.'

'You can't just change your name,' Sophia protested, 'unless you do it by deed poll.'

It was probably the best thing ever to have Sophia there after all for their first meeting in twenty years. Stig – jeez, he kept forgetting his new name – Sadiki obviously found her as funny as Tinker did. He adored his godson – Luke was kind and sweet – but he loved sparky Sophia just as much. He wondered if he'd ever get around to having kids of his own. His eyes wandered to Fiona who was at the bar, finally chatting to someone: a hot bartender.

'It's not official,' Sadiki told Sophia. 'But that's neither here nor there.' He put his hand on his heart. 'Because I've done it in here. Have you made your confirmation?'

Sophia nodded.

'So you got to choose a name then?'

'Anastasia,' Sophia said. 'She was an exorcist saint,

which seemed pretty cool to me when I was twelve and a bit over-the-top now. But, anyway, that's just a middle name.'

He nodded. 'Still, it wasn't by deed poll, right?'

Sophia looked unconvinced. 'So, why Sadiki?

'It's an African name that means "loyal" and "faithful".'

'Well, I've never heard of it,' she said. 'But don't worry. I'll still call you Sadiki.'

'Loyal and faithful,' Maya said, coming up to them. 'To whom?'

CHAPTER NINE

Maya could have kicked herself. She'd seen Tinker, Sophia and Stig chatting and laughing and now she'd ruined the mood by launching straight into the personal sphere. And she'd stared at Stig for way too long. Taken in the stress lines that crisscrossed his face, the grey suit that wasn't badly cut so much as tailored for a different man. The sleeves were too long. The pants scrunched around his black shoes that looked for all the world like the school shoes he used to wear back in the day. The studded, black and white western shirt made his look even more eclectic.

She didn't deserve the welcome Stig gave her, how he pulled her in for a hug, ignoring the question she shouldn't have asked in the first place.

'I've been getting to know your fabulous kid, Maya,' he said.

Sophia tapped herself on the shoulders in self-congratulations and Stig and Tinker smiled. That was the right way to do it. Issue a compliment. Chat about the weather, how beautiful the brides looked. Anything that helped dip their toes in the shallows instead of dive-bombing into the deepest water.

'It's so lovely to see you after all these years, Sadiki,' Maya said, hoping that the use of the silly name would make up for the early onslaught. 'You look good,' she lied. A venial sin, at most.

'You too,' he lied back.

Despite the hairdresser's assurance, Maya's curls were already drooping unevenly, and she hadn't had a chance to check her make-up. There were probably smudges on her cheeks from the mascara that had irritated her eyes all day.

Onstage, where the bridal table was set, Gino kept his signature houndstooth beret on as he tapped a spoon against his glass. Yvette was right by his side. Maya looked around for Connor and Luke but she couldn't see either of them.

'Ladies and gentlemen,' he said, 'entrées are about to be served. Please take your seats.'

There was rarely a delay between a command from Gino Galleta and action. The guests stopped mid-sentence, mid-greeting, mid-everything and began looking for their place cards. And perhaps he thought the time their group took to respond was a moment too long, because he strode up to them.

'Tinker, Maya, Sophia,' he said, seemingly not noticing the fourth person standing with them. 'The bridal table awaits.'

Maya nodded. 'Sure,' she said. 'Mr Galleta, this is … Sadiki.'

Gino gave him a cursory glance as he reached out his hand. 'Pleased to meet you,' he said.

Maya could see Stig's Adam's apple go up and down as he gulped. His face was expressionless, the return handshake robotic. He was in shock. It was unimaginable to think of what he might have been feeling, being unrecognised by the man who'd changed the course of his life.

The board had attempted to sell it as a win-win, but Stig's real friends hadn't bought it. Maya then started a petition with the hope of convincing those in power to change their minds. She'd managed to get over a hundred signatures from the girls at St Audrey's, but Tinker was the lone wolf from St Fabian's who signed it. The only staff member who did was Miss Robinson, the school counsellor. Maya had tried … and failed. And hadn't the counsellor left her job not long after? Maya couldn't recall, but regardless, they'd all been ineffective.

Stig had been lost. He'd disappeared into the ether. And now, Maya supposed she'd have to try to get used to Sadiki.

•

'If it isn't the prodigal son!' Barry said and Sadiki almost chuckled at the irony. He'd hardly been living a lavish life, as the original bible story told it. Quite the opposite. God had withdrawn his blessings rather than Stig rejecting them. But, yes, he had been absent, and that was how most people interpreted the parable. Obviously, Barry hadn't been paying attention in Religious Education. At least, not like Stig used to.

'How terrific to see you, Stig. Meet my lovely wife, Lil.'

'My name is Sadiki now. Long story, but the supposed prodigal son has returned a changed man.'

If there was one person daggier than Maya at their combined schools, Barry had been it. He'd worn Coke-bottle glasses and spoken with a stutter. Now, though, he'd grown into himself. The stutter seemed to be gone, the glasses most likely replaced with contact lenses.

He kissed Sadiki on both cheeks. 'You're sitting next to us,' he continued, 'at table eight. Can I show you now?'

Maya smiled nicely as Barry turned to greet her. But after, as she walked to the bridal table, her heart was thumping. Barry had been part of that terrible time.

Stig sitting with him, conversing with him, would likely dredge up bad memories.

•

'Stig ... Sadiki, I mean, I have a confession to make,' Barry said. His entrée was untouched.

Sadiki put down his knife and fork, signalling readiness to listen. During their school days, Barry had been a nice guy. He'd been targeted for his awkward looks and stutter, but always seemed to know how to turn the other cheek. Sadiki could have learned a lesson from him, but he hadn't. He'd always been reactionary in responding to the taunts, doubling down on his claim of innocence, but that just made things worse.

'I've been carrying something with me forever,' he said. 'Please, can you come outside with me so we can have a word?'

Sadiki braced himself as they got up.

'Honey,' Lil said, 'where are you going? Your duck pancake will get cold.'

Barry leaned across and kissed her on the cheek. He whispered something and she nodded sombrely, holding his hand until distance prevented it.

It was a lovely night but the stars weren't out. Barry put his hand on Sadiki's shoulder. For several seconds he seemed unable to speak.

'I owe you an ... apology,' he said eventually.

Sadiki looked askance. He waited for Barry to speak.

'We were friends in high school,' he said. 'I mean, I liked you.'

'Yes,' Sadiki assured him. 'I liked you too, Barry. And you never did anything to be sorry for. Not that I can recall, anyway.'

'Oh, but I did,' Barry said, sinking down onto an outdoor chair, head in hands. 'And I hope you can forgive me.'

Sadiki moved a chair so he was opposite his old friend. Barry lifted his head and took a deep breath.

'It was me,' he said. 'I took that bloody video.'

Oh god. He wasn't Sadiki. He was back to being Stig, back inside the pain. It might as well have been playing on a screen in the night sky. The zooming in on their costumes on a bench in the change rooms. Stig, naked, ripping off Joe's towel. The punch to his left eye. How it all appeared to represent something that couldn't have been further from the truth.

'But why?' he managed eventually. 'Why would you do that, Barry?'

'I'd just got the camcorder. I was filming everything. And when I saw you guys in the change rooms, it was automatic. I promise I wasn't going to show anyone. But Mackenzie got wind of it and made me play the footage. He ... well, you of all people know what happened after that.'

Stig stood up and paced across the lawn, back and forth. Barry watched in silence.

'Joe shouted that someone had been filming,' Sadiki – yes, he was Sadiki now – said, 'but my back was to you and you must've run out. Afterwards, he refused to speak to me. I just assumed it was Mackenzie.'

'I did run out. And I never fessed up to it. Especially because Mackenzie was claiming the glory of casting you as a predator. That meathead wouldn't even have known how to operate a bloody camcorder.' Barry shook his head. 'When the jocks started accusing you of groping them – and worse – they used that video as supposed "proof". I knew they were making false allegations. But I was a coward. I couldn't be more sorry,' he said finally.

There was no doubting Barry's sincerity. It was written all over his face. Sadiki reached deep inside himself, searching for forgiveness.

'It's okay,' he said finally. And it truly was. The harm that video caused wasn't intentional. He put his hand on Barry's shoulder and the relief was palpable. 'Joe punching me was his gut reaction to potentially being outed. It was a deflection. I knew that instantly.'

'I kind of did too,' Barry said. 'If anyone bothered to really look at the footage, they would have seen a glint of playfulness in Joe's eyes as you approached. But no one seemed to want to recognise that. And now – well, you've suffered. And Joe's dead.'

From inside the marquee came another clinking of glasses. 'I fear it's time for truth-telling,' came Gino Galleta's deep voice. Full of swag. Full of shit. Full of insincerity. His speech would be slick and meaningless.

Sadiki tapped the studded pocket of his western shirt.

CHAPTER TEN

'Our Lani Louisa has always been precocious,' Mr Galleta said, already drawing chuckles from the crowd. He was a man who stood tall. Confidence oozed from every pore. 'At age five, she told me, "Papa, I love you, but we do seem to have our differences."'

The line landed exactly as he'd intended. Photographers snapped away. Lil leaned into Barry, and he took the opportunity to sneak a kiss. Their love seemed so effortless that Sadiki could barely look away. It was clear that she soothed him. There'd been moments like that with Marcus. Little golden nuggets in among the downs and downs of their lives in Sydney.

'Aged eleven,' Mr Galleta continued onstage, 'Lani informed me and Yvette that she intended to take a holiday in Barbados. I told her that I'd have to check my schedule and she looked askance. "Not with you and Mama," she said. "I need to go by myself. But can you give me your credit card?"'

This one drew roars of recognition. Sadiki noticed Lani, trust-fund baby through and through, shifting in her seat. And, yes, her father was as slick as ever. Such a competent grey fox, delivering humour with a sting in the tail.

'At seventeen,' Mr Galleta continued ...

Barry looked Sadiki in the eyes. They were seventeen when the video that changed the course of Stig's life emerged.

Mr Galleta had the audience eating out of his hands, of course. That's how he played life. That's how he'd spun it with the school board. Proposing the obvious solution to St Fabian's collective dilemma. Oh, he'd done it with such finesse, with skilful manipulation. *Mr and Mrs Johannsen, a year in the army would make a man out of your son. You're intelligent people. And I believe, Mr Johannsen, you had a glowing career as a field marshal yourself.*

'... Lani came to me with a less-than-ideal school report ...'

With all that had been going on, Stig's latest Year 11 report had been appalling. Then Joe's death capped off that horrific year. But Mr Galleta was going to turn it all into a punchline.

Sadiki got up and made his way to the bathroom. He looked in the mirror. His face had once been described as 'lived-in'. It had been pretty ironic, since he was only nineteen at the time, but Marcus had been right. Life had further etched itself over his eyes, his forehead, his cheeks. He practised the circular breathing technique Acharya had taught him.

The ampoules in his pocket called out. One was a microdose, but ten? He could easily put them into a drink and watch with satisfaction as Mr Galleta's massive ego dissolved, publicly.

'Stig ... Sadiki, are you okay?'

'Barry, you should be out there,' he said. 'I just ... needed a moment.'

Barry made no move to leave. Instead, he joined Sadiki at the basin. 'I dread the day Arlo will be seventeen,' he said softly.

'Your son?'

'Yes, *our* son,' Barry corrected. 'Luckily, he has more Lil in him than me. I reckon it's eighty–twenty. I'm hoping it stays that way.'

Sadiki sighed. 'I still think about him,' he said. 'About Joe Carruthers, I mean.'

There was a hearty round of applause from the reception. Mr Galleta's speech was over.

'He was a good kid,' Barry said. 'Well, honestly, that's not true. I didn't like him. He just seemed to be another jock to me. Someone it was best to avoid.' Now it was his turn to sigh. 'He was a bloody great footballer, that much was for sure.'

Sadiki understood Barry's impression of Joe. Before they'd been cast as the Cowardly Lion and the Tin Man, he'd felt the same. But there had been so much vulnerability Joe had kept well hidden.

'He was a fitness fanatic,' Sadiki said, frowning. 'When everyone else got tanked, Joe was too concerned about how it might affect his training. Then, one night out of the blue, he sat by himself, getting so shit-faced that he stayed in the burning converted garage out the back of his parents' house and just—'

'But it wasn't out of the blue. It was because of me,' Barry interrupted. 'He was troubled because of the video *I* took. He couldn't see his way clearly to stick up for you in case he got tarred with the same brush you did. And then, he went along with the others who were getting their kicks out of accusing you of assaulting them. Anyone who didn't believe them – and there were students who didn't – were too scared to contest the jocks, especially en masse. It was all a disaster, and it started with me.'

'Without further ado,' Mr Galleta said from the next room, 'I'd like to introduce Lani's long-time partner in crime, Tim Hodges, aka Tinker.'

'We missed whatever Mr Galleta had to say about Bridget,' Barry said. 'Better get in there for Tinker's speech.'

•

Maya's kids were tearing up the dance floor. Well, Luke was. Sophia's style suggested more of a potential massacre. She'd already bumped into an elderly man with a walking stick. Lani and Bridget were braving proximity, but everyone else in Sophia's orbit was giving her a wide berth.

'Are you going to get out there and show them how it's done?' Tinker asked with his oh-so-familiar grin. 'Crazy in Love' had been a favourite, but Sadiki wasn't sure he was up for it until he saw Maya heading towards them. She'd always been like a dog with a bone. A second chat with her would most likely be an interrogation he wasn't quite ready for.

'Caught between the devil and the deep blue sea,' Tinker joked. The real devil was hanging at the bar, schmoozing with the important folk.

Sadiki wound his way through the crowd and found a space close to Luke. Sadiki was good at this. He'd always had rhythm in his bones and he could still manage to do the splits. His leap from the ground may have been a bit less graceful than it was in his youth, but he still made it back to upright.

And there was Luke, mirroring his first move with an impressive litheness. Next, Sadiki opted for a disco spin, right hand pointing up to the roof. Luke spun in the opposite direction, left hand lifted. Sadiki hadn't intended for this to be a dance-off, but here they were, and it was fabulous.

Everyone in the marquee seemed to be on, or gathered around, the dance floor. The crowd circled around them, clapping and cheering with each new move. Even Mr Galleta deigned to watch, signature whisky on ice in hand. Sadiki suspected it wasn't the one he offered at the open bar. Mr Galleta had always been a Hibiki man.

Luke did the drop first and Sadiki took his cue. When they high-fived in the centre, Mr Galleta put down his drink to clap. It was a small acknowledgement, but it was something. At that moment, Sadiki knew he was above sending the old man unknowingly on a trip. He used psilocybin with respect, with ceremony. Acharya was right. The stars weren't out tonight, but he carried a universe within him. Surely he had gained the wisdom, the integrity, to deal with this man the proper way. Surely.

Sadiki's natural rhythm seemed pretty much the only trait he'd inherited from his mother. But Maya had always been a truly terrible dancer, clunky and out of sync with the music. She'd been a good sport about it whenever they cracked up about her style. And from his peripheral view, it looked as though Connor was on par with her. But Luke was awesome. The song finished and, instantly, Luke went back to being a shy kid, awkwardly accepting Sadiki's outstretched hand to shake before slipping away.

When Sadiki looked up, Lani's father was beckoning

'You always had talent,' Mr Galleta said. So, he did remember. He'd just chosen not to acknowledge the fact. 'Your performance as the Cowardly Lion in *The Wiz* was, quite frankly, outstanding.'

Sadiki gulped. He'd had great feedback at the time, but from a professional film producer? That might have buoyed his spirits, kept him sane, when tormentors had snapped at his heels.

'It's unfortunate that you weren't ... stable, at that stage. I'd already pitched you to a casting agent and she was set to audition you for a movie I was working on.'

'Really?' Sadiki replied, his voice choking on the word. He cleared his throat. 'You really saw that much promise in me? Why didn't I know any of this? Why didn't someone tell me?'

'Obviously, I had to pull the request—'

Sadiki shook his head in disbelief. 'Did you though? Because it could have been just the ticket for me. Certainly a damn sight better than shoving a square peg into a round hole by sending me into the army,' he said.

Mr Galleta looked momentarily taken aback, but such a reaction didn't last long with a man like that.

'I stand by the advice I gave,' Mr Galleta said firmly. 'And let's not get carried away by sliding-doors rubbish. If you wasted the chance to straighten out your life, if you ran away rather than face your ... deficits, that was your call. The movie, by the way, never got past pre-production.'

'But there might have been other chances. Don't you see—'

'Hello, Sandra.' Mr Galleta greeted an attractive middle-aged woman in a stylish outfit with a kiss. And did he surreptitiously, in the darkness and at an angle where only Sadiki could see, place a hand on her arse? Yes, he did, and she most certainly didn't mind. There had always been rumours about Mr Galleta's womanising, but at his daughter's wedding? That seemed, at the very least, tasteless.

Regardless, Sadiki was dismissed with a flick of Mr Galleta's hand. And now, finally, the only Galleta who deserved his regard was striding towards him in all her bridal glory.

CHAPTER ELEVEN

As Lani wrapped her arms around her old friend and felt his own squeeze back, tears threatened. 'I'm so glad you came,' she said and, god, it seemed an understatement. Seeing Stig-Sadiki dance up a storm with Luke, then chat amicably with Papa, it was as though things were finally on the path to righting themselves. She took his hand and they walked outside and over to the gazebo where they could finally talk in private.

He sat on the bench seat and she joined him.

'Do you know how much we've missed you?' she asked, and there was the grin she remembered so well.

'No,' he said. 'You'll have to tell me. In detail.'

'It was never the same, of course,' she sighed. 'Four becoming three has made things, well, unbalanced, I guess. I mean, we've stuck together, but we've missed your energy. Your sense of fun. Your bloody ridiculously slick moves, like the ones you just demonstrated out on the dance floor.'

Sadiki's laugh was music in itself.

'It affected us all,' Lani continued. 'Maya became more ... Maya-esque.'

'I can see that,' he said. 'Good for her. That she's always known herself, I mean.'

'Oh, she certainly has, and does,' Lani agreed and the two of them smiled into their mutual understanding.

'Her kids seem great,' Sadiki said. Lani sensed the sadness of him having only just met Luke and Sophia tonight, but at least she'd been the one to facilitate that after all these years. 'And Tinker?' he asked. 'Is he okay?'

'I think so,' Lani replied. 'You know, he's just doing his thing.'

'Which is?'

'Well,' Lani said, realising Sadiki had no clue as to Tinker's lifestyle as an adult. 'Honestly, I think he's a bit lost.'

They looked across the fairy-light-sprinkled garden to where Tinker was standing with Fiona and, from his body language, obviously being lectured to about something.

'Our Tinker has a bit of a pattern,' she ventured. 'You know, with older women who tend to run rings around him.' She paused, wondering whether she might have crossed some line, but Sadiki nodded.

'Tinker was always the sweet, malleable one,' he said. 'I can see how that might have happened.'

As if to demonstrate the point, Fiona took Tinker's drink and put it down on a nearby table, shaking her finger at him. Then she appeared to walk off in a huff.

'And you?' he asked.

Lani gestured to Bridget, who was deep in conversation with Sophia. 'I think I've fallen on my feet,' she said. 'Sadiki, my wife – can you believe I get to say that – is great. We have so many plans. Even babies.'

'I love that for you,' Sadiki said. 'Immaculate conception?'

Lani grinned. 'IVF.' There was a pause. 'And you're happy?' she asked. 'You seem happy. I mean, we didn't get to talk that much just over coffee about where you're at. But I'd like to hear more.'

'Do you think we could rally the troops so I can tell you all together?' Sadiki asked, and Lani knew instantly that he meant Maya and Tinker.

'I don't think we need to,' Lani said. Because Maya had joined Tinker, spotted them, and were heading over.

•

'Did something just happen with Fiona?' Lani asked as Tinker walked into the gazebo with Maya.

Tinker shrugged. He didn't actually get what had happened between them. Fiona had accused him of drinking too much (he hadn't – he was only on his fourth beer). Then she'd gone on about how he hadn't been paying proper attention to her (which he'd been trying to do, but guessed he'd failed).

'I think she's gone home, but it'll all come out in the wash,' he said, though he really didn't think so. 'I'm not going to stress about it. Not tonight, anyway. My god, the gang's all here. Finally.'

'Thanks to Lani,' Sadiki said.

Tinker felt Maya tense up beside him and understood she still wasn't convinced that was a good thing. He sat on the opposite bench to Lani and Sadiki, patted the seat next to him and Maya reluctantly sat.

'So, Lani was just asking me about my home,' Sadiki said. 'It's a tranquil, beautiful place in Creswick called Soul Haven.'

Tinker liked the sound of 'tranquil'. Whatever it was, seemed like it might be the opposite of his own life.

'And what do you do there?' Maya asked like a schoolteacher, but Sadiki didn't seem to mind.

'What we do there is look after our spiritual selves,' he said, and even in the dark, Tinker could see Maya raise her eyebrows.

'How so?' she asked.

Sadiki smiled. 'With meditation. With workshops. With love,' he replied.

'That sounds interesting,' Tinker said, hoping that Maya would drop those bloody eyebrows. It was making a situation that should have felt good uncomfortable.

'It is, Tinker,' Sadiki said. 'It's a beautiful, inclusive space where everyone can feel belonging and grow into their true selves.' He paused, smiling. 'Which is, of course, a work in progress.'

Tinker smiled back, but it was a weak smile. At the moment, well, most of the time actually, he felt like he was a work in regress.

'After all that happened at St Fabian's, then Joe's horrific death, I was a basket case for many years,' Sadiki said softly.

With that statement, the tension between Tinker, Maya and Lani felt like an electric current.

'And how do you support yourself?' asked Maya, changing the subject at the mention of Joe.

Despite her tone, Sadiki answered without missing a beat.

'By supporting each other.'

Maya shook her head. 'I mean, financially,' she persisted.

'Maya, do you really need to ...' Lani began, but Sadiki was seriously good at staying calm. It was as though the pain was still there, but now it just hovered around him without weighing him down. Tinker could have used a dose of whatever Sadiki was doing to pull that off.

'It's a community,' Sadiki said. 'We work as a hive.'

'A hive has a queen,' Maya insisted.

'Yes,' Sadiki said. 'Exactly.'

'You mean I've been usurped?' Lani joked, tossing a frown at Maya.

'Afraid so,' Sadiki said with a smile. 'I'd like you all to come and witness for yourselves how we do things.'

Lani leaned into him and gave him a kiss on the cheek. 'I'm totally up for that,' she said.

'Me too,' Tinker agreed.

Maya stayed silent.

'Excellent. We hold open sessions every month,' Sadiki said. 'I'll send you the details.'

Tinker had no clue as to what a 'session' might be. He was about to ask, but Sophia clomping over in her pink and orange dress distracted him.

'Bridget asked me to tell you there's people she wants you to meet,' she said to Lani.

Lani got up and held out her hand. Tinker put his on top. Sadiki's came next. Finally, limply, Maya joined in.

Then the group disbanded.

CHAPTER TWELVE

'It's above and beyond awesome!' Sophia said, holding up a copy of *The Australian Women's Weekly*. The first shot was stunning. The two brides with Lani's father between them, all three looking radiant at the pinnacle of the many steps up to the grand Galleta residence. Sophia laid the mag lovingly on the kitchen table.

'That's me,' she said with a romantic sigh, pointing to the smaller photo below. 'And there you are too, Mum. Can you actually believe it?'

'You look beautiful, Sophia,' Maya said.

'I know!' she agreed. 'I'm going to show everyone at school today.'

Sophia began walking towards the bathroom then turned around and came back. From behind the seat, she draped her arms around Maya's shoulders. 'You look beautiful too, Mum,' she said loudly, right in Maya's ear, before heading off again.

Maya had promised herself she wouldn't scrutinise her own image in front of her daughter, that she should model body acceptance and rah, rah, rah. But there it was, right in front of her. She was short, stout and dowdy among the otherwise perfectly beautiful line-up. Why hadn't she realised the tip of her bra was showing above the neckline of the gorgeous gown that would've been a knockout on practically anyone other than her? She put on her reading glasses. What was that on her left cheek? Ah, it was just a speck of toast from breakfast on the page. A small mercy.

'Okay, we're off,' Connor said, coming into the kitchen with Luke.

Maya stood. As she held Luke's shoulders, she replayed the scene of him and Stig-Sadiki captivating the audience with their dancing at the wedding. She wasn't sure if her son was gay but her mind jolted with the understanding that certain talents, certain leanings, could make school a terribly rough ride. All she could do was hope and pray she and Connor had given their son the life skills to cope with the upcoming transition. Stig – goodness, she couldn't think of him as Sadiki, it was too much – had suffered.

Sophia and Luke had gravitated to Stig at the wedding. Even Sophia had put on her listening ears, obviously finding him interesting. But Maya doubted she'd accept the invitation to go and visit him any time soon. It sounded like his *alternative* lifestyle was weird. Odd jobs and a guru? That wasn't how a responsible adult should be living. And she could only hope that Lani and Tinker would leave things alone now, because more interaction with Stig meant more chance of them actually divulging their role in Joe's death.

'Good luck with orientation day, my darling boy,' Maya said.

'Yeah, good luck, Luke,' Sophia added, popping her head out of the bathroom. 'Oh, and Mum, I keep forgetting to look up a word Sadiki mentioned,' she said after Luke and Connor had left.

'What's *myopic*?'

•

'Google tells us that if both biological parents have blue eyes, there's a ninety-nine per cent likelihood that the baby will too,' Bridget said.

Kandolhu Island was everything Lani had hoped it would be for their honeymoon. Their villa was set right on the water. The languid days seemed to stretch out forever and it was just about cocktail hour. She wished that Bridget would give the donor-sperm talk a break though. Lani wanted this too, she did, but Bridget was adamant that they get started as soon as possible.

'Okay, top of the wish list,' Bridget continued. 'Caucasian, one hundred and ninety centimetres – about six foot two. That's ideal, right? D39609720 has an MBA too, so he's got to be smart. And he's Vic-compliant. It all stacks up, hey, kitten?'

'One more swim and then let's order coconut mojitos,' Lani said, diving into the crystal-clear water. Bridget followed. As soon as she opened her mouth, Lani predicted her next comment. Three, two, one …

'Guess you'd better lay off the alcohol.' Shazam. 'You know, I think I'm grateful now that Tinker didn't want to donate his sperm. I mean, the man is clearly a hunk, but he's not the brainiest of folk.'

'Tinker's smart in his own way,' Lani objected, splashing her wife. (Her wife!) 'But, yeah, I reckon we're better off going with a stranger.' It was so weird to think of a stranger's sperm inside her, merging with her egg. 'Not because of his brain capacity, but because it could get too complicated. He'd want to be actively involved. Tinker's always been a doer.'

Bridget stifled a scoff. 'Except in job seeking and keeping,' she said.

Lani felt suddenly pissed off. Her last acting role, in *Neighbours*, was almost ten years ago. Even then, she wouldn't have scored it without her papa's 'introduction' to the producer. 'You could say the same about me,' she said.

'Come on, kitten,' Bridget said, treading water. 'It's just an observation.'

Lani let out a breath. 'Your observations can seem pretty judgey, Bridge.'

'Yes, they can,' she said. 'I'll work on it.'

Lani rolled her eyes, but she was smiling. Unlike most people, Bridget actually would work on it. Whether she'd succeed was another thing, but Lani had to admire the intention.

'Sophia told me that your other old mate, Sadiki, was different but in a fascinating way. I'm sorry I didn't get a chance to talk to him at our wedding. So, are you going to keep in contact with him?'

Lani nodded. 'Actually, Tinker and I are thinking about going to see where he lives. Apparently he's part of some kind of commune in Creswick.'

'Not Maya?' Bridget asked. 'Or me?'

'Maya was invited but she's not keen,' Lani said. 'You know how rigid she is about people's life choices.'

'Judgey? Like your old ball and chain?'

Bridget's teasing was good-humoured, but there was an element of possessiveness at being left out of the invitation that filtered through. Lani dived under the water towards her, pretending to drag a heavy weight on her left foot. They'd have to shore up their boundaries. But not now. Now her wife needed reassurance.

'My poor, entangled mermaid,' Bridget said, opening her arms. They were both laughing as Lani perched on her lap.

'It's hard,' Lani said, nuzzling into Bridget's neck, 'being wed to a human.'

'Yes, sorry about that. Your tail is beautiful, but I'm guessing you'll be needing help to get back up on deck.' She got out and held out a hand to pull Lani up. 'When are you going to the commune, then?'

Stig had mentioned they might like to time their visit with a 'session', whatever that meant.

'I'll check with Tinker,' Lani said. 'But I'm thinking next month.'

'Yes, okay,' Bridget said. 'But … priorities. Can you make it sometime after our appointment at the clinic?'

CHAPTER THIRTEEN

'Welcome home, Sadiki.'

It was as though he'd been holding his breath without knowing it. He paused outside Acharya's house, filling his lungs with country air. It had only been a few days, but it seemed much longer. From her mouth, he felt the name, like a river, flow through him, a sacred christening. Stig coursing downstream and finally out of sight. Sadiki truly and forever coming into full being.

'Come, tell us the story of your visit to the past,' Acharya said, leading the way inside.

'Hi Sadiki.' Patty stood from an armchair in the lounge to greet him. She looked different. The stringy brown hair that had all but covered her eyes was washed, silky and tucked behind her ears. Now, he could see the intricate specks of brown in her hazel eyes.

'Patty's staying with us for a while,' Acharya said.

'I won't be a nuisance,' she declared. 'I promise I'll do all my own dishes and stuff. I brung food. And you still get the big room with the red velvet curtains. I've set myself up in the one with the flowery wallpaper.'

For a moment it flew over his head. Was she talking about his cottage?

'But don't you live with your mother?' he asked.

Patty snorted. She looked at Acharya, who seemed to take it as a cue to speak on the girl's behalf.

'Patty's done great work in the last few days,' Acharya said. 'She's uncovered memories that have lain dormant. But now she's safe, with us.'

With me, you mean. And didn't she insinuate her mother was supportive? Sadiki's ungracious thoughts were intercepted by Acharya. Her expression hardened.

'Yes, with you, in my cottage, Sadiki. And close by me so we can continue to do the necessary work.'

He'd been chastened, and deservedly so. Acharya had never driven the point home before, but the cottage he loved had been bestowed on him by her grace. Yes, he worked at the bakery for free and surrendered his dole, but he didn't even pay rent.

'Sit, Sadiki,' Acharya said. 'Patty, make us some chai.'

•

Sadiki talked through the visit with his mother, the Apostle teaspoons and his father's pride and joy, the Gunnar Nordahl soccer jersey. He repeated the swap-card story, with additions that hadn't featured in the age-regression workshop that had first uncovered the memory, like his father's suit.

As usual, Acharya listened closely. As usual, she empathised. When he came to the grandeur of Lani's wedding though, she paled. Ostentation sat badly with her.

'And the great Gino Galleta oversaw proceedings?' she asked.

'Yes, he did. He was like a clone of himself, Acharya, smarmy and insincere. I realised, because of you, that I must release his influence on my life.'

For a moment, her eyes rolled back in her head and Sadiki understood that she was doing the work – the letting go of past hurts – on his behalf.

Sadiki fetched her a glass of water and she recovered enough to hear the rest.

'Oh, but Maya's children were a revelation,' he told her. 'Luke's a natural performer. Acharya, it was such a spirit-lifter to dance with him. He sort of transformed, and then straight afterwards, he went back to being a shy kid. It was extraordinary.'

'He reminds you of you,' Acharya said, and there she went again, nailing his feelings. 'So, you were saying his godfather is Tinker?'

'Yes,' Sadiki couldn't keep the pain out of his voice. 'They seem really close.'

Acharya nodded, clearly deep in thought on his behalf. 'And the girl?' she asked.

'Sophia's great too, but in a different way. She's bright and funny, exuberant and curious. She certainly interrogated me about my name change. In the end, I reminded her that Catholics get to choose a name when they do their confirmation. That seemed to resonate.'

'So, the parents, Maya and—'

'Connor,' Sadiki finished for her.

'Connor,' Acharya repeated, 'are still believers in the Church of ignorance?'

'More than ever, from what I could tell.'

Acharya shook her head. 'It's such a travesty to fill curious minds with myths and falsehoods,' she said. 'Religion should be regarded as child abuse. At that age Sophia's mind should be nurtured and expanded. Teaching Catholicism to children is like training a parrot. They may speak the lingo, but it's all rote.'

Sadiki shrugged. 'Maya and Connor are good people,' he said.

'And part of the very establishment that shuts you out,' Acharya said wistfully. 'It's beyond hypocritical that Lani and Tinker, as non-believers, took on the roles of godparents. But the children sound wonderful. Tell me, Sadiki, does it sadden you that you've missed out on seeing them grow? Does it pain you that your other friends were chosen to watch over them?'

Sadiki just nodded but his eyes welled with all that he'd missed out on.

Patty returned with a pot of chai and Acharya dismissed her with a nod. 'There are ways – secular ways – of being a godparent to those children,' she said as she poured the tea. 'Ways to develop a strong connection whereby we can help young minds blossom.'

Acharya got up. From the top drawer of a mahogany cabinet, she pulled out a Mac laptop he'd never seen before and held it up. 'What are the duties of a godparent? We can keep in touch with the children,' she said. 'We can be watchful. We can be caring. We can give guidance.'

Sadiki leaned into the peaceful silence. He didn't know exactly what she meant by that, but he trusted in her processes, whatever they might be.

'Did you spread the word of Soul Haven, our alternative to the sad scourge of Catholicism, Sadiki?' she asked eventually.

'I did,' he said. 'And I invited them – Lani, Maya and Tinker, I mean – to come and witness the beauty of our being in a session.'

'Good,' Acharya said. 'Excellent work. You own your name now, my Sadiki, loyal and faithful. You've earned it.'

It was amazing to hear her say that. He hoped they'd come and experience a sample of his wonderful life.

'S'cuse me, Acharya,' Patty said, coming back into the room with her dolls. As she put them on the mantelpiece, he noted that one had a cheap-looking ring wrapped around its arm. The other, a plastic fork protruding from its chest.

'No fork,' Acharya said, soft but firm. Patty gave them a petulant look before removing it. She walked back towards the kitchen.

A knock on the door interrupted them and Acharya went to answer it. The male voice Sadiki heard sounded strangely familiar.

'Melinda went to sick bay last week,' Patty said, coming back from the kitchen. 'Apparently, she had her rags so bad she was cramping. She was clutching her tummy and moaning, and I thought, good, you deserve it. Nothing's really happened with Alice, but I reckon this'll do it.' The doll she replaced back on the mantelpiece had bandages on an ankle. 'I'd stab her if Acharya let me. But I guess I'll have to be satisfied with—'

Sadiki stopped listening to Patty's ramblings. There were two sets of footsteps coming up the hallway. He stood, knowing in his bones something important was about to happen.

Behind Acharya, looking the same except for a little grey hair around his temples, there he was. Still wearing the silver and rose-gold ring with the eternity symbol Stig had found for him at the antique store in Kings Cross, the same day he'd bought the St John with his cup of sorrow teaspoon for his mother. The love of his life. The only love of his life if he didn't count the fiasco that was Joe Carruthers.

Marcus.

CHAPTER FOURTEEN

'Have you found your utopia here, Sadiki?'
Marcus's tone was teasing. The way he stroked Sadiki's cheek just about brought him undone. Not even the sex so much, but the intimacy. The double bed was only just big enough for the two of them.

'You just ... disappeared,' Marcus said, seriously now. 'You didn't even leave a note. It was hard to track you down. I wavered between wanting to and not, I felt so betrayed. Then Rashida, from the squat, went to Ballarat for some reason and said she saw you hanging out with this strange woman she'd done a voodoo course with at Shangri-La. She spoke to her, and Bernadette Robinson said she should look them up in the next few months at a place in Creswick called Soul Haven. So, here I am.'

'I'm so glad you came,' Sadiki said, propping himself up on an elbow. 'I'm sorry for hurting you, but I had to take the opportunity. Acharya saved me. I was so close to the edge, so close to deciding not to live.'

'I know,' Marcus said.

The days and endless haze of scoring and shooting up in

the shared squat lay between them. They'd been each other's comfort for a while, but it hadn't been enough.

'But why would a stranger want to save you?'

'She wasn't a stranger, Marcus. We had history. She was my school counsellor when I was going through hell – the only adult who helped me. For her efforts, she got the sack. In a way, we were both banished. And she was troubled, too, when I ran into her at Kings Cross.'

He took a deep breath before he continued. 'It was like ... fate. She'd been through a terrible time where she'd been unfairly dismissed from her workplace. She was looking into taking legal action but didn't have the funds. Still, even at that dark time in her life, she wanted to talk about me. We sat in the backyard of the poky flat she'd rented and she reflected my life back to me. She'd given it so much thought. She remembered the rumours that had been circulating around St Fabian's about me being a predator and reiterated that she never believed them for a moment.'

'Who could ever have believed that of you?' Marcus asked. 'You're the most gentle person I've ever known.'

'Ah, but they did,' Sadiki said. 'Mud sticks, and I was covered in it. The thing is, she knew so much about me. She said she could see my aura, and that happened to her sometimes, but the signs had never been so strong.'

Marcus raised his eyebrows, but he needed to hear this.

'She told me I had internalised anger about my father coercing me into the army, and about Mother not putting up a fight for me. And that I'd been self-medicating for years to avoid working through all that.'

'Well, yes,' Marcus said. 'But haven't we all been self-medicating?'

'Maybe,' Sadiki replied. 'The major thing, though, was that she identified the fact that my father was abusive. I guess I'd never thought about it that way before. I got that he was a hard man, but—'

'I knew he'd slapped you a couple of times,' Marcus interjected. 'But it's a long bow to call that abuse.'

Sadiki sat up and looked Marcus in the eyes. 'There was more. Acharya knew – could see in my spirit – there was more and that I'd buried it in my subconscious. Even now, I still haven't got to the bottom of it, but I'm on my way. She also knew that when I was able to find it, to find the evidence, I'd be set free. So, I went back to her flat again and again. Every time, she listened. Every time, I felt more heard, more understood. And Marcus, I know you were too out of it to realise, but when I began to understand myself, I started easing up on the drug use. She could see that too. She told me how proud she was. Then, one night, we took mushies together. She asked me to do a manifestation and, for the first time, it was focused on her. We asked the universe for help so she could fight her case and right the wrongs that had been done to her.'

'And?'

'It was only hours afterwards that she got a call from her cousin. Her aunt was dying. I stayed at her place for a few days while she went to visit. When she returned, she told me her aunt had passed, leaving her farm to Acharya in her will.'

'Woo-woo,' Marcus teased. 'Ever heard of coincidence?'

Sadiki indulged him. Marcus didn't understand, yet, how powerful Acharya was. 'She helped me with the rest of the detox, and I went with it because I finally had something to get clean for. She wanted me to go with her. She said that, together, we had unlocked divine powers. It was because of me – because of us, together, and the karma we generated – that her luck had changed. We'd both been pariahs, but now it was clear to her we were kindred spirits and could finally look forward to creating a bright, spiritual future. And it all happened, Marcus. Just like she said it would.'

'I'm happy for you,' Marcus said, kissing him. 'Truly.'

Sadiki drew back so he could see his lover's face. The front door creaked open, followed by banging sounds coming from the kitchenette, cupboard doors opening and closing. They both laughed at how un-utopian it sounded.

'So, my darling cynic, why did you eventually decide to join us?'

'When I got off it,' Marcus said, not needing to explain what 'it' was, 'I realised how alone I was in this world. You'd gone. My old friends were alienated. My parents weren't ready to see me after all the shit I'd put them through, and though I was in loose contact with my sister, Pauline, she didn't trust me anymore. After I'd gone through rehab, which she paid for without really expecting I'd be successful, I started to actually *feel*. And the overwhelming feeling was that I missed you and wanted to be with you again.'

Sadiki cradled Marcus as he continued. They'd talked about all this before, but neither of them cared about the repetition. There was always a different slant on their past experiences – different ways of framing a future together.

'I started thinking about what life – a sober life – could be for us. A little patch of land to call our own, a shack, being off-grid and growing our own veggies. The whole shebang.' He paused. 'Is it possible? Is that something you even want?'

The sheer want of it was an ocean. For a moment, Sadiki couldn't respond. 'Yes,' he said finally. 'More than anything.'

Marcus grinned. 'I wrote about it in my diary – you know, as an incentive.'

Sadiki nudged him. 'Can I see it? I want evidence of your longing for me in black and white.'

'Hmm,' Marcus said, rummaging in his day bag. 'I was sure I had it in here when I arrived last week, but it seems to have disappeared.'

Sadiki pulled on shorts and a T-shirt and walked into the kitchen.

'Patty, did you happen to see Marcus's diary?' he asked. Plenty of his stuff had gone missing since they all moved in together and magically reappeared at his request. He guessed it had something to do with her poverty-stricken past.

'Hmm,' Patty said. 'Actually, now I think of it, something like that dropped out of a bag in the lounge room. I put it in a safe place. Want me to get it for you?'

'Hmm indeed,' Marcus said knowingly as he joined them, on to her ways more quickly than Sadiki had been.

It took Patty at least five minutes before she returned.

'Here it is,' she said brightly, tossing it on the kitchen table. 'You should be a bit more careful with personal stuff.'

'Oh, I will be,' Marcus said. 'You can count on that.'

For a moment, Patty's face reddened, but with the knowledge that she was about to be Acharya's special messenger, her recovery was swift.

'Acharya says she wants to see you both.'

•

Acharya pushed a wisp of hair behind her ear. She always wore the same caftan – black with silver at the end of the sleeves and hem – to the sessions. And there was always an extra twinkle in her eyes just like there was now. She motioned for Sadiki and Marcus to sit.

'It's joyous to witness the reunion of your broken souls,' she said.

'Well, I wouldn't say broken,' Marcus objected with a smile. 'More like a dent here and there, perhaps a few scratches, but the engine is fine.'

Sadiki groaned inwardly, willing Marcus to settle in and listen properly.

'*Broken*,' Acharya repeated, 'is not a dirty word, Marcus. Because it's from that state we can begin to reassemble ourselves.'

She didn't seem to catch his shrug. Or perhaps she chose to ignore it.

'I've been summoning visualisations on your behalf.' Acharya leaned back in her chair, looked up to the rafters and closed her eyes as she continued. 'I see what's best for you. A plot of land. Your own little house. Chickens. Vegetables. Love.'

Marcus gasped, but Sadiki knew this was not coincidence. It was Acharya's remarkable intuition.

'There's an area of Soul Haven I haven't known what to do with until now.'

Acharya opened her eyes and looked at Marcus. 'Sadiki tells me you're an experienced builder.' She switched her attention to Sadiki. 'And you are more than capable of assisting my visualisation to come to fruition.'

Sadiki reached out a hand and Marcus gripped it.

'There's a little half-renovated church on a parcel of land that came with my inheritance. It's close by, so you could remain connected and still retain privacy. It will of course be sanctified afresh, set apart from any religious faith, repurposed, but still, in a sense, a place of worship. And it can be yours.'

Marcus lifted his hand in a signal for Acharya to stop. 'Sadiki and I can't repay you for this,' he said. 'We're grateful for the thought, but—'

Hushed voices came from the kitchen, indicating that preparations for the session had begun. Marnie came into the lounge, wearing a brightly coloured head scarf and a red and gold caftan Sadiki fancied used to belong to Acharya.

'Please excuse the interruption,' she said. 'May I have the kitchen keys, Acharya? We only need flour and milk to prepare damper for this evening.'

'Yes, of course, Marnie,' Acharya said, taking the lanyard from around her neck. 'And please be assured your presence is never an interruption. Your work here is valued. You are precious.'

Marnie bowed her head as she took the lanyard, and Sadiki assumed it was to hide the tears that welled in her eyes.

'Thank you, Acharya,' she said, 'I'm proud that the proceeds from my house can buoy up your good work.'

'She sold her house and gave the money to you?' Marcus asked, eyebrows raised. He winked at Sadiki. 'That's some excellent manifestation.'

'Not to me. To Soul Haven,' Acharya corrected.

Sadiki could see a momentary discomfort in her eyes, and he got why. Each should give according to their capacity, but that wasn't something that required outward acknowledgement. Self-gratification should be internalised and used to expand the spirit.

Acharya stood up. 'I'll give you some space to think about it,' she said.

•

Outside, Marcus draped himself dramatically over the bonnet of his beat-up Subaru. He jumped off and held both of Sadiki's hands. 'It just seems too good to be true,' he whispered, though no one was close by. A couple were putting up their tent unnecessarily close to Sadiki's cottage. The urge for privacy for him and Marcus was acute. It had only been a week since Marcus and Patty moved in but it wasn't going to work with the three of them living in the same small cottage. Acharya had gleaned that. She understood him on such a level that words were hardly necessary.

'How could she possibly have known what we were talking about?' Marcus asked.

'Acharya's highly intuitive,' Sadiki said.

'That's a bit more than intuition,' Marcus said. 'And what do you think the catch is?'

Sadiki smiled. 'There doesn't always have to be a catch, Marcus,' he said. 'And there's a lot about Acharya that seems too good to be true. She's evolved in a way we should aspire to. And this is exactly what we want, right?'

Marcus shrugged. 'What I want is to be with you,' he said. 'What I want is to have you and hold you. But I wasn't thinking of a *group* commitment. I don't want to be beholden to Acharya.'

'It doesn't work like that at Soul Haven,' Sadiki said. 'What we take from Acharya is spiritual guidance. And she always wants the best for her—'

'Followers?' Marcus teased playfully. 'Cashed-up disciples?'

'Community,' Sadiki objected. 'Do you have anywhere else to go?' As soon as he clocked Marcus's dejected expression, Sadiki wished he could erase the words. 'I'm sorry,' he said. 'But could you just try to lean into this experience, for me?'

He wrapped his arms around his lover and felt Marcus, finally, relax against him. When he pulled away to see his face, the gorgeous half-smile that had first attracted him was back.

'Okay then,' Marcus said. 'I'll put aside my scepticism for you. To the mending of broken souls, Acharya style, I say amen. With caveats.'

CHAPTER FIFTEEN

For Tinker, it felt like a perfect mixture of old times and new. Heading up to Creswick with Lani and Maya to see the fourth member of their group fuelled his nostalgia. Especially so since Lani was stirring him relentlessly.

'Listen, Lani,' he said, leaning over Maya in the middle bench seat of his ute to shake a finger. 'You can call me anything you want, but don't insult my chariot.' His beloved car had character but no Bluetooth and the aircon was shot. 'Anyway, chicken shit, when are you going to get your licence?'

'Probably never,' Lani admitted. 'Bridget's always on at me, but hey, only one of us needs to drive now we're joined at the hip most of the time.'

'It'd be smart to do it before you have a baby,' Maya joined in. 'I mean, we've only got the Volvo but it's a safe car, and at least Connor and I can share the pick-ups and drop-offs – what?'

'Nothing,' Lani said, stifling another giggle.

'She's judging you,' Tinker said, and it was satisfying to see Lani get a jab in the arm. 'So, why the change of mind about coming?'

'Well, there's a few reasons,' Maya said. 'One, I have to be on guard in case either of you stumble into a conversation about Joe. Two, I'm interested to see how Stig – Sadiki, I mean – lives. And three—'

'Three?' Lani prompted.

'Three,' Maya said, exhaling, 'is that I suspect Sophia thinks I'm myopic.'

'Which means "short-sighted",' Lani filled in for Tinker, 'not expansive.'

'Der,' Tinker said, though he actually didn't think he'd ever heard the word. 'That couldn't be further from the truth, Maya,' he fibbed. As much as he loved her, Maya was that word – whatever it was again – down to a tee.

'So, Tinker, how's it going with Fiona?' Lani asked as he looked for exit signs from the Western Freeway, obviously sidetracking so she didn't have to fib along with him.

Tinker had thought about how he was going to spin what had happened. It seemed right to get at least some entertainment value out of what she'd told him. 'Fiona broke up with me a few days back. She reckoned there was no point in having a gigolo without the jig.'

Lani's laugh was a snort. 'Maybe you just weren't that into her,' she said in an American accent.

'True,' Tinker said, laughing along. He had zero inclination to admit the pain. The fact was that after he'd hung up the phone to Fiona, he'd felt worthless. It was best to shrink the whole experience into a joke. And he had less than zero desire to tell them she'd put five thousand dollars into his bank account as a parting gift. Which was lucky, because he'd been on the brink of having his gas and electricity cut off.

'If it's any consolation, Tinker,' Maya said, 'I think you're too good for that kind of relationship.'

Tinker shrugged as though it was no big deal. He drew Lani's and Maya's attention to the incredible full moon ahead and listened as they *ooh*ed and *aah*ed.

But when they reached the rusted sign that read 'Soul Haven', there was silence. The three musketeers were about to go on another adventure with light overnight bags.

And heavy secrets.

•

Tinker didn't know where the property boundaries fell, but whatever the case, the land seemed to stretch out forever. A dozen or so cars, some flashy, others rust buckets, were parked on a paved area. He pulled into an available space and they sat for a moment.

'So – here goes,' Tinker said.

Just then, Sadiki emerged from the large bluestone house. He was with another guy about their age and a slightly older woman with short auburn hair and a flowing black and silver robe.

'Looks like our Sadiki's found Maleficent,' Lani joked, but no one even smiled.

They got out of the car and the group approached to greet them.

'You came,' Sadiki said as though it surprised him.

'Greetings,' the woman said with a strained smile. She was unusual-looking, with green eyes set wide and her cheekbones high. Plus, she was tall – at least six foot.

'I'm Acharya,' she said, 'and I'm humbled to welcome you to this month's full-moon session.'

Tinker went for a handshake but got two kisses, one on each cheek.

Sadiki did the rest of the introductions. 'And this is Marcus,' he finished.

Tinker got straightaway that they were lovers. It was in Sadiki's eyes, Marcus's too, and it made Tinker feel like punching the air for his friend.

Lani did the rounds but seemed super focused on Acharya. Actually, Acharya seemed super focused on her too.

'I feel like I know you from somewhere,' Lani said eventually.

Acharya shook her head, but now Maya was staring at her too. She snapped her fingers trying to remember, but Lani got in first.

'Oh my god, I do know you. You're, um – Miss Robinson.'

Acharya's nostrils flared.

'You are,' Maya agreed. 'Either that or you've got a doppelganger.'

'I remember now,' Lani said. 'We consulted you a few times when Maya and I went to St Audrey's, right? You *tried* to help us help Stig.'

The emphasis on 'tried' seemed to annoy Acharya further because her brow furrowed. Only now did Tinker notice she hadn't kissed either of his female friends.

'I used to be Bernadette Robinson,' she conceded finally.

Lani threw her hands in the air. 'Sadiki, you rat,' she said kind of jokingly, kind of not. 'Why didn't you tell us our old school counsellor is your Acharya?'

'Because they are two different entities,' Acharya said. 'Yes, before my transformation I worked at St Fabian's and St Audrey's.' She paused, looking Lani directly in the eyes, almost like she was pinning her down. 'Until I realised I was no match for the toxic patriarchy, led by your father.'

Lani was so used to being instantly admired that the force of the comment made her take a step backward.

Maya stepped between the two women, hands on hips. 'Matriarchies can be just as toxic,' she said. 'I believe the name you bestowed on our friend means "loyal" and "faithful", and they're qualities to be admired for sure.' She paused, taking Lani's hand in solidarity. 'Unless, of course, the person you're pledging them to thinks themselves above others. Because the only *entities* that should be worshipped are Jesus Our Lord and the Holy Spirit.'

There was a patient smile on Acharya's face now and Tinker knew that would be driving Maya crazy.

'Well, that's a delusion,' Acharya said, standing at her full height. 'But you always were an unquestioning soul, Maya. Perhaps this session might open your mind a little. You believe in miracles, don't you?'

Sadiki looked as uncomfortable as Tinker felt with the exchange, but Marcus seemed kind of amused. There was an awkward pause. Tinker wondered how to fill it. The goats meandering up to them were a welcome distraction.

'This one,' Sadiki said, tickling the smaller black and white kid under the ear, 'is Sadie.' The larger, off-white one made a beeline for Maya. 'And your new friend is Gertrude.'

'Sorry, I'm not really a goat person,' Maya said, standing behind Tinker for protection. Everyone chuckled as Gertrude put her nose in the air and walked off, but Lani remained unfazed.

'Well, I do hope you all enjoy the session,' Acharya said, walking back towards the house, and Tinker breathed a sigh of relief that the moment of tension had passed.

'Come, we'll show you around,' Sadiki said.

The set-up was like many music festivals Tinker had been to, but on a smaller scale. A huge bonfire was burning in the centre of an open space, with people huddled around it. Others were setting up tents. Three portaloos stood in a row a short distance to one side. On the other side, a woman was arranging food and drinks on a long trestle table. A sign hung on the front: *Donations gratefully accepted. Please give according to your capacity.* Which, Tinker thought, was fair enough. All this cost money. Lani would be cool with contributing his share for him.

'The session,' Marcus said in a spooky voice as they made their way towards Sadiki's cottage, 'begins in thirty minutes.' He kissed Sadiki on the lips before turning to head back to the fire. 'Don't be late,' he said over his shoulder, 'or you'll miss the virgin sacrifice.'

CHAPTER SIXTEEN

As the guys went off to explore, Maya sat with Lani in the lounge room of Sadiki's cottage.

'I just feel like escaping from this stupid place,' Lani said. 'Miss Robinson is such a bitch. Who does she think she is, bringing my father into this?'

Maya grimaced. It was true that Mr Galleta was tricky, and that Lani had always found him relatively unsupportive as a parent, except in the financial sense. It was also true that you could criticise your own family as much as you wanted, but as soon as someone else did, you got protective.

'It seemed awfully pointed,' she said. 'I'm sorry, Lani.' She paused. 'I'm just trying to trace back to when we first met with her, I mean, when she was a school counsellor.'

Lani sank into Sadiki's sky blue velvet couch and Maya followed suit, only realising how tired she felt when its softness surrounded her. The cottage was like a cocoon. The four mismatched chairs around Sadiki's small dining table, each with handmade, knitted cushions in deep blues and golds, gave the place texture. There was barely a blank space on the walls between his collection of paintings. Maya suspected that most were amateur ones of the landscape outside their door. She handed Lani the glass of water she'd poured in the kitchenette and Lani took a sip.

'I saw her a few times alone before we went together,' she said. She put her head in her hands. 'Mostly I was complaining about my parents.'

'What kinds of things did you tell her?'

'Well, it's embarrassing now,' Lani said. 'But mostly it was about how Papa refused to give me positive feedback.' She sighed. 'I can't remember the specifics, but I do remember seeing her after our last performance of *The Wiz*. I think I was probably a bit dramatic. I'd already planned how I'd put it, you know, to get full impact.'

Maya smiled her encouragement.

'Okay, it went something like this,' Lani said. 'It doesn't seem to matter what I do. I just get criticised. Like, wouldn't you think Papa would give me some *accolades*? He was raving about Stig's performance as the Cowardly Lion. But you know what he said about my Dorothy? "You did quite well, Lani." In bed that night I replayed his comment over and over until I charged into their room, woke both him and Mama up and demanded a proper critique.'

'Did your dad give you one?' Maya asked.

'Yes,' Lani said. 'He said my performance was quite good. Again. And to go back to bed.'

Maya had to work hard to suppress the urge to laugh, especially given the whining tone Lani was putting on. 'So, how did Miss Robinson advise you?'

'She said that Papa might be trying to help my development as a performer. And I told her it was all stick and no carrot, and that my parents were both too preoccupied with their own lives to give any thought to mine. Or, you know, something like that. Then I told her – and I totally remember this because I'd already planned to say it before I went to the appointment – "It's like I'm *invisible*."'

At that, Maya couldn't resist a giggle. Lani Galleta was the least invisible person she'd ever known in her life. It was a relief that her friend could see the funny side because she laughed too.

'Then Miss Robinson – now turned Guru Acharya – gave me a bunch of sage and said I should burn it around my home to clear out bad energy. I'm sure you can remember how that went down,' Lani finished, snorting water through her nose with the hysterics that followed.

Maya did remember. Yvette had started with opening every window in their house and followed it up with a visit from a professional to get rid of what she insisted was a lingering smell.

'I only saw Miss Robinson once,' Maya said. 'In my deadly earnest way, I'd started a petition to stop the school sending Stig away.'

'Yes!' Lani said. 'I'd forgotten that.'

Maya had suspected as much. She adored Lani, but when things didn't directly involve her, she tended not to pay heed. 'We'd got about a hundred signatures from the girls at St Audrey's,' she reminded her. 'But none of the boys from St Fabian's – except Tinker – would participate in case they got ostracised by the jocks who were tormenting Stig. And I tried with the teachers too, but no-go. I figured a signature from the school counsellor could help. She was pretty nice, remember? She did sign it.'

Lani leaned forward and put her hand over Maya's. 'Ah, yes,' she said, finally twigging. 'Didn't you take it to the board and make an impassioned plea on Stig's behalf?'

There was lots of noise coming from outside now, or perhaps Maya just hadn't noticed it before. 'It didn't work,' she added. 'As you know.'

'Yeah – you gave it your best shot,' Lani said. 'But what I don't get is why she hates Papa. Or why she parked outside our place for hours one day.'

Maya thought for a moment. Maybe Lani's recollection of her parking in their street wasn't entirely irrelevant, like she'd initially deemed it. 'Perhaps he had something to do with her getting sacked?' she ventured.

'She got sacked?' Lani asked.

'Yes, I remember now. She got marched off the St Fabian's campus by security. At least that was the rumour going around.'

'Hmm,' Lani said. 'Even if that was true, don't you think it's over-the-top that she'd be hanging on to resentment for this long? If Papa was involved, he could only influence the school board, not make the decision. And I mean, all that happened twenty years ago. Now she's supposed to be this … this freaking new and improved model, right? Like, not very evolved.'

'Who's not very evolved?' Sadiki asked, coming back into the cottage with Tinker and Marcus.

'Us,' Maya answered quickly. She snuck a look at Lani, who clearly knew what it meant. Stig – or Sadiki – had been through hell and they were part of the cause. If they hadn't done what they'd done the night they went to see Joe ...

The least they could do for Sadiki now was to go through with the session he'd invited them to attend. They didn't have to buy into any of what was about to happen, but they'd both suck it up.

Lani gave Maya a sly wink. 'Yep,' she said. 'So, is it all ready to go out there?'

Sadiki and Marcus were holding hands. They seemed totally besotted with each other.

Marcus gave Sadiki a peck on the cheek. 'Take us to your leader.'

CHAPTER SEVENTEEN

I am the pure child that I was.

The full moon was playing along with the unfolding charade, looming above the gathering in the night sky. Lani snuck a look at her phone. It was almost 10 pm. She wondered if four hours on the property demonstrated enough interest in Sadiki's new life.

She refused to join the chant, but for Sadiki's sake, she moved her lips. Had she ever been a pure child? She guessed so, though in her parents' house it wasn't purity that was valued. What she'd learned, what they'd modelled, was how to get what you wanted. But that wasn't a bad thing. Was it?

I seek enlightenment. I look up to the full moon.

More like howl to it, werewolf-style.

She shouldn't have bothered touching up her make-up. These people were wild. It was a balmy night, but perhaps Lani shouldn't have left her Prada coat in Sadiki's cottage. It was a bit of a worry he'd left it unlocked.

We praise and thank and love you, Acharya.

Maya edged closer, a sour expression on her face. 'If that's not worship, I don't know what is,' she whispered. 'Just look at everyone treating Miss Robinson like she's some kind of messiah. It's ... sacrilegious.'

I am cherished. I deserve to be cherished.

Lani certainly hadn't felt cherished when *Acharya* took a dig at her. The sins of the father crap could go jump. And of course they were out in nature, but weren't there some whiffs of church here? The repeated refrains. *Lord, I am not worthy to receive you, but only say the word and my soul shall be healed.* Maybe she should recite that aloud and see if anyone noticed.

'Okay, this isn't working for me,' Maya whispered. 'Let's ditch the twilight zone for a bit and get a cup of tea.'

Lani certainly didn't want a cup of tea, but she'd spotted some beers in an ice bucket on the trestle table and she could murder one of those.

I am powerful, the others continued chanting. *The kingdom is within me.*

She didn't want to offend Sadiki, but he was over the other side of the bonfire and wouldn't know if they disappeared for five minutes. Miss Robinson – who'd positioned herself at the top of a man-made hill (and wasn't that a faux altar?) so she could lead the chant over that bloody microphone and overlook proceedings – would notice. But that just made it more tempting. Screw Acharya. Lani wasn't about to become anyone's disciple, let alone a creepy ex–school counsellor.

There was no one manning the goodies on the trestle table. Lani helped herself to some damper, opened a beer and took a large swig, while Maya poured tea from a thermos. It wasn't until Maya had almost finished the whole mug that Lani noticed the label.

'Shit, did you see this?' she asked.

'See what?' Maya looked at the sticker but it didn't seem to register with her. 'I need my specs,' she admitted.

Lani took the mug from Maya and put it on the table. She turned the thermos so the print was more visible in the firelight. 'Maya, I don't think that's regular tea,' she said.

Maya gulped. 'No, it's honey and lemon,' she said tentatively. '*Magic Tea: for ceremony only,*' she read.

'Well, at least you got the ceremony bit right,' Lani said in an attempt to lighten the situation as the chanting continued.

'Fuck,' said Maya.

•

'It's fine,' Maya said when Tinker joined her and Lani. 'I reckon I'm not susceptible to drugs. Remember the time in Year Ten when Barry convinced me to take a puff of a joint? All I felt was a bit woozy.'

Tinker studied Maya's face. Her pupils seemed to be the normal size. 'Or maybe it just hasn't kicked in yet,' he said.

'Now, partner up with someone you don't know.' Acharya's voice came through speakers as she moved through the crowd with a roving microphone. 'Please, find yourselves a seat or cushion and we can begin our important self-discovery work.'

'Go,' Maya told them. 'If I need you, I'll call out, but I can tell nothing's going to happen.'

Tinker and Lani shared a nervous grimace before finding available spots where they could keep Maya in their sights. Tinker had been sitting cross-legged for a minute or so when a woman around his age joined him on the opposite cushion. She had long dark hair, parted in the middle. The bonfire light flickered across her face, highlighting a beautiful open smile.

'Tell this new person, with every ounce of honesty you can muster, why you're here,' Acharya said.

Tinker's mind went blank. There were too many reasons why he was here. How could he possibly untangle them to get close to the truth?

'My name's Zanni. Would you like me to begin?' the woman asked, and Tinker nodded with relief. He snuck a glance at Maya, who seemed to be okay, though the way she was chatting to a young man with multiple face piercings seemed a little unmyopic.

'I want to do this properly,' Zanni said. 'The thing is, I rarely do anything properly. I mean, it's not that I don't toss myself into the mix. The problem is ... I toss myself into the *wrong* mix and spin around like I'm in a bloody rinse cycle.' She paused, rolling her eyes. 'Well, that was truly eloquent, wasn't it? Do you mind if I start again?'

Tinker smiled and nodded. Zanni might not have thought her words were well chosen, but he got it. He really did.

'You're very good-looking, aren't you?' she said. 'I wonder sometimes, what that might feel like. Jesus, I'm sorry. Can I get a third take?'

'It's okay,' Tinker said. 'I know it's an advantage. But I also feel like it's … well, stunted my development. It's as though the other parts of me get kind of stuffed down to base level.'

'Really?' Zanni replied. 'That's so interesting. And thank you for not denying you're hot. That would have been disappointing.'

'Take three?' Tinker reminded.

Zanni leaned forward. 'I was walking past Cosmic Counselling the day after Warren broke up with me, so I decided to go in. I should have seen the split coming, the red flags were everywhere, but I'm a master of denial. It's one of my superpowers.'

'Congratulations,' Tinker joked. That beautiful smile returned, but he could see the sadness too.

'Another talent I possess,' she said, 'is choosing emotionally unavailable partners, on repeat. If it was a sport, I'd be an Olympic gold medallist.'

'Oh, I don't know,' Tinker found himself saying. 'I reckon I'd give you a run for your money.'

'My subcategory would be married men,' Zanni said.

'Mine would be older women.'

'I walk in with my eyes firmly closed.'

'Is there another way to do it?'

Zanni grinned. 'So, what is it about older women that appeals to you?' she asked.

Tinker shrugged. 'Their experience, I guess. They know who they are.'

'But do they?' she challenged. 'Or have they just learned how to *look* like they know? That's what I thought about Warren.'

She folded her arms. 'But it occurred to me later that I was an experiment. Some dalliance to tick off his bucket list. I'm not even sure I was a real person for him.'

Tinker reached out and touched Zanni on her cheek. 'Yep, flesh and blood, I'm afraid,' he said. And, yes, it was corny but, fuck, it felt good to make Zanni laugh. And maybe this conversation wasn't the whole truth, but at least it was gnawing around the edges of honesty.

'I'm staying here for a few days,' Zanni said, pointing to a one-man tent across the other side of the fire. 'Acharya and I are doing an intensive on my daddy issues. Mine was a very charming player. Being under his gaze was a rare gift that he bestowed and then removed at whim, like a magic trick.' She lifted a pretend hat. 'See the rabbit?' she asked. She put the hat back on and drew it down again. 'Gone!'

The way Zanni spoke was so … original. Tinker hoped he could keep up, but he also had the feeling that, for once, he was. 'If it's mummy issues for me, I'm not seeing it,' he said. 'Mine's solid as a rock. The only thing I can think of is that Mum thought everything I did was beyond amazing. I didn't need to chase her for attention, that's for sure. But maybe—'

A tap on the shoulder interrupted his thoughts. 'Hey, Tinker,' Lani said, nodding a quick hello to Zanni. She put a hand over her mouth, but her eyes told him she was trying to stifle a nervous giggle.

Tinker looked over to where Lani was pointing and saw why.

CHAPTER EIGHTEEN

Gertrude was not, in Sadiki's experience, a friendly goat. The many times he'd tried to pat her, she'd headbutted him and not in a playful way. She tolerated Acharya in the sense that she liked to walk beside her, but even then, refused to be touched. So, it was a small miracle to see Gertrude and Maya lying flat on their bellies in the grass, foreheads together as though they were in deep conversation. The unusual scene had interrupted the session for a few minutes, but as the minutes ticked by, most people resumed their one-on-one chats.

'Maya's under the influence of Magic Tea,' Lani explained as Sadiki approached. The three of them stood back. Maya's mouth was definitely moving. He wasn't sure whether Gertrude's was, but it wouldn't surprise him. 'Do you think we should do something?'

It was a beautiful sight to see Maya opening up this way, getting to explore parts of herself as yet undiscovered.

Tinker seemed to view it similarly. 'I think we just leave her be,' he said. 'She looks happy enough.'

They watched in silence. As Maya rose to her knees, Gertrude mirrored her position, sitting back on her hind legs. Maya made prayer hands and kissed the goat's snout. As she got up and walked towards them, her movement was leaden, as though her brain had forgotten to send a message to her feet. They went to meet her.

'I've found it,' Maya said, moving her arms in an expansive, circular motion. 'It's here! We're all *here*.'

'Yes, we're all here,' Lani agreed. 'Just like in the old days.'

'No,' Maya said urgently. 'I mean we're *all* here. Joe is Gertrude. Gertrude is Joe.'

Sadiki started at the mention of Joe. Yes, mushroom trips could be wildly unpredictable and elements of the past might merge with the real and the imagined, the past and the present, but Joe hadn't really been part of Maya's life. So why was this happening? Was there some kind of sign he should be taking from this?

'There is no death,' she continued, 'just change of form. Can you see it?'

What Sadiki could see, mostly, was Lani's and Tinker's discomfort at seeing Maya so … abandoned. Or perhaps the mention of Joe was part of it?

And now he saw it. Joe's death had rocked his world to the core, but the nature of it, the brutality, had been a shock for all the students at St Fabian's and St Audrey's.

'We are forgiven,' Maya said, reaching up to the moon and spinning in circles. 'Feel it. Can you feel it? I can feel it. Release. Release. Release.'

'Forgiven for what?' Sadiki ventured.

'Maya's hallucinating,' Lani reminded him. 'She doesn't have a clue what's going on.'

'Still, it could mean something,' he insisted. 'Something outside our current plane.'

'Or it could be gobbledygook,' Lani said.

'Yes, that's what it is,' Tinker joined in. 'Maya's just … raving.'

As if to demonstrate the fact, Maya fell to the ground and started simultaneously laughing and crying. 'Let's say it. Let's sing it. Let's pray it,' she said through the hysterics.

Lani and Tinker tried to help her up but she pushed them away.

'Forgiveness is freedom,' Maya declared.

A group had gathered to watch her personal epiphany. Some grabbed hold of her final words, improvising as they went along.

Forgiveness is freedom. Soul Haven is the path. Forgiveness is freedom. Soul Haven is the path.

When Maya threw up though, the group disbanded.

'I think we need to get her home, Sadiki,' Lani said, and it was odd that her voice was wavering and that she was so keen to cut short Maya's experience.

But immediately, Tinker backed her. 'I know the rest of us have had our fair share of trippy experiences,' he said. 'But not Maya. She'd be … I mean, the real Maya would be—'

'Horrified,' Lani finished for him. 'I'm sorry, Sadiki, but we have to go.'

•

'Fuck, that was close,' Lani hissed as she cleaned Maya up in Sadiki's cottage. 'Tinker, let's get out of here before she can say anything else. I've left some make-up in the bathroom along with the crucifix that fell off Maya's necklace when she was puking.'

'I love you,' Maya swooned, seemingly unperturbed by the foul breath she blew on Lani. 'We all love each other. Truth is good. Forgiveness is good. Where's Gertrude? Where's Joe? Ah, they're here.'

Gertrude wasn't there, and Joe as sure as hell wasn't, but Lani made some cooing noises to calm her. 'Please, Maya, don't say anything more about Joe,' Lani tried. 'Think about the impact it would have on your family – on Luke and Sophia. Remember, you were the one who was most afraid Sadiki would find out what we did.'

'The earthly self is bound but the spirit soars.'

Jesus, Lani wished she could still Maya's 'soaring spirit' at the moment.

'Hurry up, Tinker,' she called, and finally he was at the door with their bags.

•

When they left the cottage, people were packing up. Gertrude strode through the dwindling crowd like an aggro bouncer calling last drinks, but thankfully Maya seemed to have moved on. Instead, she was dancing to some inner music, hands in the air and hips swaying in a very un-Maya way.

'It's customary to say goodbye and thank Acharya for her wonderful work,' Sadiki said as he wandered up to them.

Fronting up to Acharya was the last thing Lani felt like doing. The reinvented school counsellor, who'd switched pencil skirts and court shoes for caftans and sandals and decided that made her some kind of guru, was behind the trestle table with a queue of devotees before her. As Sadiki went to join Marcus, Lani backtracked to get Tinker for support. He was joined at the hip to the woman he'd been talking to during the one-on-one session. He introduced her as Zanni. From the long black plaits and multiple pleather bracelets, Lani assumed she was a session regular.

'So, what's the preferred amount for donations?' Lani asked her.

'Whatever you can afford,' Zanni said, focusing completely on Tinker. 'I've been having private counselling with Acharya that she hasn't charged me for, she's so generous. But I have money now, so I'm going to donate a hundred dollars towards tonight's' – she grinned at Tinker before she continued – 'enlightening session.'

'Then that's what we'll do,' Tinker said.

Since she knew she was the one who would pay, Lani itched to call him out. But as the queue moved forward, he lagged behind with Zanni.

Eventually there was only one person in front of her. He keyed in one thousand dollars. She wondered how much Acharya would rake in tonight. How much did this prophet profit? It would have been a good line to pass on, but there was no one to receive it.

Lani took a deep breath, pulled up the banking app on her phone and stepped forward.

'Thank you for the session, Miss Robinson,' she said, and honestly, she hadn't fully intended to call her that. But it was pleasing to wipe the beatific smile off her face.

'You're welcome,' she said. 'I understand that you, of all people, could benefit from stepping outside your little circle of privilege.'

Though her heart was thumping, Lani kept her voice even. 'Really?' she asked. 'How so?'

That bloody smile returned. 'Here, with effort, we cleanse ourselves of sins from the past.' She leaned forward, hovering her hands over Lani's shoulders and dropped her voice to a whisper. 'The universe will conspire so that you don't pass on your father's legacy.'

Around Lani, this fucked-up little universe kept spinning. Tinker flirting, Maya dancing.

'Are you trying to curse me?' Lani demanded.

'*Trying* implies I may not succeed. But I always do, as has been proven by how I ultimately saved Sadiki. You see, unlike you, as a spoonfed, eternal infant, I make my own way in the world.'

Lani felt herself disintegrating. Tonight, in a way she'd never experienced, people were walking all over her. She couldn't find words.

The witch closed her eyes and tapped her temples. 'As I enter your psyche,' she said, 'I see many manifestations of your transgressions. Oh, and now I see Joe Carruthers. I see a bottle ... no, two, no, three empty bottles of Hibiki. Isn't that the whisky your father drinks?'

Lani stifled a gasp. Reports of the fire didn't mention alcohol and they sure as hell didn't mention that Lani, Maya and Tinker were there earlier that night. Papa had seen to that. So, how could Acharya have known? Did the witch really have some of the powers Sadiki credited her with? Lani doubted that. But whatever she was up to sent a shiver down her spine.

With herculean effort, she roused herself. Already, Lani knew that she'd never tell anyone about the hex. To do so would give it validation.

She refreshed her banking app and typed in the amount she was willing to contribute. One dollar. She arranged her face into an angelic smile that would trump Miss Robinson's by a country mile.

'That's on behalf of Tinker and Maya too,' she said. 'You're welcome.'

•

'Sadiki reckons Acharya has those kinds of … visualisations,' Tinker said as they pulled out of Soul Haven. Except for the moon, the night was jet black and his ute's headlights weren't as bright as they should be.

'I don't buy that for a minute,' Lani said. 'Her telling me that she sees bottles of Hibiki at Joe's the night he died is just too close to home. Maybe she knows something?'

'Like what?' Tinker asked. Lani was obviously in a strange mood after everything that had gone down.

'I don't know,' she snapped. 'Maybe she has inside knowledge. Anyway, aren't visualisations supposed to manifest something good?'

'I'm good,' Maya said between them on the bench seat. 'And you are,' she continued, leaning on Tinker's shoulder.

'What about me?' Lani prompted.

'Eye of the needle,' Maya cooed.

'Oh, shut up,' Lani retorted and Tinker laughed, happy for the diversion.

'I think the regular Maya is coming back to us,' he said. 'Anyway, Lani, don't get stuck on the whole "bottles at Joe's place" thing. Tonight was interesting.' Zanni's number was in his phone – the very last one on his list of contacts and it felt like a sign that things might be about to change for him. 'Thanks for putting the hundred bucks in for me. I'll pay you back.' He wouldn't, but Lani was always cool about stuff like that.

Lani folded her arms. 'I didn't put in a hundred for you,' she said. 'I put in a dollar – between the three of us, because that's what Miss bloody Robinson deserves.'

'Money is a symbol,' Maya said.

Tinker took a left onto the highway. This wasn't good. Sadiki would be upset if he found out. And Tinker didn't know whether he was keen to do another session, but he'd like to keep his options open. What he did know was that he wanted to see Zanni again. Lani could be so selfish.

'Yep, money is a symbol all right, Maya,' Lani said. 'It's a symbol of fuck you, Miss Robinson.'

'Gertrude loves me,' Maya said. 'Joe forgives.'

The driver's window was rattling. Tinker pressed the button, but it still refused to go all the way up. 'Okay, maybe she's not quite herself yet,' he said as Lani wrapped the rug Fiona had given him, the one she made sure he knew was cashmere, around Maya. 'What will we do with her?'

'She can come home with me,' Lani said. 'Connor thought we were going to stay the night anyway.'

'Good,' Tinker said. 'And I'm guessing we'll keep the shroom trip to ourselves.'

'Yes, for sure,' Lani said.

Maya lay her head on Lani's shoulder. For the rest of the drive, they were quiet. After Tinker dropped them off, he checked his phone. It was 3.25 am and there was a new message.

He turned the ute around and drove back to Creswick.

CHAPTER NINETEEN

'We choose you to be our baby daddy,' Bridget said, coming up behind Lani and looking at her through the bathroom mirror as she brushed her hair with her new Mason Pearson. Thank god Tinker had, at least, picked up her Prada coat from a stand in the bathroom in Sadiki's cottage because he sure as hell hadn't retrieved the other stuff they'd left in there. She was also down a tube of her favourite lipstick, which, to her chagrin, had been discontinued. And Maya was missing the small silver crucifix she wore on a necklace that night, which wasn't necessarily a bad thing since crucifixes gave Lani the creeps.

'Heston of the brown-green eyes, straight hair, O-positive blood type. Heston of the MBA, full lips and light brown eyebrows, you're our hero and we salute you,' Bridget continued. 'This child will be so well loved, blessed with a beautiful life.'

Lani forced a smile. The genetic testing had gone without a hitch. The latest blood test and ultrasound had shown her hormone levels to be fine. And yesterday, the nurse had informed them there was a single mature follicle ready and waiting.

But even after more than a fortnight, Acharya's curse dominated Lani's thoughts.

The universe will conspire so that you don't pass on your father's legacy.

'Lani, are you okay?' Bridget asked.

'I'm just a bit jittery,' she told Bridget, deliberately letting her misjudge the cause.

'I'll be right there by your side,' Bridget said. 'They say it's no more painful than a pap smear. It'll be done and dusted in a flash, and you'll be fabulous.'

'Of course I will,' Lani said, trying her best to lock the curse out of her brain. 'So the vial of sperm from our knight in shining armour will be washed in the clinic? Better clean sperm than dirty. Though sperm in general has always struck me as distasteful.'

'Not these little darlings, these are glorious,' Bridget said. 'And we have two vials, remember? It could take a few rounds before we get our bundle of joy. But Heston's been on the register for ages, so it looks likely we'll be able to try for a genetic sibling down the track.'

Lani bit her lip, nerves, excitement and apprehension battling for priority. They'd considered all the possibilities and both she and Bridget were convinced the intra-uterine insemination method would yield the best results. They might have to go through the process a few times, but the doctor seemed confident.

Fuck you, Miss Robinson.

'Kitten, we're going to be the best mothers ever,' Bridget said.

Lani wasn't sure she'd be the best mother ever. She wasn't even sure she'd be middling, but she was as ready as she'd ever be. She turned around and kissed her wife. The passion was building when they were interrupted by a loud knock on the door, followed in a split second by another.

Sophia was in her checked school dress, backpack slung over one shoulder. Every time Lani saw her, she seemed closer to being a fully-fledged woman. She wore her new fringe with chutzpah, but her goddaughter's attitude seemed to be changing too. Right now, she looked surly.

'Lani,' she said, 'will you swear to tell me the truth?'

•

'Mum and Dad were fighting,' Sophia said. She drank a bit of the smoothie Bridget had made for her before going upstairs to give them privacy.

'What about?'

Sophia wiped her lip. 'It started out with Dad saying it might be time for Mum to get a job. And she said, "I have several. I'm a taxi driver and a cook and a cleaner and a psychologist."'

Lani had heard it all before. She shrugged. 'Well, I guess it's true, in a sense,' she said. 'But, Sophia, that sounds like a pretty normal arg—'

Sophia put her hand up in a stop sign. 'It wasn't though,' she said. 'Dad was telling Mum she was in a rut. You know, tennis on Mondays, coffee with other mums on Tuesdays – that sort of thing.'

Lani nodded and poured the rest of the smoothie from the blender.

'Then, Mum spat the dummy and said this.' She picked up her phone and read from her notes. '"Maybe you don't know me as well as you think, Connor. Maybe you're myopic. Because guess what? When we went to see Sadiki for that session, I had a magic mushroom trip and it was amazing. I talked with a goat called Gertrude and she talked back. The whole experience was mind-blowing. And, you know what, I might even do it again."'

Lani gulped.

'Mum's always going on about drugs,' Sophia said angrily. 'She's all, "Just say no."'

She threw her hands up, almost knocking over Lani's Dior blue Cannage glass. Lani pushed it towards the centre of the counter for safety.

'So, what I want to find out is, did she really have magic mushrooms?'

Lani sighed. 'Isn't that a question you should put to your mum?'

'I did! She told me I must've heard wrong, but she was lying. I was at the top of the stairs, writing it down word for word. Lani – you swore you'd always tell me the truth.'

Lani closed her eyes tightly. She felt the push–pull – being someone Sophia could confide in versus loyalty to her friend.

'The truth,' she started slowly, 'is complicated, Sophia. Your mum didn't know there were mushrooms in the tea she drank. So the answer is yes, she had some, and yes, she did have some out-there experiences. But it was an accident. Your mum is still anti-drugs.'

Sophia whacked a hand on her forehead. 'She said she might do it again,' she reminded Lani. 'Mum's a liar and a *hypocrite*,' she continued after a pause. 'And not just about drugs.'

'Oh, sweetheart,' Lani said. 'I know it's hard to understand. But when you get older life gets more and more complicated. Sometimes, things you thought were set in stone, ideas about yourself and other people, can go in unexpected directions. The thing is, everyone's a hypocrite in some ways. But your mum just wants to protect you.'

'Well, she can't,' Sophia said.

The poor girl was crying now. As she put her head in her hands, her fringe lifted.

'Sophia, you're bleeding,' Lani gasped. 'My god, what happened to your birthmark?'

'I hate my birthmark,' Sophia said between sobs.

'Oh, darling, no! Your birthmark makes you—'

'I don't *want* to be unique,' Sophia said, pre-empting what Lani was going to say in a small voice. 'I want to be *normal*.'

Lani held back her own tears. She stood and wrapped her arms around her goddaughter. 'It's okay,' she soothed, over and over.

There was, clearly, a lot going on for Sophia. Part of Lani wanted to get to the bottom of it, but another part wanted to run for the hills. *We're going to be the best mothers ever.* Yeah, right. If she ever did manage to get pregnant and give birth after Acharya's curse, she'd better study a ton of parenting books.

She retrieved a box of tissues from the bathroom. Sophia pulled out a long line of them and blew her nose.

'I tried to get rid of it,' she said. The laugh she gave next was incongruous. 'With a scourer.'

It must've been the shock that set her off because Lani found herself laughing too. She lifted Sophia's fringe and took a close look at the birthmark. There didn't seem to be too much damage, just grazed skin. 'Sophia, is someone being mean to you?' she asked eventually.

'Like, *everyone*,' Sophia replied.

Lani's phone buzzed on the counter. She put a hand on Sophia's shoulder as she answered the call. There was no hello.

'Please tell me Sophia's with you,' Maya said, her voice frantic. 'I've checked everywhere. She was supposed to be home two hours ago. I'm utterly beside myself. Oh, Lani, I keep thinking of what might have happened to her!'

Sophia shook her head, but there was no way Lani could keep Maya in the dark about her daughter's whereabouts.

'She's here, Maya. Don't worry, Soph is here and she's safe. Bridget will drive her home now.'

•

As Bridget and Sophia left, Lani picked up her phone. The romance between Heston's luckiest sperm and one of her prime, juicy eggs might be fraught, but the only way through was to close her eyes and jump.

CHAPTER TWENTY

'I'm so glad you want to be a permanent part of Soul Haven,' Acharya said. 'This will be your introduction to a better Tinker, a better life. What do you see as parts of yourself that require evolution?'

Tinker grimaced. This situation – lying down on a massage bed in Acharya's darkened lounge room waiting to be transported to who-knows-where while she lit candles and waved burning sage above his head – was awkward for him. But he did want to belong at Soul Haven for good. After more than three months of coming and going, he knew that now.

'I think, in some ways, I'm a bit, I don't know, immature I guess,' he tried.

'Yes, I can see that,' Acharya agreed. 'Your emotional development has been stunted, which is why I've chosen Age Regression for your first therapy. I could see, in the Meet Your Inner Child workshop, that you're repressing difficult memories. Tinker, are you ready to surrender yourself to the experience? Are you ready to trust my processes?'

Tinker gulped as he nodded.

'Excellent, excellent,' Acharya said. 'Now, close your eyes.'

The words she chanted were unfamiliar but soothing. Tinker felt himself drifting into what felt like semi-sleep.

'Invite your mind to become a projector screen. You're going back through time, walking through a forest, under a knotted vine,' she said eventually.

It was almost like he was both inside and outside himself, but a young Tinker did as she asked.

'Now you're emerging,' she continued, 'into an enormous library. A beautiful library, stacked with books, floor to ceiling. There will be nourishment for your brain in here. There's a book – a special book that's beckoning to you,' Acharya said. 'Can you see it? Can you identify it?'

The book that reached out to him was on the top shelf, bound in fawn leather. Phantom Tinker saw the ladder up to it, but he didn't need it. Instead, he floated skywards and the book, which looked heavy but was as light as a feather, fell into his hands.

'Now, pick a piece of furniture, or a cushion on the floor, where you might feel most comfortable.'

There was a giant fluffy green beanbag right in the centre of the library. Young Tinker nestled into it.

'Open the book on any page.'

Tinker recognised the technicolour image of an imp spinning straw into gold on the silky page. His mum had read that story to him many times as a child.

'It's *Rumpelstiltskin*,' he said.

'Lean into the book. Enter it. Wiggle your way through the pages and land in your childhood. Have you arrived somewhere, Tinker?'

It was just as she said. Tinker was chubby-faced, perhaps eight years old. His mum and dad had both come into his bedroom to kiss him goodnight.

'How do you feel?'

'Loved. They think I'm perfect and tell me so.' Tinker paused. There was something else about being eight. Something just on the periphery of his memory.

'Mum's reading it to me. She loves this story. She wants me to love it too, but I'm scared of the bit when he tells the miller's daughter he's going to exchange gold for her firstborn child.'

'What does your mum say when you tell her that?'

'She says it's just a story and that I have nothing to fear.'

'Right, there's nothing to fear,' Acharya said. 'But you're upset. I can see that.'

'I am. Because Dad's laughing at me for still being afraid of the imp in the *Rumpelstiltskin* story.'

'And what does he do?'

'He says he'll read it to me. He says I'm a big boy and have to learn to face my fears.'

'Oh, my poor Tinker. And how does that make you feel?'

Tinker wasn't sure.

'Just run with whatever comes to mind. It's important not to censor yourself. Is your father angry now?'

'I don't know.'

'You do. Reach back and ask your eight-year-old self.'

'Yes, he's cross. He's telling me not to be a baby.'

'Ah, so that's when it started, this feeling of inadequacy. Keep going, Tinker. You're doing good work.'

He didn't want to keep going. His father's expression kept changing. Was he cross? Maybe that was a misrepresentation? Maybe he was just teasing, and that was a different thing, a trait that had been passed through the generations. But still, Acharya was right. His feelings of inadequacy had to have come from somewhere.

'Now you are ten, now fourteen, now seventeen ...'

'No,' Tinker objected, though he wasn't sure whether he was speaking aloud. 'I don't want to be seventeen.'

'But you are, because this is where the real work begins,' Acharya insisted and objecting was no good. He was the age she'd led him to. It was midnight at the park. Stig was there, Maya and Lani too.

'We're not us without you.' He was talking aloud now. As he surveyed the scene in his mind, on the massage table Tinker's head moved from side to side.

'Leave there now,' Acharya said after a while. 'You know where you must go. You must face the darkness within. You must find yourself where you need to be, and you know where that is.'

They were at Joe's place, in his cool, converted garage. He, Lani and Maya were determined, so determined, to get Joe to fess up. They were desperate to make him admit that he'd been in a relationship with Stig. But they were getting nowhere. They were drinking Lani's dad's whisky, but not as much as Joe believed. Not Maya, but he and Lani. They were tipping refills down the sink when Joe wasn't looking. Oh god, no. Tinker didn't want to be here. But there he was. Maya was crushing up three of her mum's valiums, a grimace on her face as she put them into Joe's drink.

'Tell me what's happening.'

'Joe's passed out on the couch. He won't – or can't – talk anymore. And I'm ... I'm doing wrong. I'm doing a bad thing—'

'Face that guilt. Stare it down. You know you're where you need to be. You know that's where you need to start your healing.'

Tears pooled in Tinker's ears.

'The garage door opens by remote. I've taken it with me. And now, there's fire. I'm far away, but I know it's my fault Joe's stuck there. And he's burning. I don't want to see this. I don't.'

'That's good work,' Acharya said. 'Bless that scene. Wrap it up and hand it to me. I will take your burden.'

'You will? You would do that for me?'

'Yes. Yes, I make that vow. I'm wrapping up the scene.' Tinker's eyes were closed as he lifted the heavy package with difficulty and held it up. Then, there was lightness. Acharya had taken it from him. And he was so grateful. So, very grateful. His seventeen-year-old self and his thirty-seven-year-old self were equally indebted.

'You're coming back through the library,' Acharya said. 'Back through the years, through the forest and under the knotted vine. Back to the present. Back to me.'

When Tinker opened his eyes, Acharya was above him. She placed a warm hand on his forehead.

'Thank you,' he said.

Acharya smiled. 'I will always shoulder your burdens,' she said. 'All I ask for in return is your loyalty and adherence to my rules at Soul Haven. Zanni will lead the way into your new maturity and demonstrate how to commit to my processes, trust in them. Can you trust in me, totally? Can you do that, Tinker?'

'Yes.'

'You are free now,' Acharya said. 'Free and unencumbered to grow and become who you were always meant to be.'

Her smile was kind. She was generosity itself. Tinker hadn't felt this light for years.

'Welcome home, Tinker,' Acharya said.

CHAPTER TWENTY-ONE

'Look who found us,' Marcus exclaimed. Gertrude looked annoyed at the interruption as she chomped. The block was 700 metres or so from the centre of Soul Haven but tucked away with only dirt-road access.

'I think the appeal is more around those blackberry bushes than our company.' Sadiki laughed and, if a goat could roll its eyes, Gertrude was doing it.

'Well, our enterprising friend might have discovered it,' Acharya said. 'But others won't find it so easily. Your home will be a little slice of reprieve from the hustle and bustle.'

Sadiki reached for Marcus's hand. This was beyond anything he'd ever dreamed of: undulating hills, lush foliage and even a small dam. All courtesy of the wonderful Acharya.

The white weatherboard church Acharya had transported onto the land was quirky. The metal roof was rusty and the floorboards threatened to fly up, cartoon style, with every few steps, but they've fallen in love with it. Someone had obviously started the renovation from the inside out because the upper walls were freshly painted cream, as was the wainscoting that ran underneath, clearly an attempt to strengthen the structure.

'How can we ever repay you?' Sadiki asked.

'You already do repay me,' Acharya replied. 'With your support and commitment, with the workshops you run in our community and with your happiness. You demonstrate faith by investing in' – she waved her hand around to encompass the entire block – 'our shared future. Each should contribute according to their capacity.'

At this, Sadiki felt a wave of fury. Even though almost three months had passed since Lani, Maya and Tinker had come to the session, it still rankled that Lani had chosen to give a single dollar in return for the experience. That's what she thought about all they were trying to achieve at Soul Haven. In her endless grace, Acharya had chosen to forgive, but Sadiki wasn't there yet. Maya had been tripping, so she wasn't accountable. And Tinker was always broke, but he'd shown his belief in their community by returning to them several times. He was at the main property right now, staying in the new yurt Zanni had moved into permanently.

'I'm glad Tinker can appreciate what we offer,' Acharya said. 'It's lovely having him around. I gather Lani and Maya haven't seen fit to visit again.'

'I don't know about Lani, but I think Maya's a bit overwhelmed with parenting duties.' Sadiki paused and shook his head. 'Tinker tells me Sophia's having some issues and putting Maya through her paces because she found out her supposedly straight-as-a-die mum took mushrooms here.'

'Hmm,' Acharya said with a smile. 'Well, we can hope Maya's little adventure has helped her lateral thinking because that's what's needed to manage a child in crisis.'

Sadiki hadn't really interpreted whatever Sophia was going through as a crisis, but perhaps it was. Acharya had a sixth sense for those kinds of things.

'I gather that Maya's inclined to be rigid,' she continued. 'A curious child should be encouraged to question. I'm seeing to that. Taking action.'

Sadiki did a double take before realising Acharya meant action on the spiritual plane. A sage cleansing ritual, for instance, performed on Sophia's behalf might help. It certainly couldn't hurt.

What continued to hurt, to rage within him, was his old friends' dismissiveness.

'There will always be some who are unable, or unwilling, to step up to a higher level of consciousness,' Acharya said, a mind-reader again. 'Some whose evolution is thwarted by slavery to the almighty dollar. It's often the most privileged who cannot access a sense of generosity, who are stuck in the cycle of personal ego. Others who cannot – or will not – question dubious religious teachings. But we must pity and not blame.'

Sadiki shrugged. Lani had the gall to leave messages, even insinuating her shitty donation was a harmless joke, but he hadn't replied. And Maya had gone silent after the session.

Sadiki walked around the perimeter of the church with Marcus and Acharya, Marcus pulling off flakes of paint as he went.

'I don't foresee it will be a regular event, but there will be times when clients require intensive and private work. In those instances, you will return to the cottage.'

'Are you talking a few hours, or days?' Marcus asked.

'Marcus, I have famous clients,' Acharya said, her voice perfectly even. 'They require anonymity. There are others who are experiencing domestic violence and mustn't be found by the perpetrator. And my work will take the time it takes. Do you agree with the terms? Because if you don't, you should speak now.'

'Well, I think if the church is ours, the decision should be too,' Marcus said. 'I guess we look at it on a case-by-case basis. I mean, Sadiki and I don't want to be ousted just on a whim.'

Sadiki felt his body tense. Surely, adhering to Acharya's wishes was a small price to pay for this opportunity. Or had he missed something? 'How can we ever repay you?' he asked.

Marcus frowned. 'We've already been through that, my darling goldfish,' he said, giving Sadiki a little jab in the arm.

Acharya's raised eyebrows sent a confusing message. Maybe she was just annoyed with Marcus's seeming lack of gratitude? But this stuff ... this forgetting what he'd said recently, losing track of keys and conversations, was happening more and more frequently.

Acharya was poised to speak again when her pager beeped.

'There's an emergency,' she said. 'I need to get back to the cottage.'

•

It was a ripper day. Sunshine made their community and its surrounds even more appealing.

'So, what exactly are we doing in Sadiki and Marcus's backyard?' Zanni asked. 'Desecrating the soil?'

'We?' Tinker teased, leaning on his shovel. So far, Zanni

hadn't touched the one he'd brought along for her. She lay back on the grass, letting the sun kiss her face. He gestured to the holes he'd already dug and then kept going on the largest one that seemed to be taking forever. 'This, Betty Sue, is the beginnings of a mighty fine veggie patch,' he said in his best hillbilly voice. 'Acharya has planned it as a lovely surprise for the lads.'

'It's quite far from the church,' Zanni observed.

'Yes, well, Acharya says that the soil's best here. She also reckons that spring's the best time to plant okra – whatever that is – when it's at home, and that it needs to be planted deep.'

Zanni rose and walked over to him. 'In Australia, it's known as "lady fingers",' she said, tickling him with her own. 'It's used in heaps of stuff. Okra water is great at reducing blood-sugar levels, supporting weight loss and improving digestion. It's also good in cooking and skin products. Speaking of which, I've gotta go pack some orders, Billy Bob.'

Tinker groaned. 'You've done seven days straight. I wish you didn't have to work right now. It's kind of perfect here, just alone in the bush – with you.'

'Ah, but it's my job fulfilling orders that helps fund our extravagant lifestyle,' she joked.

No one at Soul Haven earned wages. Their yurt was comfortable but basic, consisting of their bed, a lounge suite, a couple of chairs and a floor rug. Still, Tinker wanted for nothing and he was grateful.

'It's true I'm working too much,' Zanni said. 'Soul Haven Inc. is getting so busy, I'm going to need more help.'

'Really?' Tinker replied. Acharya never failed to impress.

Apart from all her other skills, she seemed to be a gifted entrepreneur. 'Like, how busy? You think it's making money?'

'Well, I'd say it's making a lot. I don't get to see the figures because Thomas handles that side of things, but I do know it's all non-taxable income.'

'How does that work?'

'Apparently it's registered as a religious group, so it's exempt.' She must've clocked Tinker's expression because she went on. 'It just makes sense to register the business that way. I mean, we all benefit, right? Why give the government the proceeds of our labour when it's Acharya who does for us what they should? Besides, I'm sure every cent we make goes back into developing Soul Haven.'

'That just feels a bit—' Tinker couldn't find the words to say how unsettling this was to him. His parents had often spoken about taxes, however annoying, being the backbone of civilised society. Soul Haven wasn't a religion. It was a way of life. And he was no financial whiz, but it did seem that Acharya must be making more than it cost to run Soul Haven.

'Darling, the products we make – the gorgeous candles and incense, and especially the Anointed Earth Organic Moisturisers – we release into the world with love. Soul Haven Inc. shows the world what it can be.'

When Zanni hugged his sweaty body, he felt calmer. She was right.

Tinker kissed her. He'd never felt so in step with any other woman. Zanni was his true north. He wasn't used to sleeping the whole night with anyone. She snored. She even dribbled onto her pillow a bit and talked in her sleep, but none of that seemed to matter. They'd made a 'no sex until we really know each other' pact. And, as difficult as it had been, Tinker had kept his end of the bargain. He really did feel like he knew her. Zanni was sweet and funny. Her laughter came easily and often. And she never looked down on him.

He hadn't told Lani and Maya he'd been visiting Soul Haven frequently over the last few months. If Lani found out – especially about Soul Haven Inc. – she'd be brutal. She was still hanging on to resentment for the true things Acharya had said about her dad. She couldn't seem to let go of Acharya saying there'd been Hibiki bottles at Joe's the night he died either.

And Maya had been freaking out about Sophia finding out she'd taken shrooms. Sophia was running rings around her on the back of it.

No, neither Lani nor Maya would understand the sense of belonging he'd found here. They'd never get why he'd decided to become a permanent fixture.

'I've asked if I can finish at five today so I can make it to Sadiki's session,' Zanni interrupted his thoughts.

'I hope it's not tantric,' Tinker said and Zanni laughed. He hadn't really meant it to be funny, but if he had to endure that and not ...

'I reckon it's about time we consummate this blessed union,' she said.

Tinker's heart skipped a beat. He could have taken Zanni up on that offer right away.

But into their peace and quiet and connection came a scream.

CHAPTER TWENTY-TWO

'You never protected me,' Patty yelled as Tinker reached the cottage. 'You let your boyfriend burn me with a cigarette. What mother does that?'

Patty rolled up the sleeve of her caftan, showing a red dot on the underside of her wrist. Her mum, Claudine, looked to Tinker like how he imagined Patty would look in twenty years. Like she would if she'd come straight from one of those apps that age you backward and forward.

'Oh my god, Patty,' Claudine said. 'Yes, that did happen, but I didn't *let* Snake do it. It was an accident. You were just a toddler and you picked up his fag from an ashtray, not getting that it could burn you. Snake was upset. He didn't understand that you need to have eyes in the back of your head when you're looking after a kid. He put cream on it and wrapped it in a bandage and was super sorry about the whole thing. But I never let him babysit you alone after that.'

Something about that rang true for Tinker. There could be different ways of interpreting the same event. Purpose was important. Like his dad chiding him for being afraid of a fairytale was, he was sure now, gentle ribbing and not fury, because his father didn't have a mean bone in his body. He was thinking about mentioning his thoughts, but he was too slow to get the words in order.

'Which means you're admitting you let him look after me alone in the first place,' Patty hissed.

'I had to work,' Claudine objected. 'I was doing eight shifts a week, cleaning other people's houses. Your father never gave us squat. No child support. Nothing.'

'Yeah, good choice. Thanks for choosing me to be born to a deadbeat dad. Lyle's been a ripper, hasn't he? Never missed a birthday, there for my important moments – all of it. Oh, remember when he taught me to ride a bike? All them times he took me fishing? How he always called me "princess"? No? That's 'cos it never happened. None of it did.'

'I'm sorry Lyle couldn't ever wrap himself around being a proper dad,' Claudine said. 'You deserved more. But, Patty, I done the best I could with what I had.'

'Yeah, right,' Patty hissed. 'Well, Claudine, it wasn't very bloody good.'

Claudine flopped on the couch. 'You kind of got a father in the end,' she said. 'I know it was a bit late, but Butch has been with us since you were eight. And he's been good to you, right? He's been good to both of us. He's kind to you. He adores you.'

'What's going on here?' Acharya demanded and Tinker couldn't have been happier to see her. He was way out of his depth. She would handle this way better than he ever could.

'I'll tell you what's going on,' Claudine said, rising to her full height, which would have been five foot four at most. 'You're bloody well trying to steal my daughter.'

'I think you need to calm down, Claudine,' Acharya said in a silky voice. 'No one's trying to steal anyone. Patty came to Soul Haven of her own volition, and you need to respect that.'

'Yeah, let's talk about respect,' Claudine scoffed. 'I took my kid to get help from you at your office in Ballarat 'cos I was worried about her. I figured you – someone – might be able to teach her how to handle the shit that was going on at school. Someone who knew better than me.' She paused. 'Someone who had proper skills and, you know, insights, I guess. And I was just walking past and I saw your banner, *Cosmic Counselling – free introductory session*, and I thought, *Why not? How could it hurt?* But I didn't know then what I know now. That so-called introductory session was an introduction' – she waved her hand around to encompass the cottage and beyond – 'to this, whatever it is. It was a way for you to recruit people. Next thing I know, Patty's got voodoo dolls she's doing all sorts of nasty stuff to and she's hiding things from me, and nothing really gets resolved at school except that some of the students who'd been mean to her got sick and my Patty took it as some kind of sign that she'd turned a corner. And, oh, she'd turned a corner all right. She'd jumped out of the frying pan and into the fire.'

Claudine turned to Patty, her eyes pleading. 'Look, I know I've made mistakes,' she said. 'I know I'm not the perfect mother. But you were about to finish high school – you're just months away. Patty, I had a rotten time at school too, but you're smarter than I ever was. And, afterwards, your whole life changes. You just have to stick it out, then there are things – opportunities – that will make high school seem like a blip in your life. Patty, you have a home. Butch and I love you.'

'Yeah, Butch really adores me,' Patty said. 'Probably in all the wrong ways. 'Cos I've been fucked up since I was a kid. I dunno exactly what happened yet, but whatever it was, Acharya will help me recover the memories.' She tapped her temple. 'Because it's in here, somewhere,' she whispered.

Claudine let out a wail that sent shivers up and down Tinker's spine. She walked right up to Acharya. Then she spat at her.

Acharya didn't react. On autopilot, Tinker went to the kitchen and retrieved paper towels, handing a sheet to her. She wiped the offending glob off her cheek.

'You're a peasant, Claudine,' Patty mumbled. 'You're disgusting.'

'Maybe,' Claudine said. 'Or maybe that's just what this bitch deserves,' she added, still staring Acharya down. 'Patty, if you don't come home with me, I'm calling the cops.'

'Please, go right ahead,' Acharya said. 'I'm sure they'll be interested because spitting is assault. And Butch's associations with the Harley Knights is bound to give them something juicy to investigate.'

'Come home with me, Patty.' Claudine looked broken now, all the bravado gone. 'Please. Finish your education. That's how you'll find yourself. Not here with this whack job and her cult.'

'It's cheap and easy to call any group you don't understand a cult,' Acharya countered. 'But that doesn't make it true. We are … a spiritual family.'

'Yeah,' Patty agreed. 'And guess what, Claudine, I am home. If you want any communication with me from now on, don't call me *Patty* ever again. My real name, the name Acharya has gifted me, 'cos of my sacred evolution, means "awakenment" and "enlightenment".

'I am Bodhi.'

CHAPTER TWENTY-THREE

Maya stood with the other mums in the hip-hop studio, opting to be as far away from Stella as possible. Even though the class hadn't commenced, Stella's daughter, Alana, was already twerking provocatively and gawking at herself in the floor-to-ceiling mirror. As she showed off, one of her fancy barrettes fell to the floor.

'Just a quick rundown on the recital next Sunday,' Rosie said. 'I need everyone to be at the hall exactly one hour before start time, so eleven forty-five am sharp. The girls' hair should be done at home, in any version of French braids as long as there's nothing covering their faces. If you have bangs,' she continued, smiling at Sophia, 'gel and bobby pins will do the trick.'

'No, Rosie,' Sophia said. 'I'm not doing that.'

Alana turned around, smirking. As a ringleader at their school, Maya suspected she was behind Sophia's new self-consciousness about her birthmark. After all, it had started soon after *The Australian Women's Weekly* photo spread a few months ago. Jealousy could cause huge rifts in relationships between fourteen-year-olds, but Sophia refused to talk about it.

Maya pined for her daughter's confidence, but there were no two ways about it. She'd lost face over the mushroom-trip fiasco. Sophia had begun rejecting house rules. She'd put a password on her laptop she wouldn't share and she was spending more time on it than she was allowed. Plus, when she went out, she often switched off her phone so Maya couldn't tell where she was.

As Rosie went to Sophia to speak with her privately, Stella made a beeline for Maya. 'Alana's been tirelessly practising her solo,' she said. 'I was a dancer myself, so I can tell she's bordering on professional. And Rosie says there are going to be talent scouts in the audience, so cross your fingers for us.'

Maya had zero inclination to do that. Wasn't it enough that her daughter was the only girl who had a solo? 'Alana seems to be tirelessly professional in other areas too,' she said.

Stella looked askance and Maya wrestled with the urge to say more, but Sophia would be furious if she found out, so she bit her tongue.

'Is there something on your mind?' Stella asked. 'Would you like to join me for coffee while the girls rehearse?'

It was tempting, but once she started, she'd probably go the whole hog, so Maya took the buzz of her phone as a sign to decline. She walked outside into the car park to answer.

'I'm pregnant,' Lani squealed. 'With child. Up the duff. First go and we nailed it.'

'Oh, Lani,' Maya said, 'that's brilliant. I'm so happy for you. It's just … well, it's the best news I've heard for ages. How many weeks are you?'

'Eleven,' Lani replied. 'Bridget wanted me to wait until we got to twelve, but I'm busting.'

There was a long pause on the other end of the phone.

'I'm freaking terrified,' Lani said then, and Maya knew it was meant to sound jokey, but there was something in her friend's voice that suggested she really was. 'Can you have a word with the guy upstairs, you know, to look out for us heathens?'

Maya smiled. As an atheist, what Lani was asking didn't make sense, but of course she'd pray for a safe birth and a healthy baby. Along with her other prayers.

'Speaking of heathens,' Lani said when she'd recovered composure, 'did you know Tinker's been visiting the funny farm?'

'No, I didn't,' Maya replied. 'He hasn't breathed a word of it to me.'

'I only got it out of him because he turned up for lunch the other day wearing pleather bracelets. Do you remember meeting a woman called Zanni at that crazy session?'

'Only vaguely,' Maya admitted. 'Though I do recall having several epiphanies that now escape me.'

Lani's laugh was a cackle. 'And has Sophia forgiven you?'

'I don't think so,' Maya said. 'She's … well, she's hardened towards me. I guess it's a penance I've got to accept.' Through the studio window, she watched the girls dance. Her daughter was lagging behind the beat and it made Maya sad to see. 'Sophia's obviously got some stuff going on at school, but she won't tell me about it.'

'Well, she'll get there,' Lani said. 'I guess it's just that developmental stage where she's pushing back against her mum. Isn't it kind of textbook stuff?'

Given that Lani knew nothing about parenting yet, that seemed a dismissal of the topic. Maya fought an urge to lash out.

'I think Tinker's smitten with Zanni,' Lani continued obliviously. 'Honestly, she seems nice enough. And she's around our age for once. But he's so cagey about Soul Haven. I'm worried he'll get sucked into the cult.'

'Hmm, I'm not sure it's a cult as such,' Maya said. 'Maybe more like a commune. I mean, there's nothing religious about it.'

'Maybe,' Lani conceded. 'But Maya … I get really bad vibes from Acharya.'

Suddenly, the music in the studio stopped. Maya looked back through the window to the girls. Alana was holding her leg and crying, a pool of vomit on the floor beside her. Sophia looked strangely unaffected.

Maya hung up on the call and rushed inside.

'It's a wasp sting,' Rosie said incredulously. 'How on earth does that happen?'

•

'Earth to Tinker,' Lani said, a grin spreading over her face after she shared her big news. On the other end of the phone, she heard a sharp intake of breath. He seemed totally overwhelmed.

'Come and hang with me right now?' Lani asked. 'I'm desperate to bore you with the minute details.'

'I'm so happy for you and Bridget,' he said finally. 'Of course you got results on your first try because you're a legend. I reckon you'll have a dream pregnancy and give birth to the most perfect baby ever. I can't wait to see you. But it can't be today because …'

He paused, and Lani instantly knew where he was.

'Oh no, Tinker, you're not at Soul Haven again, are you?' she asked.

'Yes,' he replied, and Lani could hear the defensiveness even in that small word. 'Lani, you've got to understand something. I really like it here. I did an age regression and it was ace. I feel like I'm really moving towards forgiving myself for what I did to Joe. And the group workshops are amazing. Like, Meeting Your Trauma Head to Head.'

Lani flinched. 'Did Sadiki go to that?' she asked.

'Sadiki ran the workshop. Acharya puts a lot of faith in him.'

'Yeah, but surely that's playing with fire after what he's been through.'

As soon as she'd said it she wished she could erase her words.

'Well, you could say that,' Tinker said after several seconds. 'But here are the choices – you either do the work or you remain spiritually immature.'

Lani's own inner child felt inclined to puke. 'Jesus,' she said. 'Who stole Tinker and replaced him with an alien?'

There was a long pause where Lani expected at least a chuckle. Tinker was always up for a bit of gentle ribbing. Surely he wasn't taking this rubbish seriously?

'That was a joke,' Lani tried. 'Remember those?'

There was no response.

'Sadiki's still not taking my calls or answering my texts,' Lani said, changing tack. 'Sounds like he's holding a grudge over my dollar donation to She Who Will Not Be Named. If you're there schmoozing, maybe you can tell her I'll transfer a few grand today?'

Actually, that was a good idea. Lani should have thought of it earlier. Because even though she didn't believe in curses, not really, what that woman had said to her seemed more terrifying now that she was pregnant. This could be a, well, a peace offering of sorts.

'I don't think Acharya would accept it,' Tinker said.

Lani had never known Tinker to be such an arsehole. He should be whooping with joy about her news. Clearly his allegiances were shifting more than she'd thought.

'Hey, my darling, we don't want to be late for Releasing Soul Ties.' Lani recognised the voice as Zanni's. 'I can't miss this one. Oh, sorry, I didn't realise you were on a call. I'll meet you at the house in five.'

'Tinker, all this hocus-pocus – it isn't you,' Lani said. 'I think it could even be dangerous. Whatever it is …'

She had more to add. Much more.

But Tinker had hung up on her.

CHAPTER TWENTY-FOUR

There were ten people in Acharya's sprawling living room. Sadiki was glad she'd accepted his plea that she lead the Releasing Soul Ties workshop. It would have felt fraudulent to do it himself.

'Give yourself time and space to focus on one person you need to disconnect from. It may be a friend, colleague, parent, partner. Maybe living, maybe passed. Whatever the case, it should be someone you've trusted with your soul. But that trust has curdled. Perhaps it was them, perhaps it was you. Breathe in that person. Let them circulate through your body one last time.'

This was Sadiki's third try. It was always Joe he visualised.

'Allow, for a moment, your love,' Acharya continued. 'Allow the feelings that made this relationship transcend.'

He was in Joe's bedroom, in his converted garage, seeing his many trophies on the bookcase. There was a breeze blowing through the open window. 'Nights in White Satin' was blaring as they explored each other's bodies.

'Slowly summon the hurt. Introduce your love to your pain. They're entwined. A rope plait. Love is hate.'

In the school corridors, Joe's denial. His palpable fear of being outed. His betrayal.

Back to Joe's bedroom.

It's a metal chain, not a rope plait.

Concentrate, Sadiki. Transform it into a more malleable medium.

Metal becomes – water becomes wine. Sin. Love God.

Open eyes. Zanni standing, swaying. Beside her, an old friend. Name?

Fire. Screaming. Joe's face, his beautiful face contorting, melting.

Breathe, Sadiki. Walk. Escape.

Breathe.

Nothing.

•

'I'm taking him to hospital.' Marcus was above Sadiki, eyes glistening.

'What happened?'

'You were crying,' Tinker said.

Tinker! Of course, his real name was Tim but that was the nickname that had stuck.

'You were lurching around. You tripped up the stairs, fell and hit your head on the coffee table.'

'There's no need for hospital,' Acharya said. 'Sadiki, you just got up too quickly. You had a dizzy spell – maybe a panic attack. We can monitor you right here.'

'Here' was Acharya's couch, moved into the corner to maximise space for the workshop. Everyone was gone except Acharya, Bodhi, Marcus and Tinker.

'Oh, so you have a medical degree, Acharya?' Marcus snapped. 'I'm taking him to hospital to get checked out.'

'Western medicine is a furphy,' Acharya said, her voice firming. Bodhi stood close by her side, mirroring Acharya's stance, hands outstretched, palms up. 'You understand that, don't you, Sadiki? We've discussed it many times. Tell Marcus *no*.'

'With respect, Acharya,' Tinker said, 'I think we should take him.'

'It would be against my will,' Acharya told them. 'And what has been given, the joys each of you have been gifted, can be taken away.'

'It would be against my will too,' Bodhi echoed feebly.

'You know what, Acharya?' Marcus said as he and Tinker lifted Sadiki upright. 'You can shove your joys and your gifts. And I don't care about your will.'

•

As he walked through the automatic doors of the hospital, Marcus beside him, Tinker couldn't think what to say.

'Look at her, claiming ownership,' Marcus sniped as Acharya guided Sadiki to reception. 'She didn't even want him to come to hospital in the first place.'

'Well, Marcus,' Acharya said, turning around, 'I'm respecting your wishes, but I still don't think it's what Sadiki needs. He had a dizzy spell and a fall—'

'But that's not the whole of it,' Marcus said through clenched teeth. 'You'd think, with your *intuition*, you'd see that something else is going on. Something's wrong. Sadiki's been forgetting things, getting disorientated. I know because I'm the one who's with him all the time. I'm the one who looks after him.'

Acharya sat on a plastic chair next to Marcus, blocking out Tinker's view of Sadiki.

'Really?' she replied. 'Interesting how you've cast yourself, Marcus. The way I see it, you've waltzed into a good thing without having to plough through the tough stuff. Was it you who was there during Sadiki's withdrawals? Were you the one mopping his brow?'

'You mean when you rescued him and joined your karma together, like that's even a thing?' Marcus snarled. 'Who are you really, Acharya? Who the fuck are you?'

'The one who'd do anything for my Sadiki,' Acharya answered in a heartbeat. 'We are bound in a way you'll never understand. Lovers are transient.' She looked over the top of Marcus's head at Tinker. 'I don't see you, Marcus,' she said under her breath. 'Nobody does.'

Tinker leaned forward so he could see around Acharya. Sadiki looked too exhausted to deal with the tension. Tinker inhaled deeply.

'Please, stop all this. You both love Sadiki,' he said. 'For his sake.'

The sound of an ambulance broke the silence. The receptionist walked up to them.

'A doctor will see you now,' she told Sadiki. 'You may take one support person with you.'

Sadiki reached out for Marcus.

•

There was time to get a load of washing done before dinner preparations. Maya went upstairs to strip the beds, starting with Sophia's. She sat down for a moment and looked around. Sophia was almost unrecognisable these days, but at least her room was just as it always had been. The only things Maya hadn't seen before were three skin-coloured felt dolls in the middle of her bookcase.

'Why are you always in my room?' Sophia asked as she burst in.

Maya chose to ignore the attitude. She picked up one of the dolls. 'What are these?'

Sophia narrowed her eyes. 'Do you need to know?'

'For goodness sake, I guess not,' Maya conceded. 'I'd just like to talk to you about *something*. Are they for an art project?'

Sophia took the doll from her and put it back on the bookcase. 'Why are you always in my room?' she repeated.

'Well,' Maya said, trying to keep the frustration from her voice, 'for starters, I'm not always in your room. I'm currently in here to strip your bed. And hello to you too, Soph.'

'I can do it myself,' Sophia said.

'Okay,' Maya said. 'I'll teach you how.'

Sophia tilted her head to the side. 'Mum, it's not exactly rocket science.'

Maya was about to defend herself when her phone pinged with an email. Sophia read over her shoulder.

From: rosie@hiptohopdanceacademy.com
Subject: Changes to dance recital

Dear parents
Unfortunately, Alana Dupont has been in a skiing accident and broken her femur. She will be unable to perform at our dance recital. To fill in the space from her solo, please be advised that the whole group should re-familiarise themselves with the choreography we've rehearsed for 'Millionaire' (Chris Stapleton).

Kindest regards
Rosie
PS: Get better soon, Alana.

'Karma's a bitch,' Sophia said with a smirk.

'That language is unacceptable,' Maya chided.

'*That language is unacceptable*,' Sophia mimicked. 'But when the shoe fits—'

'Sophia,' Maya interrupted. 'I know Alana isn't your friend, but we don't wish accidents like that on anyone.'

Sophia picked up another doll from the bookcase and squeezed it. Perhaps it was one of those stress toys?

'Well, *I* do,' she said. 'Jeez, Mum, you have no idea how horrible she is.'

Maya took her glasses off and put them on the bedside table. 'I'm listening.'

Sophia sat down heavily on her bed. 'She's always giving me grief about my birthmark, and now her sidekicks are doing it too.' She shrugged. 'So, are you going to tell me to shake it off?'

Maya frowned, a wave of fury at Alana's cruelty threatening to swamp her. She breathed deeply.

'No,' she said as she sat down beside her daughter. 'That is definitely not okay. Sophia, let me talk to your home-group teacher? Or the counsellor?'

'That'd just make things worse,' Sophia replied. 'Anyway, guess what? I *am* learning to shake it off. Who the hell is Alana Dupont anyway?' She paused. 'Mum, stop.'

Maya hadn't even been conscious of the tears rolling down her cheeks. She retrieved a tissue from her pocket and wiped the offending droplets.

'I just ... Sophia, I feel helpless. I want to take action on your behalf,' she said.

'It's okay. I'm taking action for myself.'

'How?'

Sophia paused, gathering her words. 'I'm thinking differently,' she said. 'Alana and the rest of them can't hurt me if I don't care.' She tapped her temple. 'It's all about what goes on up here,' she said. 'I have control over that. And it makes me ... powerful.'

Maya frowned, trying to understand where Sophia was going with this.

'Mum, you don't have to know everything about me,' Sophia said. 'Just get that I'm my own person, and I need to be allowed to have my own thoughts.' She paused. 'And beliefs,' she added.

'Okay,' Maya said. 'What kind of beliefs are you talking about?'

Sophia tilted her head. 'I don't want to go to church anymore,' she said.

Maya gulped. Had this come out of nowhere? Or had she been too preoccupied worrying about Luke changing schools to notice Sophia's doubts?

'But, Sophia – your faith?'

She shook her head. 'I'm not feeling it, Mum. Some of the stuff … I've been googling all the weirdness of being Catholic. I mean, do you know there was a thing called "the confirmation slap", where the bishop smacked people on the cheek so they'd get used to suffering in the name of Jesus Christ? That's pretty wack.'

What was 'pretty wack' was sitting on Sophia's bed hearing her daughter talk like this. Maya urged herself to tread carefully. 'Darling, that didn't happen at your confirmation. The ritual was abandoned before you were born,' she said. 'And regardless, it was symbolic.'

'I don't care if it was,' Sophia replied. 'The thing is – I don't want to be a servant of the Lord. I don't want to be anyone's servant. Mum, I don't even know if I *believe* in God.'

Maya stood up quickly. 'Of course you do,' she said, the words coming out forcefully. Sophia was a *child*. She was having doubts, yes, but that didn't mean she was going to abandon all she'd been taught.

'Why, "of course"?' Sophia demanded, standing too, towering over Maya. 'Because I'm supposed to go along with everything you tell me to think and feel? I'm supposed to have the same, buttoned-up mind as you?'

Maya hadn't even thought about doing it. But her arm was raised, hand poised to slap Sophia's cheek.

Sophia glared at her. 'Would that be a *symbolic* slap too?' she demanded.

'I wasn't—' Maya went to object, but it was too late and the gesture too transparent.

Sophia grabbed her backpack, charged downstairs and slammed the front door behind her.

CHAPTER TWENTY-FIVE

It was a beautiful day. Sunlight streamed in through the windows and a breeze made the jacuzzi water look like chipped glass. Lani had ordered a delivery from Tinker's favourite burger place. And there he was, finally, coming down her driveway in his ute. No matter what, no matter that they hadn't spoken many times or in much depth after he'd hung up on her almost two months ago, she was going to make this day special.

'Just look at you,' he said when she opened the door.

Lani grinned. 'Look at my cankles, you mean?' she replied, lifting the bottom of her silk trousers.

'Your cankles are lovely, Hubbell.' He laughed, making her recall endless evenings of popcorn and old movies – *The Way We Were* had been a favourite for both of them. 'And what about this?'

Tinker didn't ask permission, he didn't need to, before placing both hands on her belly.

Once inside, they stood facing the window, Tinker nursing a light beer and Lani a Perrier.

'Eighteen weeks,' Lani told him. 'You wouldn't believe the acrobatics going on in there.'

'Well, given that it has your genes, I don't doubt that for a second. This bubba is bound to be a mover and shaker.'

'I've missed you,' Lani said softly. 'You've been in Creswick so much lately.'

Tinker shrugged. 'I've moved into Zanni's yurt permanently,' he said.

In the decades before Soul Haven came into the picture, Lani would have known something as fundamental as where Tinker was living. Now she felt like giving him a shove, making him stagger backward like he used to.

'Oh,' she said cautiously. 'When?'

'Some time ago.'

'That's good news,' she lied, taking in a deep breath. She wasn't going to have this moment spoiled. 'Timothy Alan Hodges, I've spoken with Bridget and we're in agreement. We'd love you to be this one's' – she pointed to her stomach – 'godfather.'

Tinker walked over and sat on the couch, patting the seat next to him, and Lani obliged. He leaned back, hands over his eyes, most likely overwhelmed. She could practically see him with their little girl, tossing her up in the air and catching her, teaching her to change a tyre on a bike, all the blokey stuff that would mean she'd have a substitute dad as well as two mums.

When he uncovered his eyes, they were glistening. 'I'm sorry, Lani.'

She frowned. The baby moved inside her. She needed to pee. Maybe he meant he was sorry for hanging up on her?

'I want to be a big part of this child's life,' he said, 'but not as a godparent. Lani, you're not even Catholic. Me neither. It's ... hypocritical.'

Lani got up. This was unbelievable. Why was he being such a prick?

'Hang on, Tinker,' she said. 'I think you're forgetting something. You're *already* a godfather. Remember a kid called Luke Donnelly?'

'Of course I do,' he said. 'But I made that decision before I found ... enlightenment.'

'Oh, for fuck's sake.'

Surely the tears in his eyes showed he was conflicted. There had to be a chance that he'd see sense.

'What if ...' she said, trying and failing to keep her voice even. 'What if what you're experiencing isn't enlightenment, but manipulation and coercion?'

'What if your whole life had been about those things?' Tinker countered. 'Would it colour your views if you're still being spoonfed by powerful, wealthy parents? Would you even be having a christening for this baby if it wasn't for Gino and Yvette?'

Tinker wasn't being fair. Yes, she had to admit they supported her financially and that she hadn't been a practising Catholic for many years, but her parents didn't run spooky workshops and lure disciples. They didn't require her to worship them. Her friend had been brainwashed, pure and simple.

The doorbell rang and Lani let Tinker answer it, trying to use the time to calm herself. He collected the burgers and fries.

'Thanks for the thought,' he said, putting them on the kitchen bench. 'But I don't eat this stuff anymore.'

'I guess not,' Lani said sharply. 'You're swallowing enough shit as it is.'

Tinker sighed deeply. 'Sadiki and I will ask Acharya to perform a ceremony to place universal blessings on your child,' he said, like he was some kind of martyr.

At the mention of Acharya, a feeling of foreboding prickled her skin, forced its way into her limbs, her organs. The baby suddenly stopped fluttering. Or was she imagining it?

'You can shove your blessings,' she hissed. 'And Acharya can go to hell. Sadiki too.'

Tinker looked winded. Tears trickled down his cheeks and, again, Lani reached for the hope that he'd see what was actually happening.

'Sadiki's dying,' he said eventually. 'It's stage-four brain cancer.' He stopped and looked around like it might be his last visit to Lani's house. His expression was so resentful, so hardened, he might just as well have accused Lani of making Sadiki ill. 'Coming here was a mistake,' he said. 'This time, I'll learn from it.'

•

Maya hadn't bitten her fingernails since she was a teen. Now though, she couldn't help it. She attacked one after another.

'Tell me again about the argument you had with Sophia,' Connor said.

Maya squeezed her eyes shut. Every little thing that went wrong in their house was attributed to her. She tried to steady her thoughts, but the words came out through gritted teeth.

'Sophia expressed that she didn't want to go to church anymore. And that she didn't believe in God.'

Connor nodded. 'And how did you … receive that information?'

'I said I'd throw a party for her.'

'This isn't the moment for sarcasm.'

'Seems like the best option to me.'

It was after 8 pm and the spaghetti bolognaise was still on the stove. She hadn't told him about the slap because it never happened. The more she thought about it, the more Maya knew it wouldn't have eventuated anyway. She'd never hit her kids. It had been a kneejerk reaction, a venial sin she'd confess to the priest. But Connor had his own faults.

'Look, it's disappointing,' he said. 'Of course we want our children to believe as we do. But the way you go about it—'

'Okay, how about I be more like you?' Maya interrupted. 'How about I ignore the fact that Sophia's going out without our permission and doesn't answer her mobile? Act as though her rudeness is no big deal? Accept her grunts in place of communication? Actually you probably haven't even noticed since they're not directed at you. It's your leniency that's the real problem.'

'It's not leniency, Maya.' Connor's eyes were narrow. 'It's giving our daughter leeway to find out who she is. It's understanding and tolerance.' A vein in his temple was standing out, a tell of the anger he'd never admit to.

At least Maya was honest with herself. 'We've been worrying about the wrong twin. All this hoo-ha about whether Luke would be able to fit in at a new school – whether with his differences, his quirks, he'd be accepted. Our fears have been misplaced.'

There were footsteps at the top of the stairs. Maya couldn't bring herself to turn around.

'Why were you so worried about me?' Luke asked, his voice wobbling. 'Is it because I'm small for my age? Do you think I'm weak? Or do you just think I'm weird?' He paused then answered for himself. 'I guess it's all of the above.'

Maya's heart sank into the pit of her stomach. It lay there, leaden, while Sophia joined her brother. She must've snuck back in from wherever she'd disappeared to after she stormed out.

'Come on, Luke,' she said, looking straight at Maya. 'Mum's being a bitch. Let's order Uber Eats – my treat.'

With that, the twins went into Luke's room and closed the door.

Connor retreated to his study.

And Maya was left alone with a kilo of uneaten spaghetti bolognaise.

CHAPTER TWENTY-SIX

All the permanents – Thomas, Marnie, Bodhi, Zanni, Tinker, Marcus and Acharya (everyone except Sadiki) – were gathered around Acharya's dining table. The mood was sombre. Tinker held Zanni's hand and she squeezed back.

'The purpose of today's meeting is to decide what's best for Sadiki,' Acharya said.

'What's best is that he and I relocate to Melbourne where he can get treatment in a city hospital,' Marcus replied. 'That's our only chance of extending his life expectancy.'

At the head of the table, Acharya stood up.

'No, Marcus,' she said softly. 'Sadiki should live out his days in peace and tranquillity, here at Soul Haven.'

'Exactly right,' Marnie said, clacking her knitting needles. 'I endured chemo and radiation for over six months. I know how gruelling it is, and I certainly wouldn't wish that on Sadiki.'

Tinker turned to her. 'But Marnie, don't you think that's the reason you're in remission?'

Marnie shook her head. She put down the pink baby thing she'd been knitting. 'No, I don't,' she said emphatically.

'I'm doing well because I've chosen to live, just as Acharya said, in peace and tranquillity. I have survived with belief and love and support.'

'How can you possibly know that's the reason you're still alive?' Marcus demanded. 'I can tell you one thing: it's worked out well for Acharya that you sold your house and gave the proceeds to her. Does anyone here ask themselves what she does with all that money? Thomas?'

Thomas sighed. 'As you know, I do the books. I can guarantee that Acharya puts every cent back into making Soul Haven the place it is.'

'Of course I do,' Acharya said. 'I think you'd better calm down, Marcus.'

'Right,' Marcus said. 'How about we all calm down so much that we don't think at all? Let you do it on our behalf. Is that what you'd like to see happen?'

Acharya smiled, but Tinker could tell how annoyed she was. She strode to the mahogany cabinet, came back with a folder and put it in front of Marcus.

'As you can see, Sadiki has appointed me as his Enduring Guardian. Which means I'm empowered to make medical decisions on his behalf.' She paused, waiting for that to sink in.

Tinker moved chairs to sit in the empty one next to Marcus. 'Sadiki loves it here,' he said. 'And the prognosis is so dire that, at best, medical treatment will only buy him some time.'

Tears ran down Marcus's cheeks, but the fury was still there. 'However long treatment buys us, however much more time I get to spend with Sadiki, I'll take it.'

'You're not fully understanding,' Acharya said. 'But let me indulge you for a moment. All those in favour of Sadiki staying put and seeing out the remainder of this life with dignity, raise your hand.'

Marnie's and Bodhi's shot up instantly. Thomas's followed. Then Zanni's.

Tinker hesitated.

'You can put all your hands in the air till kingdom come,' he said. 'It means nothing to me.' He stared Acharya down. 'And you know where you can stick your Enduring Guardianship, Acharya? Sadiki chose me to support him when we first went to hospital. He will choose me again. Every time.'

Bodhi got up and stood beside Acharya. 'You're not seeing this right, Marcus,' she crooned. 'You're all about Sadiki's body, and Acharya's about his soul.' She looked up at Acharya, who nodded her approval. 'It's kind of a no-contest,' she finished.

'Too right it's a no-contest,' Marcus said. 'It will be me who's by my lover's side. It will be me who cares for him and cherishes him right until the end.' He paused, then stood. 'As soon as I get things sorted, Sadiki's coming with me.'

•

'We need to get him out of Soul Haven,' Acharya said when Marcus had left. 'Tinker, can you sort that out for me?'

Tinker grimaced. 'Maybe just let things settle for a while,' he suggested. 'Marcus might view things differently when he sees that, together, we can make Sadiki comfortable and as happy as possible.' He looked to Zanni, who smiled weakly. 'Acharya, I don't think Marcus leaving would be in Sadiki's best interests. I think if I was in Sadiki's situation and Zanni left, for any reason, it would be devastating.'

Zanni kissed his cheek. 'Perhaps there's another way to deal with this,' she said. 'Quality of life is the most important thing for Sadiki and it's obvious to most of us that it will be maximised here. Tinker has a point. Marcus will come to see that, in time.'

Acharya let out a breath and looked around the table. 'We don't know how much time we have,' she reminded them. 'But I'll think on it. At the very least, we can all agree that there is to be no more communication with Marcus unless I give the green light for it. If he doesn't come around, he will remain a disease we must root out of our beloved community.'

'I'm not going to talk to that dickhead again,' Bodhi declared, standing so close to Acharya that they were almost joined. 'Not unless you tell me to.'

'I think you're being very kind, Acharya,' Marnie said. 'I have no desire to talk to Marcus either. He is faithless.'

'He's an ingrate,' Thomas added. 'Second-guessing you about finances was the last straw for me. Your transparency is as unquestionable as your generous spirit.'

Zanni put her hand on her heart. 'We praise and thank and love you, Acharya,' she said. Then, the others joined in the chant. Including Tinker.

CHAPTER TWENTY-SEVEN

'Where's Marcus?'

Sadiki had slept – for how long? Light to darkness and back again. Moments of peace interspersed with the repeated jolt of recognition. He was dying. He had months to live, at best.

'Marcus?'

Acharya pressed a button and he rose with the bed (not his and Marcus's) to a seated position.

'Darling, we've been through this many times. Marcus is gone. He left. Remember, my sweet, you read the email from him.'

She tried to give him his laptop. He pushed it to the floor, but the contents of the email came back to him like carriages on a sushi train. *Love. Beautiful mind. Can't bear witness.*

Acharya stroked his hair. 'Unfortunately, some are afraid of the great unknown,' she said. 'But we know it's just another element of the soul's journey. One that should be embraced as a wonderful transformation.'

Her mouth kept moving but the words were like steam, evaporating before he could process them. Sadiki rolled over.

'Marcus,' he said into the pillow. Acharya was mistaken. Marcus wouldn't leave him to face this alone.

Clanging noises came from the kitchen. Bodhi emerged with sandwiches and chai, putting them on his bed tray. Did she bow her head to Acharya? It seemed so, but how to trust his judgement when his impressions were so jumbled?

Acharya gave him some pills. She waited as he swallowed them.

'Can I get you anything else?' Bodhi asked, as if this was her home and she was the host.

'Go away,' Sadiki snapped. The way she smiled at him was like she was indulging a bratty child. No, it was more than that. It was a cheap imitation of Acharya's smile. Wasn't it?

'Sadiki is upset about Marcus leaving,' Acharya said. 'Bodhi, I think it's time he knew the truth.'

Bodhi nodded and went to their shared cupboard, bringing back Marcus's favourite yellow overalls. Why would he leave them behind? She handed them to Acharya, who reached into the front pocket and took out a familiar kit.

'Marcus is using again,' she said, showing him the spoon, lighter and needle. 'He didn't have the spiritual capacity to deal with your illness. But I'm here to guide you into the next dimension.'

'Me too,' Bodhi said.

Acharya placed a cool hand on his forehead, emanating strength and love. She cherished him. But she was wrong about Marcus. Sadiki could feel his presence, somewhere close by.

Somewhere just out of reach.

•

The sound of a revving motorbike splintered the Soul Haven peace and woke Tinker up. He looked at his phone. It was 12.32 am.

'What is it?' Zanni asked drowsily.

'I don't know,' he said, stroking her hair. The poor thing had been working all hours to get Soul Haven Inc. orders out and she'd only come to bed an hour ago. 'I'll just check everything's okay. You go back to sleep.'

He pulled on his boxers and a T-shirt and walked out into the night, following the motorcycle's high beam. The man was dressed in leathers. In the torchlight of his phone, Tinker could see him turn off his lights and take off his helmet. He watched as the man strode towards Acharya's house. Tinker burst into a run and caught up to him just as he banged on the door.

'Hey, what do you think you're doing, mate?' Tinker asked.

Up close, he could see the man was small. He had a greying handlebar moustache and brown eyes with deeply etched crow's-feet. He looked dishevelled, as though he'd been drinking. He didn't respond. Instead, he banged again on Acharya's door.

This time, she opened it. She wiped the sleep from her eyes and looked from one man to the other, clearly confused.

'Can I help you?' she asked.

'Too right you can. You can give me back my girl.'

'Your girl?'

'Patty,' the man declared, and now his face seemed to collapse and Tinker saw that he was more upset than angry. 'You give me back my Patty,' he said, very softly.

'Tinker, please deal with … whatever this is,' Acharya said. She moved to close the door, but the man put his foot in the gap.

'I'm Butch,' he said. 'Claudine's partner. I've been Patty's stepdad for ten years. I know the kid's got problems, but I love her like she's my own flesh and blood. And you've been putting things in her head …' He paused as his voice broke. 'You've been telling her things that, well, they just aren't right.'

Acharya sighed. 'I haven't been putting anything into Patty's head,' she insisted. 'She's been discovering things for herself.'

'But they're bullshit things,' Butch said. 'They're—' He stopped and rubbed his eyes. 'Whatever you've been dredging up, you gotta know that. I never touched my baby in that way. I never would.'

The sob that escaped his mouth was heart-wrenching. It made Tinker suddenly feel like hugging him rather than kicking him out. Still, he took Butch by the arm.

'Time to go, mate,' he said.

'I know what it's called,' Butch said, shaking off Tinker's hand. 'She's having false memories. I've been researching them, trying to figure out what to do – how to help my Patty.'

'Bodhi is getting all the help she needs right here, with me,' Acharya said. 'All will be revealed in the end. Now, goodbye.'

'Her name is Patty,' Butch said, recovering himself a little. 'And yes, all will be revealed. Because I've been doing research into you, Bernadette Robinson.'

Even though she still looked calm, Tinker could tell Acharya was rattled. It was in the way she shifted her feet and the slight clenching of her jaw. Butch turned to Tinker.

'Does she tell you people about her past?' he asked. 'Do you know she was sacked from her job as a counsellor at St Audrey's and St Fabien's about twenty years ago for unethical behaviour? Or that she landed at a retreat called Shangri-La in the Blue Mountains, working there for years until her psycho ways got her marched out of there too?'

Tinker shook his head. 'Mate, even if it's true, none of that is relevant now.'

Butch tapped the helmet under his arm. 'Ah, but that's where you're wrong,' he said. 'Because she's still doing the shit that got her kicked out of Shangri-La. I rang around – the people who worked there while she did wouldn't even talk to me. It was like they were scared of something. It took me ages but I finally found someone who was willing to speak.'

Butch turned to Acharya, a renewed strength in his eyes. 'Remember Linda Crossley?' he asked, and this time, Tinker definitely saw a reaction. Acharya seemed momentarily cowed. 'She's retired now, but she was the head of the wellness centre at Shangri-La.'

'I don't recall any Linda Crossley,' Acharya said. 'But if I did—'

'If you did,' Butch interrupted, 'you'd remember that she discovered you were running workshops behind her back. Dark-witch stuff, she reckoned. She said the board's vote to boot you out was unanimous, but you carried on like a wild thing, cursing them all as you got booted out, wishing them all sorts of doom, personalised to their supposedly private details. But when you suggested one of the board members was going to miscarry her child, and she retaliated, things got hectic. Linda told me they had to have you hauled away by security guards. Just like they did at St Fabian's. Now, does that ring a bell at all?'

He paused and shook his head. Then he fixed his eyes on Tinker. 'You really want to be taking life lessons from a witch?'

Tinker flinched. 'Sometimes, when people don't truly understand Acharya's processes—' he began, but Butch cut him off.

'You mean, the process of fucking with people's minds?' he demanded. 'Like she's fucking with Patty's? And yours. And everyone else's at this godforsaken place. As far as I can tell, that's what she does here. Soul Haven my arse. Linda Crossley says that your Acharya is, and I quote, "a psycho who needs to be stopped".'

Butch turned to Acharya again and pointed a finger at her chest. He lowered his voice. 'The cops may have let you get away with your shenanigans,' he said. 'But guess what, Bernadette Robinson? Claudine, me and our friends won't. That, I can guarantee.'

Tinker walked Butch to his bike. 'Acharya won't do any harm, but I'll keep an eye on Patty,' he said in a hushed tone. 'I mean, along with my girlfriend, Zanni. You know, just to make sure she's okay.'

Butch started to put on his helmet but lay it on the seat instead and reached into his pocket.

'You seem like a good bloke,' he said. 'Maybe you've got sucked into this thing like Patty has.' He reached into the pocket of his black leather riding pants, pulled out a piece of paper and handed it to Tinker.

'Linda Crossley's contact details,' he said.

CHAPTER TWENTY-EIGHT

'Tinker, here's the thing,' Sophia said on the other end of the phone as he sat in his ute outside the yurt where Acharya had given him a special spot to park. 'I'm not sure I believe in God anymore. I mean, I get there was an actual Jesus and stuff. But the whole Heavenly Father thing? Like, it's a pretty good story, but so's *The Hunger Games*.'

'Well, Sophia, you're at an age where it's normal to question things,' he said. 'Have you spoken to your mum and dad?'

'I tried to talk to Mum and she obviously told Dad. I reckon they probably want to do an exorcism or something, make my head spin around three-sixty. Which is ironic, when you think of it, because Anastasia is my saint name. It'd be like exorcising the exorcist.'

Tinker stifled a laugh. 'I think you're underestimating them,' he said. 'I get it, though. You're curious. You want to check out different options of what to believe in.'

'Exactly,' Sophia said. 'I mean, I have no clue what Lani subscribes to. But she reckons what you're doing is bonkers. And mum's just … small minded. I get the feeling that she actually learned something when she did shrooms up there. All she'd tell me was that she had a conversation with a goat, which is cool. Like, whoa. But she's so stubborn that, since then, she seems to be trying to undo whatever it felt like 'cos it's kind of competition with the old, bearded man in the sky.'

Sophia sighed deeply. 'The weirdest thing is that I still say my prayers before bed, even though they don't work.'

'That's okay,' Tinker said. 'I reckon prayers can operate in different ways. Acharya says that you can emanate your will into the universe – that's what a lot of our workshops are about.'

'Tinker, you really get it,' Sophia said.

It was amazing that she wanted to discuss the big issues with him. Despite his misgivings about Marcus disappearing, surely it was a solid testament to the evolution he'd experienced at Soul Haven. Wasn't it?

'There are powers out there we don't even understand, and they can make the universe conform to our will,' Sophia continued.

It was strange to hear those words coming from Sophia's mouth. Tinker guessed she'd been doing some spiritual-style googling.

'I say a prayer for you sometimes.'

It was so touching that Tinker's hand went to his heart.

'What else do you believe in?' Sophia asked.

'Well,' Tinker said, using the pause to think about his reply. 'I reckon that connecting with yourself, really thinking about who you are and who you want to be, is where it's at for me. I'm learning that when you focus on the spiritual part of yourself, you find a deeper connection with other people. Does that make sense?'

There was a long pause on the other end of the line.

'Are you okay?' Tinker asked.

'Yeah,' Sophia said eventually. 'I guess I'm just having problems connecting with kids at my school. There's a lot of mean-girl stuff about my birthmark going on.'

'Oh sweetheart,' Tinker said. 'Do you want to tell me about it?'

'Well, thanks for the offer, but I don't care what they say anymore because I've found a true friend online. She talks about real stuff, you know? And she's even got a birthmark just like mine. She's proud of it, and I'm getting there too.'

'Just be careful,' Tinker warned. 'People online aren't always who they say they are.'

'Ah, but she sent me a pic, so I know she's for real. And I'm not supposed to say this, because it's a secret, but the best bit is that you're friends with her too.'

Tinker frowned. 'I'm glad you're being so strong,' he said. 'But, Sophia, I can't think of anyone who has a birthmark like yours.'

'Oh, Tinker,' Sophia said with an exaggerated sigh, suddenly the parent to his child, 'you don't always know when people have them. I mean, if they're on the forehead they're often covered by hair.'

Tinker shrugged. Sophia had a point, but still ...

'I want to come visit you at Soul Haven. I want to find more people who think differently. Like you and Sadiki. I just don't feel like I belong here anymore. You get that, right?'

Just then, Zanni came out of the yurt, running towards him, arms outstretched with a goofy smile on her face. Tinker hugged his partner.

'Absolutely,' he said.

•

'I don't feel right about this,' Zanni said as they pulled into a suburban street in Camberwell a couple of hours after the call with Sophia. 'Marcus has abandoned Sadiki in his hour of need and deserves nothing from us. It's wrong; it's deceitful to go against Acharya's wishes. We should, at the very least, have asked her permission to look for him instead of skulking off like this.'

Tinker reached across the bench seat of his ute. He felt he was in the best relationship of his life. Their sex was beautiful, almost as though they were reaching the deepest, most spiritual parts of each other. There hadn't been a single performance problem on his part. He'd never told Zanni anything but the whole truth. Until now.

Because, as much as he wished they weren't, doubts were seeping in.

He'd told Zanni about the late-night visit from Butch and his accusations about Acharya's past. She'd instantly dismissed them, saying that all visionaries have haters trying to take them down on false pretexts.

He hadn't told her about his attempt to contact the ex-head of the wellness centre at Shangri-La. Zanni would be furious with him if she knew.

He'd hesitated for almost a week, toing and froing. But last evening, he'd called the mobile number Butch had given him. That the automated message had told him her number was out of order had given him pause.

There'd been a physical address on that piece of paper too. When Tinker had googled it, he'd seen it was a large apartment building in Brisbane with a central number. A concierge answered and Tinker asked after the resident of apartment 625, saying he was desperately trying to contact her about a death in the family. Underhanded perhaps, but the ploy had worked because the concierge informed him there'd been a fire just two days before. Apparently it had been contained to that particular apartment and Linda Crossley had vacated the property without giving forwarding contact details.

It was a lot to process, and Tinker wasn't sure he really had. But the feeling it gave him was, well, he didn't know exactly, but it sounded kind of suspect. He'd left his details in case she went back to the building.

'I get it's a conflict, Zanni,' he said now. 'I feel it too. But if we could just find Marcus, talk to him, maybe he'd change his mind. Sadiki is lost without him.'

Zanni shrugged. 'It seems like Marcus's own needs have trumped Sadiki's,' she said. 'And we don't know anything about his sister other than a minimal profile on Facebook and a message that she was willing to meet with us. What we do know is that Marcus is using again. Tinker, what if it's a crack house we're walking into?'

He looked at the garden with its neatly trimmed lawn and flowerbeds in bloom. 'You reckon?'

Zanni gave a nervous chuckle. 'Okay, let's try this, just the once, for Sadiki,' she said. 'But you have to promise to let it go after this.'

Tinker forced a smile. He understood that her love for him was the reason – the only reason, really – that she would be doing this. Zanni's commitment to Acharya was absolute. And his was too. Mostly.

'Promise?' Zanni reiterated.

'Promise,' Tinker said.

CHAPTER TWENTY-NINE

'I have no idea where he is. Marcus has been in and out of touch for years.'

From the birthday cards lined up on the mantelpiece, Tinker could see that Pauline had only recently turned thirty. But she had an air of seriousness about her, a maturity Tinker certainly hadn't had at that age, nor perhaps still.

She poured them tea from a large pot. 'I mean, until now he's never missed my birthday,' she said sadly. 'But he's unreliable, generally. Marcus broke our parents' hearts when he started using. Mine too.'

'We're sorry,' Zanni said. 'That must've been hard.'

Pauline's eyes glistened. '*Hard* doesn't begin to describe it,' she said. 'The worst of it was that he'd been such a great son – and big brother – before that. He was smart, sometimes even scathing, but always his own person.' She sighed. 'I looked up to him. Then he became a thief and a liar.'

'Marcus told me you paid for his rehab,' he said.

Pauline nodded. 'It cost half my life savings.'

'Well, he was clean when he came to join our … community,' Tinker said. Mentioning the name of Soul Haven, he'd found, even with his closest friends, tended to alienate people. 'I mean, unless he was good at hiding it, he seemed totally sober.'

'Well, I guess that's something. It was always obvious when Marcus was using,' Pauline said. 'One can only hope.'

Zanni shook her head and Tinker understood she was thinking about the paraphernalia Acharya had found in the overalls he had left behind. But was that proof? A remnant of the past?

Or had it been planted?

'Did you know Marcus was in love?' Tinker asked.

Pauline put her hand on her heart. 'Really?' she replied. 'That hasn't happened for my brother before, though I do remember him waxing lyrical – I mean, a stoned kind of lyrical – about someone he'd met in Kings Cross. He used to send me poetry about this guy.' She sighed again. 'You know, I could tell he'd written it while he was high, but it was still beautiful. The poems were always dedicated to someone with a Nordic name I can't recall.'

'That would have been Stig,' Tinker said. 'The man he's in a relationship with now. He's our friend.'

'Yes, that's it,' Pauline said. 'Well, good for Marcus.'

'His name was originally Stig,' Zanni said, 'until he found his calling at Soul Haven and Acharya gifted him with his evolved name, Sadiki.'

Tinker could see Pauline shifting in her seat, but Zanni seemed determined to shed more light on a topic best left undiscussed.

'It means "loyal" and "faithful",' she explained.

Pauline frowned. 'Loyal and faithful to what?'

Maya's question to Stig at Lani's wedding echoed in Tinker's ears. *Loyal and faithful ... To whom?*

'To our spiritual leader, Acharya,' Zanni enthused.

Pauline put down her cup and Tinker could see the cringe factor written all over her face.

'Even when he was as high as a kite, Marcus wouldn't have gone for anything like that,' she said. 'He always maintained that no one was better than anyone else, and he certainly would never have claimed allegiance to anyone who purported to be on a higher spiritual plane.' She paused, and the look she gave them was biting. 'That sounds like a cult. Maybe my brother was just smart enough to get out while others got sucked in.'

'You're misunderstanding the situation,' Zanni tried to explain. 'Soul Haven is a community, and a community needs a leader.'

Pauline stood up. 'If it walks like a duck and quacks like a duck ...' she said. 'I think it's time for you to go.'

'Pauline, Stig is dying,' Tinker said softly. 'He's yearning for Marcus. Which is why it's so important we find him.'

'Well, I'm sorry to hear that,' she said but her voice was steely now. 'As you might imagine, it's pretty important to me too, and to our parents. But as I said, I have no clue where he is.'

Tinker stood up and Zanni followed suit, looking bewildered as to why things had gone pear-shaped.

'So you didn't hear from him on your birthday?' he asked.

'I told you that already,' Pauline said sharply. 'Not a word.'

•

In all her school years, Maya had never been sent to the principal's office. But here she was, at thirty-eight, on the wrong side of Ms Diamond's desk.

'Sophia's home-group teacher has reported turbulence among the girls,' Ms Diamond said. 'Which in itself isn't unusual, but her behaviour has been erratic. She's been … adversarial, in general.'

Ms Diamond put down her pen, eyes on Connor and Maya. 'Are there problems at home we should know about?'

'No,' Maya insisted.

Since there was no way she could possibly mention the backlash from her taking a mushroom trip almost eight months ago, it was necessary to lie. And it was a venial sin, at most. But she was still annoyed that Connor raised his eyebrows.

'It seems that Sophia has been misappropriating some other students' belongings.'

Maya stopped herself from gasping. She sat up straight. 'Are you saying our daughter is a thief?' she demanded. 'Let me guess, could it be Alana Dupont who made the allegation? Because she also accused Sophia of letting a wasp into their dance class, which was beyond ridiculous. That girl has it in for my daughter. She's jealous and spiteful and—'

'I won't name the students,' Ms Diamond interrupted. 'Suffice to say a barrette was found in Sophia's locker.'

'Was it diamond-encrusted?' Maya knew she should keep the snark out of her tone, but really? A barrette?

'Maya,' Connor chided. 'Let's be calm about this.'

Maya was anything but calm. Connor reached for her hand, but she shook it off.

'Perhaps the student dropped it and Sophia picked it up and put it in her locker for safekeeping?' she suggested.

'We considered that possibility,' Ms Diamond said. 'It's true that all jewellery must be removed for sport. But, Mr and Mrs Donnelly, I'm afraid there were other items.'

She reached into her desk drawer and brought out the offending barrette, along with an asthma inhaler and a butterfly pendant.

No one spoke. The barrette, with a cubic zirconia *A*, was the one Alana had dropped during her twerking episode in dance rehearsals several weeks ago. Maya had no idea who the butterfly pendant belonged to, but it was the asthma inhaler that was most disturbing.

'Whose is it?' Maya asked, pointing.

'We haven't established that,' Ms Diamond admitted. 'There are several students who use Ventolin, and many would have a spare. But, Mrs Donnelly, I think that collecting these items might be a reflection of Sophia's state of mind. We'd like her to have a few sessions with the school counsellor.'

CHAPTER THIRTY

'Here,' Lani said, placing Maya's hand on her stomach. 'Did you feel that?'

'Yes, totally,' Maya said. 'It's beautiful, Lani. You're lucky you escaped most of the morning-sickness jazz. I had it bad with the twins. Twenty weeks already?' She scooched closer to Lani on the couch. 'Are you going to find out the gender? Or have you already?'

Lani put a finger to her lips. 'You have to promise not to tell a soul,' she said, 'because I swore I wouldn't. But Bridget couldn't make it to the last ultrasound and I just … well, I couldn't help myself. It's a girl!'

'That's wonderful,' Maya said, but her reaction and the small smile that accompanied it was underwhelming.

'I know,' Lani enthused, hoping to stir up a bit more emotion. 'I'm beyond stoked. I keep hoping she'll be cool and funny like Sophia.'

'Be careful what you wish for,' Maya said, and it was a joke of course, but the timing seemed way off. 'Looks like you have everything a baby could possibly need already.'

Lani turned around. The delivery from her parents had arrived a couple of hours before. She'd unpacked the SNOO bassinet and Orbit pram but was waiting for Bridget to take them upstairs. 'Mama doesn't know which one, but she swears a Kardashian has that pram,' she said with a chuckle. 'And, Maya, if you think that's over-the-top, you should see the nursery. Mama and Papa are both super excited. I reckon they think they're getting a second chance at having the perfect child.'

'My parents were pretty thrilled when we had the twins too,' Maya said snappily. 'But ninety-nine per cent of the population don't have the wherewithal to fill a nursery with elite products to welcome them.'

It felt like a punch in the gut. God, wasn't this supposed to be Lani's special time? She'd expected so much more love and attention than Tinker was giving now he was entrenched in that fucked-up cult, and now, was Maya withdrawing from her as well? Lani couldn't bear that.

Maya got up and poured two glasses of Perrier, handing one to Lani. 'I haven't told you, but Sophia's been stealing,' she said, so softly that Lani wasn't sure she'd heard right.

Lani sighed. 'Oh, darling,' she said. 'I know you never did, but when I was Sophia's age, I nicked a whole lot of random stuff. It was exciting, I guess. A phase. Whatever it was, I grew out of it.'

'Maybe it's because we don't have as much as other people,' Maya said, and Lani got that the 'other people' she was referring to had her at the centre. 'Truly, I don't know why, but Sophia hasn't been taking stuff from shops. She's been stealing from classmates.'

Lani frowned. 'What kind of stuff?'

'Just stuff, okay,' Maya snapped again. 'I'm sorry, Lani, I'm just not going to be good company today.' She got up and gathered her handbag, 'Thou shalt not steal,' she mumbled. 'One of the most important commandments.'

Lani stood up and touched Maya's arm. 'Has Sophia fessed up?' she asked, moving past the religious reference as quickly as possible.

'Kind of,' Maya said. 'She won't – or can't – tell us why she did it, fobbed it off as a practical joke. But at least she's seeing the school counsellor. And she's been speaking with Tinker quite a bit, which seems to be helping her mood, but she won't tell us much of what they discuss.'

It was a double whammy. The mention of a school counsellor would have been enough to knock Lani sideways. But that Sophia was choosing to talk to Tinker over her was gobsmacking. Jesus, she was the kid's godmother. Why was she being locked out of everything?

The friendship between Tinker, Maya and her had been solid. Now, everything seemed fractured.

•

'Marcus's choices are none of our business,' Zanni said as they began the trip back to Soul Haven. 'It was stupid to go and see his sister. All it achieved was betraying Acharya's trust and getting accused of being in a cult.'

Tinker tried to hold her hand, but she shook him off.

The all-too-familiar feeling of rejection, of being thought of as dense, settled upon him. Before this, there'd never been a cross word spoken between him and Zanni. He would have tried to smooth over the tension, but this felt too important. He took a deep breath.

'Don't you think it's weird that Marcus missed Pauline's birthday for the first time in their lives?'

'No. He's a junkie. What I think's weird is that we risk ruining the lives we've built for ourselves. Let's put this behind us, Tinker. I agree with Pauline that Marcus was never about to give himself over to a higher power. And Acharya was right, he was only at Soul Haven for his own benefit. The one thing he contributed to was renovating the church. He wasn't loyal to her, and obviously, not to Sadiki. Come on, let's go home.'

'I don't think I can. What if Marcus didn't just up and leave? What if something happened to him?'

Zanni's eyes narrowed. 'What are you suggesting?'

'I don't know what I'm suggesting,' Tinker admitted. 'But Marcus vowed he'd be by Sadiki's side until the end. Remember what he said in the meeting about Sadiki? However long treatment bought him, Marcus wanted to spend it with his lover. And Sadiki's convinced he's still around. He asks me to find Marcus all the time and it breaks my heart.'

'That's the brain cancer talking,' Zanni said. 'Tinker, promising and doing are two very different things. You've got to be able to separate intent and action. Marcus upped and left. I mean, his car's gone. His mobile's off. Wherever he is, he doesn't want to be found.'

Zanni's frustrated sigh sounded like something that used to come from Fiona. And Tracey. And Dina. Tinker pulled the ute into a rest area off the highway, shut off the engine and looked Zanni in the eyes.

'I've got a bad feeling about this, Zanni. And that bad feeling includes Acharya.'

'You came to Soul Haven lost, like me. And now we have each other, we have Acharya and our community.'

'But it's all conditional on following Acharya's guidelines,' Tinker said.

'She has her reasons. Tinker, we've given ourselves over to her because she's making our lives better.'

'But at what cost? Zanni, I respect Acharya and I know what she's done for us. But I also don't want to be told who I can or can't see.' He paused on the brink of making or breaking their relationship.

'I tried to contact the woman Acharya worked with at Shangri-La,' he said quietly.

Zanni's normally warm eyes were cold, but Tinker went on. 'The phone number Bodhi's stepdad gave me has been disconnected, but he only spoke to her days ago. The concierge told me there'd been a fire, an isolated one, just in Linda's apartment, and that she'd gone without leaving any forwarding details.'

'Jesus, Tinker,' Zanni said. 'You know what? Shit happens in life. To you, to me, to bloody Linda Crossley—'

'Listen to me,' Tinker urged. 'When I first met you, you said you toss yourself into the *wrong* mix and spin around like you're in a rinse cycle.' He paused. 'Maybe you've done it again. Maybe we both have.'

'No,' Zanni yelled. 'This time, finally, I've got it right. Maybe it's just the Tinker element I got wrong.'

Tinker's gut churned with the string of relationships he'd failed in. His reaction was kneejerk.

'Why? Are you hanging out for someone like your daddy? Someone who'll give you love and take it away without a second thought?'

'Fuck you.'

Tinker threw up his hands. 'I'm sorry, Zanni. I didn't mean that.' But Zanni was already pulling on the handle of the passenger door. Tinker held her arm.

'Let go of me,' she warned, her voice low and furious. 'You know nothing. All you have are speculations and doubt. We are apprentices at Soul Haven but you lack faith, Tinker. And you've made me complicit by agreeing to look for Marcus with you. You run with this ... conspiracy theory, you'll ruin our lives.'

She paused and the look she gave him was icy.

'You know what, go ahead, decide it all for yourself. Risk everything we are – all our learnings – for a junkie. We'll see how that works out.'

Tinker stared blankly as Zanni opened the car door. He watched her walk towards a parked truck and speak to the driver through his window. Within moments, she was stepping up to the passenger seat.

Then she was gone.

CHAPTER THIRTY-ONE

Despite being exhausted, Lani couldn't go back to sleep. She tried to relax in the jacuzzi with a peppermint tea, but even with the buoyancy of the water, the pressure on her pelvis was constant.

'Breathe, kitten,' Bridget said. 'Where does it hurt?'

A cramp prevented Lani from responding. 'Something's wrong,' she moaned.

'Maybe you're having Braxton Hicks?'

For a couple of minutes, except for the pressure on her pelvis, Lani felt okay. She leaned into Bridget's open arms. On the deck beside them, Maya's profile pic appeared on the phone, then beeped with a voice message they ignored.

'Oh fuck.' A new contraction made Lani double over. 'I don't think they're Braxton Hicks,' she said. 'I think it's happening.'

Bridget gulped. 'It can't be,' she said in a wavering voice. 'We're only at twenty-three weeks.'

'Oh no,' Lani cried. 'I think I just felt my waters break.'

Bridget sprang into action, trying to help Lani out of the jacuzzi, but another contraction stopped her progress.

'Breathe through it,' Bridget reminded Lani, but her words meant nothing. Because all Lani could hear was Acharya's curse, on repeat.

The universe will conspire so that you don't pass on your father's legacy.

•

'No, I don't want a caesarean. We've planned for a natural birth. Bridget, tell them.'

The contractions weren't so bad now the epidural had kicked in. Lani could feel them, but they were a shadow of what they'd been over the past few hours. Her father had sorted it so she had the best obstetrician and anaesthetist in Melbourne, but that didn't mean he got to decide how her baby was going to be born.

Bridget had been holding Lani's hand, but Gino cut in while Yvette busied herself unpacking Lani's toiletries.

'We've been assured it's the best way to deliver our baby, considering the situation,' Gino said.

'All the way through the pregnancy, we've been told a natural birth is safer,' Bridget said.

'Well, that's not the case when the baby is premature,' Gino said. 'Look, Bridget, we're in a specialised maternity hospital and that means the best possible outcome. But there's so many issues we might encounter. It makes no sense to create more.'

'We don't want the little love having to fight their way down the birth canal, do we?' Yvette called without turning around. 'The poor little thing will have enough to contend with.'

'Don't say that, Yvette,' Bridget exclaimed. '*Our* baby, as in mine and Lani's, is going to be fine. We need only positive vibes in here right now. If the pair of you don't think you can provide them, maybe it's best that you leave.'

The reality of the situation hit Lani suddenly with full force. She'd come across the figures in the birthing books. The chance of survival at twenty-four weeks was only around eighty per cent, at best. She hadn't even hit that milestone yet. In terms of health and development, there were many risks involved. Their lungs, heart and brain aren't ready to survive alone outside the womb.

The universe will conspire so that you don't pass on your father's legacy.

Her scream caught everyone by surprise. Especially so when it was followed with a flood of tears.

'My baby's been cursed,' she managed between sobs.

They all eyed her as though she was going mad.

'It's true,' she insisted. 'By the cult leader of Soul Haven, who has Tinker under her spell. You know her, Papa. She was the school counsellor when Stig got sent away. I don't know why she hates you so much. I don't know why she hates *me* so much. I don't know why it feels so personal. But I've been freaked out ever since. And now, with the baby coming early ... Papa, I'm afraid.'

Her words seemed to propel him backward. She could tell he was trying to conceal his shock, but the expression on his face showed otherwise.

Yvette turned around, hands on hips, and glared at her husband.

'Tell me you didn't,' she demanded.

But Lani couldn't hear his response because the doctor strode into the birthing suite and took control.

CHAPTER THIRTY-TWO

'It's not right,' Bodhi said, scooping hot soup into Sadiki's mouth too quickly so that he could feel it dripping down his chin. 'Acharya's got this random girl at the house with her right now to do a reverse blessing ceremony, and I wanted to stay and keep helping 'cos, you know, I love putting curses on shitty people. And I'm good at it!'

Sadiki lifted his hand, trying to get her to slow down on feeding him the next mouthful, but she seemed not to notice.

'You know, it was me who prepared for the ceremony. I lit the thirteen candles, set up the altar, burned the sage and all that stuff while Acharya was picking her up from the train station.'

Sadiki closed his mouth and Bodhi put down the bowl. 'Open up,' she demanded as she tried to pry his lips apart with her fingers. 'Acharya says you need to eat the whole lot before I give you your meds.'

She seemed so determined that Sadiki considered it best to go along with her. He reluctantly opened his mouth again.

'Anyway, I met her. She seems like a wanker. She's acting as if she knows Acharya properly when all they've been doing is talking online. That's totally not the same thing. And spending an afternoon at Soul Haven doing a ceremony is nothing compared to all the work I done. Like, girl, have you had a gazillion age regressions with Acharya? No. Have you been given a special name 'cos you've earned it? No. Have you proved your loyalty, day in, day out? No, you're on a freaking day trip. You're just a tourist at Soul Haven!'

Bodhi pulled over the tray table and put down the bowl, stuck a straw in Sadiki's mouth and motioned for him to drink the soup.

'This chick's clueless. I mean, she's got this big birthmark on the left side of her forehead and Acharya painted the same one on her own, but on the right.'

Something about a girl and a birthmark struck a chord with Sadiki, but he couldn't figure out why. 'Acharya meets people where they're at,' he said, remembering the phrase from when she'd performed the reverse blessing for Bodhi when she first came on the scene.

'True that,' Bodhi said. 'But I wouldn't have fallen for something so … obvious. This dummy did though – hook, line and sinker. Anyway, I done all the right things. I asked to see what she brung to use in the session and laid them out for Acharya to inspect.' She paused. 'What's-her-name had three dolls, a lock of hair, a photo of a boy and a beanie. Acharya had set out much better tools than she lets me use. She had a whole bunch of things, like gardening shears and a frigging saw. I told Acharya that wasn't fair because all she ever gave me to use was pins and bandages, but she reckoned the chick had to have access to more power 'cos her enemies were far from here.'

Bodhi sighed deeply. 'I done everything right, and that girl's being all hoity-toity. Acharya asked her to summon the spirits of her ancestors – you know, to band together and make the curses strong. And she gets all, "I don't know if I can do that." Said it seems kind of wrong to use past generations that way. Like, she doesn't even properly believe in Acharya, when I'm a hundred and ten per cent in.'

Bodhi shook her head in disgust. 'What's-her-face could've had a field day. But, no, she was too chicken. She pulled out of the ceremony without cursing any of them. Which was so disrespectful to Acharya. But instead of giving her what for, Acharya tells the bitch she likes her questioning mind and let's enter a debate about what's right and what's wrong. So I go, this ceremony isn't supposed to be a debate. It's supposed to be about devotion! About putting your eggs in Acharya's basket. Which was sticking up for our spiritual leader, right?'

Thankfully, Sadiki finally finished the soup and Bodhi pushed the bed tray away.

'Right,' Sadiki said. He and Bodhi had both placed their allegiances with Acharya.

And, of course, he still did. She had taken his suffering and made him a life. Hadn't she? Well, for a few years that had been true. But now he was dying; without Marcus by his side, it felt as though the whole idea of Soul Haven was tarnished.

'You'd reckon Acharya would be chuffed with me,' Bodhi said. 'But that was when she insisted I go and look after you, like she wanted me out of there so she could *debate* with that stupid girl.'

Bodhi sighed deeply. 'Sometimes I feel ... well, kind of unappreciated. I mean, I'm sorry you're dying. It sucks. But since that's definitely going to happen, it's kind of obvious that I should be Acharya's second in charge. No offence, but you weren't a perfect choice in the first place,' she said. 'You're kind of ... well, soft. And to run a place like Soul Haven, you gotta be tough. Like, you've gotta have rules and consequences and I don't reckon you'd be much good at that.' She leaned in. 'I'm good at that,' she whispered, though there was no one else but them around. 'Really good.'

Sadiki tried to sit up straight, but it was an effort. 'What do you mean?' he managed.

Bodhi smiled. 'Wouldn't you like to know?' she replied. 'Geez, poor thing, you're not really in the loop anymore now you're sick. You hardly know anything that's going on. But don't worry, I'll tell you *some* things. Other things are top-secret. Just between me and Acharya.'

Sadiki frowned. 'Please tell me what you can,' he said.

Bodhi leaned back on her chair. 'Well, for one thing, your friend Tinker's in big trouble. Zanni dobbed on him. Apparently she confessed they went looking for Marcus without Acharya's blessing.'

Sadiki started at the mention of his boyfriend's name. 'Did they find him?'

A strange, almost smug look flitted over Bodhi's face. 'Of course not,' she said eventually. 'Seems like Marcus is pretty good at disappearing. Anyway, we're not supposed to talk about that.' She wagged a finger at him. 'Naughty,' she admonished.

'Can you send Tinker over when he gets back?' Sadiki pleaded. 'Maybe he has news on Marcus.'

'Dunno,' Bodhi replied. 'Depends on what Acharya says. Tinker might get booted out of Soul Haven. That's what I'd do if I was Acharya. But, Sadiki, there won't be any news on Marcus. You gotta give up on that. Your boyfriend's long gone. Now, take your painkillers so I can go back to the house and see what's going on.'

Bodhi put the pills in his mouth and he swallowed them with the okra water she gave him.

Then Sadiki fell into a deep sleep, plagued with nightmares of Marcus crying out to him.

CHAPTER THIRTY-THREE

'Good afternoon, Mrs Donnelly, it's Tarni Bradshaw from the Radcliffe High General Office.'

Maya braced herself. A call from Sophia's school at 4 pm on a Thursday was never going to be good news. 'Is everything okay?' she ventured.

'Yes. Oh, I'm sorry. I guess I should've begun with that given all of Sophia's recent ... troubles,' Tarni said, the upward inflection at the end of the sentence making it sound like a question. 'I'm just inquiring whether she'll be well enough to attend the Year 9 excursion to the NGV tomorrow?'

Maya frowned. 'Why wouldn't she be?'

There was a pause. Maya counted the seconds.

'We received an email from you on the absentee hotline this morning stating that Sophia was recovering from a virus?'

'I sent nothing of the sort,' Maya snapped. 'Sophia should have been at school today.'

'Let me check. Perhaps there's been a mistake.' Again, with the upward inflection.

With each second that passed, Maya felt more agitated. Surely there was enough actually going on with Sophia that the school didn't need to invent more issues. She grabbed her laptop, checked her sent mail and her heart dropped. Because there was the email sent to the absentee line. So now she was going to have to add truancy and forgery – though of course an email didn't require a signature – to her daughter's new skill set.

'Sophia was marked as absent from all her lessons today,' Tarni said. 'Can you please clarify—'

Maya hung up. Coral Paxton's father's details were on the class list. As she dialled the number, she could already feel Sophia's wrath at checking up on her. It had seemed a nice surprise that she'd been asked for a sleepover. But now—

'Mr Paxton? Hi, it's Maya Donnelly. Just checking whether everything went smoothly last night?'

'Sorry, Maya. I'm not sure why you're asking.'

'Sophia stayed with you and Coral last night.' Though her pulse was racing, phrasing it as a statement seemed to be the best way to hedge her bets.

'No,' Mr Paxton said. 'Coral was here, as she always is on Wednesdays – but she was by herself. Maya, is there something wrong?'

She gulped. 'No, everything's fine,' she lied. 'Just some crossed wires.'

There was a pause on the other end of the phone. 'I hope this isn't betraying Coral's confidence, but, Maya, there's some nasty stuff going on at school. If Sophia didn't go today, maybe there's a good reason.'

'Where could she be?' Maya asked, surprising herself at the plaintive tone her voice carried.

'I don't know. But if you need some help finding her, I can help.'

His kindness was making things worse. For a moment, Maya was speechless.

'I'll check with Coral and let you know if she has any clues,' Mr Paxton continued. 'But I'm sure Sophia will be safe.'

Maya said her thankyous. But, on the back of that comment, her trepidation blossomed into fully-fledged fear.

Sophia was missing.

And she'd been god-only-knew-where for twenty-four hours. There was panic in her voice as she called Connor and asked him to come home from work immediately.

•

'Has Sophia gone missing before?'

The policewoman who removed her cap and put it on the dining table looked too young, like a kid in dress-up. Maya deferred instead to the older woman accompanying her.

'Yes,' she admitted. 'Only for an hour or two here and there, but never overnight.' Beside her, she noticed that Luke was shaking. She put an arm around her son and pulled him close.

'And is there anywhere she would normally go? Boyfriends? Girlfriends?'

'There's something I have to tell you,' Luke said in a wobbly voice. All eyes were on him as he continued. 'I think Sophia was with Darcy Jeffries last night. I know she told you she was going to Coral's and she told me that too, but I overheard her on the phone to him.'

The information hit Maya like a ton of bricks. Sophia was still a kid. For goodness sake, what if she was sexually active already? That would be—

Luke intercepted her thoughts. 'It's not what you think, Mum,' he said. 'Darcy is just her friend. But he doesn't show it at school 'cos it would make him unpopular. You know, by association.'

Shades of Joe denying his relationship with Stig ran through Maya's mind.

'So,' said the younger policewoman, 'I think it's time to put in a call to Darcy Jeffries.'

Maya gulped and nodded. Sophia's motive for staying with Darcy Jeffries last night might be dubious. As was her email to the absentee hotline. But there was something else at play. She could feel it.

'I've already spoken to Darcy,' Luke said. 'Sophia snuck into his room and stayed with him last night and they just talked. But they walked to school together, so she should've been there today.'

'Is Sophia having problems at school?' the younger woman asked.

'Yes,' Luke said. 'Some kids are being mean to her.'

'And what about at home? Any blow-ups?'

'Just the regular teenage variety,' Maya said, and she wasn't lying. Was she?

'Is there anywhere Sophia normally goes when she feels down?'

'Plenty of places. But this isn't normal,' Luke said softly.

The younger woman pulled out a chair and sat, focusing on Luke.

He stepped away from Maya and took a deep breath. 'We're twins.' He put his hand on his heart. 'I can feel it here, like I did when she was in a bus accident three years ago.'

Maya resisted the urge to pull him into her embrace. To never let him out of her sight ever again. Luke was right. He'd been at home sick when the school bus rounded a corner too fast and rolled over. He'd screamed out from his bed, told her something was wrong with Sophia just seconds before she got the official phone call. Luckily, there were no injuries from that accident. But it had always seemed that the twins knew when each other was in trouble. They said it was a feeling that couldn't be explained in words. Maya had thought it quaint, but now Luke's sensibility sent a shiver down her spine.

'It's worse this time,' he said, his hand glued to his heart. 'My sister's in danger.'

'It's okay, Luke. She wagged a day of school is all,' Connor tried to reassure him, but Luke wasn't having it.

'I get that, but where did she go? And where is she now?' Luke asked.

Maya put her hand to her forehead.

'And you've tried to call her?' the older policewoman asked.

'Of course, several times,' Maya snapped. 'Her phone is either off or she left it behind. And I've rung just about everyone we know.' Neither Lani nor Tinker had returned her call, but really, what help could they be? Both her friends were so wrapped up in themselves these days – Lani acting as though she was the first person ever to be pregnant, and Tinker with his devotion to bloody Soul Haven. Although knowing that Sophia had been speaking with Tinker quite a bit lately, perhaps he could help.

'Do you know what Sophia was wearing?'

'The last time we saw her, yesterday morning, she was in her school uniform,' Connor said. 'But she had an overnight bag with her.'

'Okay, and have you checked her room? Maybe we can do that together.'

Maya led the police officers upstairs into Sophia's bedroom. It was neater than usual. The bed was made and there were only a few clothing items on the floor. Somehow, this made Maya's heart sink further.

'Her puffer is gone,' she told them. 'Her school uniform and shoes, of course, since that was what she was wearing when she left yesterday morning.' She paused, looking at the bookshelf. It seemed irrelevant to mention it.

'Is anything out of order?'

'Mum,' Luke said at the doorway, 'there is something else, isn't there?'

Maya sat on Sophia's bed. 'Sophia had three dolls there.' She pointed to the shelf where they'd been for weeks now. 'Ordinary dolls – just felt with no features. I supposed she was doing an art project. But they're gone too, which makes zero sense. Why on earth would Sophia take them with her?'

The policewomen looked as confused as Maya felt.

Luke went to the bookcase. He closed his eyes and touched the space where the dolls had been.

'I don't know,' he said. 'But those dolls have something to do with Sophia going missing.'

•

At 5.30 pm on Thursday evening, Maya knocked on the door of Stella Dupont's house. The police weren't taking Sophia's disappearance seriously enough. Yes, as they now knew from Maya's strained conversation with Darcy, Sophia had stayed the night at his house. But no one had seen her since just before 9 am. Which still meant she was missing.

'Come in,' Stella said, leading her down a hallway with impossibly high ceilings to a sitting room. 'Would you like a drink?' she asked, motioning for Maya to sit on the couch.

Maya shook her head. 'Please, can I just talk with Alana?'

Stella frowned. 'Maya, I'm sorry to hear that Sophia's missing,' she said. 'But, really, I don't see how Alana can help.'

'Well, that's not for you to say,' Maya snapped. 'I'm sorry,' she followed up. 'It's just that … imagine how you'd feel if it was Alana.'

Stella stood up and, for a moment, Maya was terrified she'd be shown the door. Instead, Stella called up the stairs. Alana came down slowly on her crutches. She stood in the doorway as though ready to make an escape.

Maya tried to keep her voice even. 'Could you tell me what's been going on at school?' she pleaded.

Alana looked at her mother, who nodded. 'It all just got a bit out of hand,' she said.

'Go on,' Stella encouraged her daughter. Maya could see the concern in her eyes. Perhaps she'd misjudged Stella. 'What got out of hand?'

Alana sighed. 'Well, it started when Sophia brought the magazine to school, you know, the one where she was a bridesmaid at Lani Galleta's wedding. Like, she was gloating, acting as though she was famous or something.' Maya gritted her teeth as she waited. 'Look, at first it was just an insult I thought of to, you know, bring her down a peg.'

'What was it you thought of?' Stella demanded.

Alana looked up at the ceiling.

'Listen,' Maya urged. 'No one's going to get cross. This isn't about that. This is about finding Sophia.'

Alana gulped. 'Okay, I said it first. It was just … I googled insults about birthmarks and came up with shitstain. And, you know, it was just alliteration to call her Shitstain Sophia. I mean, it was a joke.'

Maya couldn't help but gasp at the cruelty. But she quickly calmed herself. It was important to keep Alana talking.

'I'm sure it was just a joke,' she assured her, and the way Alana leaned on her crutch, as though her exit might be a little less imminent, made Maya feel this was the right approach.

'The thing is – it kind of caught on. Honestly, I stopped saying it. But then Casey and some others started. They thought it was funny to see Sophia's reaction, because she'd go nuts every time. And Darcy Jeffries – well, he liked Sophia but then he went off her. I think he just didn't want to be seen with her in case he got pulled into the situation. I didn't expect it all to blow up.' She paused. 'I'm sorry,' she said softly. 'I really am. But Sophia got her own back.'

For a moment, Maya felt like she might faint. 'How?' she asked.

Alana covered her eyes, then pointed to her crutches.

'I have no idea what that means,' Maya said.

'Mum,' Alana said. 'I want to go now.'

Stella went to her daughter. As Alana's tears fell, she put an arm across her shoulder. 'Darling, how could Sophia have had anything to do with your skiing accident?'

Alana wiped her eyes with her hand. 'It's so creepy I don't even want to say it,' she said.

Maya waited, trying to hide her impatience. Alana frowned. 'Sophia had these dolls,' she said. 'Like, really weird ones.'

Maya shuddered. 'Felt dolls?' she asked. 'With no features?'

'Yes,' Alana replied. 'She sent me a photo of one with my barrette on it just before I had the accident.'

CHAPTER THIRTY-FOUR

'Oh god, no. No more,' Lani wailed.

'Gather your strength,' the nurse said. 'That's good, now bear down.'

'No,' Lani screamed. At this most crucial moment, the epidural had worn off and there was no time to resummon the anaesthetist. The pain was like nothing she'd ever felt before. Raw and primal and, in the midst of it, Acharya's curse kept swirling around, all pervasive. It ran on loop in her head. Floated around the birthing suite. Got stuck in the nooks and crannies of her bed. Manifested in the nurse's concerned expression. In Bridget's palpable fear. In the obstetrician's frown. In the forceps and other Gothic-looking tools on the tray beside her.

The universe will conspire so that you don't pass on your father's legacy.

Lani was going to die. Her baby too. They'd never meet. And yet ...

'I can see the head. The baby's crowning.' It was Bridget's voice. 'Kitten, you've got this. You have.'

Lani didn't have this. She didn't want this. She wished her eggs had never met Heston's sperm. Wished ...

'We're going to help baby out, okay? You're doing so well,' the nurse encouraged. 'Another push, Lani.'

There was no stopping it. Lani was being torn apart by a herd of wild animals. She screamed. What the fuck were they doing to her? They were murdering her. Murdering her child. Who could she trust? Was there a way to keep this baby safe, keep her inside the womb where Lani could protect her? Yes, that was it. She'd keep the baby inside her. She would not let Valentina enter this strange world with its fear and longing and curses.

But no. The urge to push was overpowering. A whole body was emerging from her. Slipping, sliding out of her. Coming into the terrifying world.

So, why wasn't there crying? Wasn't that what was supposed to happen?

'It's a girl.' Bridget was bawling now. 'Kitten, it's a girl. It's our—'

But her voice was drowned out by action. So much action. Was the baby even alive? Yes, she must be, but the doctors were speaking in low, urgent voices that Lani could only hear snippets of.

No time for skin to skin.

Neonatal.

Urgent.

Tell them to prepare.

'Go with her.' Lani's voice was small, but Bridget was listening. 'Go with our baby. Don't leave her side.'

Bridget nodded. A flood of tears was rolling down her cheeks. Then Lani sunk back into the bed. Into oblivion.

•

Tinker drove around aimlessly for hours, trying to feel something, but he was numb. He'd messed things up. Again. He shouldn't have been trying to find Marcus. He shouldn't have been asking questions, doubting the status quo. If he'd only been able to trust in Acharya the way Zanni did, he could stay happy and content.

It was already dark when he got back to Soul Haven. He was tentative when he entered the yurt, ready to make the grand apology he'd rehearsed in the car. He couldn't see Zanni, but he could hear the water running.

The bathroom had steamed up. Zanni was naked, sitting on the shower floor as water rained down on her. What was she doing? Oh no. What was she doing? Her hair, her beautiful long black hair lay in chunks around her. She held up another handful and cut it randomly, close to her scalp.

'Zanni, no,' he cried, opening the glass door, but it was too late. There were only a few strands that remained long. The rest was sheared.

'Acharya knows about our betrayal,' she said, looking at him with glistening eyes. 'I've been vain, self-centred, too focused on you and our relationship. I've neglected my duty to her, and to Soul Haven, trying to chase personal satisfaction. But I'm making amends.'

She lifted up the last chunk of long hair and stared at him as she cut it off.

In his pocket, Tinker's phone rang out and then started again. He ignored it, crouching down on the other side of the door.

'What happened?' he asked.

'What happened is that I confessed,' Zanni said. 'I nearly lost belonging, because of you. I nearly lost my home and my heart. I nearly lost everything I've worked for in my evolution.'

The laugh that came next was guttural, as though it was emerging from the deepest part of her.

'But Acharya is forgiving,' she continued. 'She is light and empowerment and she knew what I had to do. This is the start of my repentance.'

Tinker put his phone on top of their vanity. He was fully clothed, but he got into the shower. He pulled her into him. She hugged him back and he felt the connection that still hovered between them.

'Maybe she can save you if you truly give yourself over this time,' Zanni said. 'Because you don't believe in anything. You're lost, Tinker.'

'Perhaps we both are,' he ventured. 'Zanni, think about it. How can cutting your hair do any good? How can it be any form of repentance? And repentance for what? We were trying to help Sadiki.'

The look she gave him was empathetic. She stroked his cheek.

'You still don't understand, do you?' she said. 'My hair is – was – my ego. In order to move forward, to evolve, I needed to let it go. And, as Acharya explained, Sadiki is better off without the poison of Marcus, the doubter, the junkie. She will be his spiritual partner. She will be beside him, guiding him into the next plane.'

'I will.'

Between the running water and the conversation, neither of them had heard Acharya enter the bathroom.

CHAPTER THIRTY-FIVE

'Where's my baby? Where's Valentina?'

Lani woke up exhausted and confused. The hospital room was already full of fresh bouquets and balloons, signalling congratulations, but wasn't that premature? Was her baby going to be all right?

Only her father was with her. He held her hand. It looked as though he'd been crying.

'She's in the NICU, honey,' he said. He paused, head in hands. 'She's doing okay. The doctors are hopeful. They can't assess for all potential problems yet. Lani, she's tiny, but she looks perfect.' A sob escaped from his mouth.

Suddenly, the terror of Acharya's curse hit her again with full force and her father must have seen it writ large on her face.

'Bridget and Yvette are with her,' he assured her. 'I did the shift before that. I promise you Valentina won't be left without a trusted member of our family. There's no chance anyone – I mean, anyone – outside us and the hospital staff, can get to her.'

Lani tried to sit up but it hurt. Everything did. Her body, her heart, her soul.

'But my innocent baby shouldn't need to be guarded,' she said. 'It must have something to do with you. Tell me, what happened between you and the school counsellor all those years ago?'

He let go of her hand, stood up and began pacing back and forth beside Lani's bed.

'Everything,' Lani demanded with as much gusto as she could summon. 'Papa, it could be important.'

He let out a massive sigh, then nodded.

'As you know, Bernadette Robinson was the school counsellor at St Fabian's and St Audrey's.'

'Yes,' Lani said impatiently. 'And?'

'She was handling the situation that had come up with Stig Johannsen and Joe Carruthers.' He sighed. 'She was supposed to be enacting damage control. Mitigating the effects of the video that was circulating that showed Stig preying on Joe.'

Lani winced at his perception, the common perception, that Stig was at fault in the footage, but decided not to contest it. At the moment, she needed new information.

'I went to see her, to figure out whether she understood what was required of her,' he continued. 'It was imperative for the reputation of St Fabian's that Joe, as captain of the football team that looked likely to win the premiership, was protected from any fallout. Scouts were to be at the game and all signs pointed to him going on to a brilliant career. At that stage, I was satisfied the rumpus would die down if it wasn't given any more oxygen.'

As she adjusted her position in bed, Lani groaned. 'Keep going,' she said. 'No omissions.'

He nodded. 'It was after hours but Bernadette was still working in her office. I took a bottle of Hibiki with me,' he said. 'Of course I shouldn't have taken the whisky,' her father continued, 'but Bernadette was an uptight character. A few drinks later she'd loosened up.'

'What does that mean?' Lani pressed. 'Papa, I don't want hints or suggestions. I need answers – *transparent* answers.' She paused. 'Swear on your granddaughter's life that you'll tell me the whole truth.'

'I swear,' he said. 'As I recall, she was advocating for Stig,' he said. 'And at that stage, I didn't see the harm in it. As we talked, and drank, one thing led to another.'

He frowned and, for the first time, Lani noted he was getting old. He looked almost as spent as she felt.

'I'm sorry, Lani. We slept together. She was a striking, albeit unusual-looking, woman, and we were two consenting adults. I know it wasn't fair on your mother, I know it was wrong, but in those days, I took the chances that came my way.'

Lani shook her head. She'd always thought her papa strong, but what he did – his opportunism, the absolute weakness of it – revolted her at that moment.

'Honey, I didn't think much of it,' he continued. 'In fact, I hardly saw Bernadette Robinson after that. But Stig kept prolonging the situation, refusing to accept responsibility for the unwanted advances that were recorded and clear to everyone who watched the video, including me.'

'But they weren't unwanted advances,' Lani objected finally. 'Stig and Joe were in a relationship. They had been ever since they performed together as the Cowardly Lion and the Tin Man in *The Wiz*. I told you that, Papa. I told you that at the time.'

He shook his head as though he didn't remember. Or because he hadn't given it any credence.

'Lani, there were plenty of other boys pointing the finger at Stig,' he reminded her.

'They were lying,' Lani insisted.

Papa shrugged. 'Regardless of the veracity of their claims, it was a poor reflection on the school. So the board, with my influence, made an executive decision to expel Stig. Sending him to the army, with the support of his parents, seemed like a win-win.' He sighed deeply. 'Your friend was troubled. Having to suck up some discipline for a year or so could have seen him clean up his act.'

'But that's not how things worked out,' Lani said. 'After what happened to Joe, he ran away instead.'

'Yes,' her father agreed. 'But you wanted the whole story, right?'

Even nodding hurt. Lani needed to pee but she quashed the thought. It was bound to be painful. Plus, having her father finally spilling the beans, she was afraid to interrupt with what she expected would be a long bathroom break.

'It would all most likely have passed by without incident,' he continued, 'except that Maya, like the do-gooder she's always been, started a petition to keep Stig at school.'

Lani felt a yearning for her do-gooder friend. Why on earth wasn't she here, supporting her? Seeing her new baby? In this entire shit fight that had emanated from Soul Haven, had Lani managed to lose her two best friends at this most crucial point of her life?

'If you recall, Maya organised a meeting between the school and student councils, in which she made an impassioned plea on Stig's behalf. She named the students she claimed were slandering him. They were our four greatest players, Lani. Liam McKenzie, Jasper Knightly, Rupert Coffey and Joe Carruthers.'

He paused, poured himself a glass of water and took a sip.

'Maya had managed to get a lot of signatures from the girls at St Audrey's, but the boys at St Fabian's – except Tinker – were smart enough to stay out of the situation. As were the staff she tried to coerce. That is, all except one. Bernadette Robinson. Well, she'd signed her own death warrant, so to speak. We had no choice but to let her go.'

'You mean, sack her? On what grounds?'

'On the grounds of violating the school's moral code by encouraging homosexual activities between minors.' He ran his hand through his silver hair. Tufts stood up, making him – usually so immaculately groomed – look shabby.

'She was marched out of the school grounds by security in front of the students, right?' Lani said.

He nodded, and the understanding of the anger she must have felt, the anger that lingered to this day, lay between them.

'I thought that would be the end of it,' he said. 'But she started sending me messages along the lines of "you fucked me in my office and now you've fucked up my life". Then she started parking outside our house, sometimes for hours. She'd wait for me to come out and then hurl vitriol. It was crazy stuff, Lani. She was acting as though we'd been in some kind of relationship. As though we'd been fully-fledged lovers, when it had never been anything but ...'

There was no avoiding it now. Lani would require help getting to the bathroom and she needed, desperately, to go and see her baby. Her vulnerable, tiny, cursed Valentina. She pressed the buzzer and a nurse came immediately.

'That's why Acharya hates you,' Lani said. 'That's why she has a vendetta against us. And Valentina. Papa, what have you unleashed?'

CHAPTER THIRTY-SIX

'You came to me to learn and grow, Tinker,' Acharya said, her even voice at odds with the situation. The black lace veil she used for ceremonies covered her face, making her look sinister to Tinker for the first time. 'I nurtured you and you repaid me with betrayal.'

Zanni wrapped a towel around herself, her now cropped, uneven hair sticking out at all angles.

'Tinker's sorry,' she said. 'He had this idea that he could find Marcus for Sadiki.'

'When you'd both been specifically instructed not to look for the wayward, treacherous man,' Acharya said.

She lifted the veil and Tinker could see her simmering fury.

'You are like Marcus,' she said, shaking a finger at Tinker. 'I had good things ... great things planned for you, but you choose to remain stunted. You're a boy-man.'

'I wanted to find Marcus for Sadiki's sake,' Tinker objected through the pain of her piercing comment. 'I thought you wanted the best for him in his hour of need.'

'That I do,' Acharya said. 'And the best for my Sadiki doesn't involve ingrates and doubters. I will see him to the other side.'

She looked at Zanni. 'You may stay,' she said. 'Given that you're willing to pay penance for your transgressions and work towards dissolving the ego that stifles your growth. You have strayed from the truth, but in lenience and light, I invite you back into the fold. Zanni, you must recommit to me and to the tenets of Soul Haven. I will show you the way.'

'I praise and thank and love you, Acharya,' Zanni said, her head bowed.

'Tinker, are you also sorry?'

Tinker could see himself in the steamed-up mirror, wet and bedraggled and pathetic. Perhaps he was going to stay a boy-man forever? But he wasn't sorry about looking for Marcus. He intended to keep going.

'There are things you need to explain to us, Acharya,' he said quietly.

'There is nothing to explain to you, other than what you need to know,' she scoffed.

'Linda Crossley,' Tinker said, and he could see the name resonating across her face in a wave of – revulsion? Fear? He wasn't sure. 'She was the head of the wellness centre at Shangri-La where you worked for several years.'

'And another stunted soul,' Acharya said, tut-tutting.

'There seems to be a lot of us,' Tinker said. He picked a dry towel off the handrail and wrapped it messily around Zanni's head in a small gesture of defiance. 'She told Bodhi's stepfather, Butch, that you'd gone renegade up there in the Blue Mountains. That you started some kind of unauthorised splinter group.'

Now Acharya seemed vaguely amused. 'Of course I did,' she said. 'That's how I started my practice. That's how Soul Haven was born. But, Tinker, it's obviously too big for you to understand—'

'Is it too big for me to understand she had a fire in her home, just after Butch revealed his communication with her to you?' he asked.

'What are you suggesting?' Acharya countered.

As the towel fell from Zanni's head, Tinker knew he was alone in this. Abandoned. Again. But this time he was going to push back.

'I'm suggesting you were involved,' he said. 'With your black magic, perhaps. Or with a bit of physical help.'

'You're a fool,' Acharya said. 'For all your good looks, your pretty face, you are a fool. You could have had it all here, Tinker. I even had a lovely surprise prepared for you this very day. But clearly you've made your choice, and I've made mine. You're out of Soul Haven. Pack your bags, say goodbye to Zanni and resume your aimless, meandering life. I'm in the middle of something important and must go now. You have fifteen minutes.'

•

'Marcus? Marcus, come to me.'

Sadiki's lover was there. In his dreams. In the sweat that drenched his bed when he woke. If he could reach out, just a little bit further, he could touch him.

'Stop it,' Bodhi chided. The black cloud she brought with her was palpable. 'Oh, for Christ's sake, look at you. You're a bloody mess, Sadiki.'

She pulled back the top sheet roughly. 'You've wet the bed, you nasty thing. And what am I supposed to do about that? Let me guess, I'm supposed to work miracles. I'm supposed to move you over and strip the sheets and bloody well clean you up somehow.'

She looked at her phone and sat heavily on the armchair next to his bed. 'It's not fair, Sadiki,' she whined. 'I went to Acharya's and got kicked out again, 'cos they're still going! Do I look like bloody Cinderella? Do I have to do all the shitty jobs while what's-her-name on her stupid day tour gets the longest reverse blessing in history?'

Sadiki tried to sit up. If only he could convince her Marcus was here.

'I can feel him, Bodhi,' he said. 'I can feel Marcus. Can you?'

'*I can feel him, Bodhi,*' she mimicked. '*I can feel Marcus. Can you?* Well, guess what. You probably can. Maybe he's right here, in your room?'

Bodhi made a show of looking in the cupboard and the chest of drawers. 'Nope, not here,' she said. 'Or here.' When she leaned down to look under the bed, the plaited leather necklace she wore dangled forward. And it was – yes, it was Marcus's eternity ring hanging from it. The silver and rose-gold one Sadiki had given him all those years ago.

She stood up again and there was only the necklace showing.

'Marcus's ring?' he asked.

'No,' Bodhi said, tucking the necklace down further inside her caftan. 'You're delirious, Sadiki. You're imagining things.' She leaned in close and whispered in his ear. 'Don't say anything about this to Acharya,' she warned. 'She wouldn't be pleased.'

She clomped into the bathroom. When she returned, it was with a warm washer and a softer expression. She pulled his shirt over his head and began sponging him, quite gently as far as Bodhi went.

'When Acharya comes, if she ever finally manages to finish up with the great debater over there, not a word,' she said.

CHAPTER THIRTY-SEVEN

Through the glass of an incubator in NICU, Lani stared at her baby.

'I know she's tiny but she's perfect,' Bridget said, kissing Lani's head. 'Valentina's having some trouble breathing. The machine you see there, the one she's hooked up to with the blue cords, is a mechanical ventilator and it's helping her little lungs get the oxygen she needs.' She paused and Lani could tell she was doing her best to stay strong. 'The doctors say there's hope, kitten. Lots of hope. Oodles of it.'

It was a struggle to stand. Lani thought her insides might escape from her body, but she needed a hug from her wife.

'Is it my fault?' she mewed into Bridget's neck. 'Is it because of me our baby is going through this?'

'Of course it's not your fault,' Bridget soothed. 'Lani, we just need to take this step by step. We need to pace ourselves.'

'Have you let Maya and Tinker know?'

'Yes, I've sent a group text,' she said. 'Your parents have gone home for a rest but they'll be back in a few hours.'

Lani was considering whether she actually wanted her father to be in the same room as Valentina anymore when she saw

Maya wave to her from the window. As Bridget sat down to continue the vigil over their daughter, Lani shuffled slowly outside the NICU.

Maya's arms were open and Lani fell into them. 'I have a friend who works in neonatal care,' she said. 'Lani, she says that Valentina is in the best hands. She says …'

The sobs took over and Maya couldn't seem to find her voice again, but the squeeze she gave Lani told her everything.

'I've been praying for her,' Maya said eventually. 'I've been praying for you and Bridget and little Valentina.' She paused. 'And for Sophia,' she added.

Lani drew back so she could see Maya's face.

'Why?' she asked. 'What's wrong with Sophia?'

The wail that came from her mouth was as guttural as Lani's had been in labour.

'She's missing,' Maya howled. 'Your beautiful baby is in intensive care, and mine is gone. Lani, what did we do to deserve this?'

'Nothing,' Lani said, summoning Bridget's words from a moment ago. 'It's not our fault. Are the police looking for her?'

'They're paying lip service to it,' Maya said. 'I can tell they think Sophia's just an errant fourteen-year-old and she'll turn up when she's ready.'

A sudden pain shot down Lani's abdomen, but she didn't have time for it. She didn't have time for anything but looking out for Valentina – and Sophia.

'Give me your phone, Maya,' she said. 'I'm going to call Papa. He'll get things moving.'

•

Tinker tried to kiss Zanni, but she turned her cheek. He had one bag, one measly bag full of possessions, at the door of the yurt. He picked it up.

'I really did love you.'

It was so soft that Tinker didn't know whether he'd heard right. The past tense was a killer when it was still present tense for him.

All he could do was nod his acknowledgement.

Zanni didn't wave goodbye. She just gently closed the door behind him.

As Tinker got into his ute, he could hear chanting coming from the main house. Acharya's, and someone else's. And maybe it was just his agitated state, but he thought he recognised the voice.

Whatever was going on in there, whoever's voice that was, had no relevance for him now.

As Tinker closed the door of his ute, his phone rang again. He looked at the screen. There was no way he could stomach speaking to Maya at the moment. But there she was, calling again.

His heart heavy, Tinker drove past the Soul Haven sign and onto the dirt road, out of the life he'd found with Zanni and Acharya. Back into his aimless, meandering existence.

Fifty or so kilometres down the road, he pulled into a truck stop. He wasn't sure how long he was lost in his grief, but it had been enough time for Maya to try reaching him again and again.

He scrolled through his phone and found a message from Bridget.

> We are thrilled to announce the arrival of our daughter, Valentina Sykes-Galleta, born at St Vincent's Private Hospital at 3.25 pm on Thursday 23 November 2023. We are very grateful for our little beauty (weight: 630 g, length: 31 cm). Although it's been a surprise that she was keen to come into the world at 23 weeks and must spend some time in NICU, the signs are positive. Lani is recovering well.

The photo attached almost made Tinker cry. The little creature was in an incubator, cords attached at all angles. He took several deep, circular breaths, the way Acharya had taught him, and called Maya. She answered on the first ring.

He'd expected her to lead with gushing news of Lani's newborn, but Maya sounded frantic.

'Tinker, do you have any idea where Sophia might be? We've looked everywhere. And I know this is insane, but Luke thinks it has something to do with these little felt dolls she's been hanging on to. Doing weird stuff with. We're out of our—'

'Slow down,' he said. 'Maya, darling, slow down.'

'I can't,' Maya said. 'I can't eat. I can't even think straight. Tinker, Sophia didn't turn up to school today. I only found out at four o'clock. Now it's past nine.'

'Oh, Maya,' he said, 'I'm sorry. No, I don't know where she is. But if I think of anything—'

He was about to continue but Maya had hung up. He looked back at the message Bridget had sent and the word *surprise* leaped out at him. Hadn't Acharya said she had a surprise for him, this very day, that he'd missed out on because of his 'betrayal'? And could the chanting he'd heard coming from her house have been Sophia?

Perhaps he was destined to be a boy-man forever. But this was important. For once in his life, he was going to trust his own instincts, make his own decisions.

Tinker turned the ute around and drove back to Creswick.

But this time, he parked outside the property and snuck in on foot.

CHAPTER THIRTY-EIGHT

'Oh, my Sadiki, it's been a day, but I haven't forgotten about you,' Acharya said, stroking his forehead. 'I regret to tell you that your friend Tinker has proved himself unworthy of belonging in Soul Haven.'

'Tinker? How?' Sadiki managed. He didn't know why she was wearing a veil, something to do with a ceremony? But it felt good to have Acharya touching him so tenderly. He could almost have gone straight back to sleep, but he resisted.

'Never mind about that,' Acharya continued. 'The important thing is that I have a surprise. You, my darling, are about to have a visitor to lift your spirits. I've just been spending time with her. And you're absolutely right. She's not only bright and funny, exuberant and curious, she's also inquisitive, interesting and clever. I've enjoyed every minute with her.'

From the kitchen came banging sounds, and Sadiki suspected that Bodhi could hear their conversation through the open door of his bedroom.

'I think our Bodhi is in a mood,' Acharya said with a smile. 'But no matter. Let's focus on the task at hand. You're so pale, so pallid, my lovely man.' She reached into a backpack and brought out a make-up bag. 'I'm going to fix you up. A touch of foundation, a bit of rouge, and you won't look so frightening to our young guest.'

Bodhi was at the door now. 'It's okay for me to see Sadiki at his worst,' she whined. 'What's special about *her*?'

'Oh, for goodness sake, Bodhi,' Acharya chided. 'Make sure there's a snack ready, please.'

As Bodhi harrumphed back to the kitchen, Acharya lifted her veil.

'What's on your forehead?' he asked.

Acharya smiled broadly. 'I'd forgotten about that. But it's a clue. Can you guess who your visitor might be?'

'Marcus?' Sadiki whispered, wishing for the only visitor he wanted. The only visitor he yearned for. Oh, but his head hurt. 'Marcus's ring. Bodhi has it.'

'Nonsense,' Acharya said, too quickly, as though she was dismissing his claim outright. But he'd seen it with his own eyes. Hadn't he?

Despite her lack of acknowledgement, Acharya stormed into the kitchen. There was an argument going on out there. Sadiki couldn't quite make out the words – *memento?* – but Acharya's low, growling tone was telling. Then he thought he heard a slap, but he could be mistaken. Given the pain coursing through his head, it was hard to trust his own judgement.

When Acharya came back into the bedroom, she was smiling broadly, so he must've been wrong. She pulled a sponge out of the make-up bag and began to apply the foundation with it in soft, smooth strokes.

'I was going to leave her with Tinker while I got you ready,' Acharya said. 'Unfortunately, given his betrayal, that hasn't gone to plan. But rest assured she's safe and sound with Zanni and I'll fetch her when you're all gussied up.' She paused and tilted her head back to get a better look at him. Then she held up a hand mirror. 'See, my darling, you're looking better already.'

It had been a while since he'd seen his own image. His face was so thin. Almost skeletal. In his heart, Sadiki knew it wouldn't be long before he left this world.

But, first ...

'Marcus is coming,' he said. 'He'll see me the way you do and he won't be afraid anymore.'

Acharya put down the brush. 'Marcus is not your visitor,' she said sternly. 'Marcus will not come, Sadiki, you need to understand that. You need to understand that he was never your true partner. He abandoned you. But I won't, darling. I'll be with you every inch of the way.' She leaned in so she was just centimetres from his face. 'Darling, before you pass, we need to do a psychic transfer. I know you'll want your soul data to merge with mine, because that's how I'll be able to continue all the good work I do here.'

Her smile seemed strained now, the tension all wrong. And maybe it was his illness, but Sadiki had no clue what she meant. If there really was such a thing as psychic transfers or soul data, and there was another life after this one, wouldn't it follow that he'd have to start from scratch karmically? But if it meant finding out where Marcus was ...

'Tell me now?' he pleaded. 'Please tell me what happened with Marcus. Because I feel him, Acharya. I feel him close by.'

Acharya patted his head. 'I saved you, is what happened,' she whispered. 'I saved you from Marcus. And from Joe. Everything I've done has been for you.'

She stood up. 'Now, it's time for me to fetch your wonderful visitor.'

Bodhi plonked herself on the bed beside Sadiki. 'You know what?' she said. 'What's-her-name's not that bloody wonderful. She didn't even have the balls to put a proper, strong curse on her worst enemies. But I have the balls. I've proven it.'

She paused and Sadiki could see utter frustration in her expression. She leaned in closer and untucked the leather necklace from her caftan. Sadiki could see it clearly now, so clearly. He hadn't imagined it. It was Marcus's rose-gold and silver eternity ring.

'I dunno who the hell Joe is, but it wasn't Acharya who saved you from being Marcus's bunny, from drawing you away from all that's wondrous and true. He was a fraud, Sadiki. Marcus reckoned he was a builder, but he never even found the special, secret part of your church. Like, really? One day, when I was cleaning, I leaned against a panel in the wall, and voila, there it was – a hidey-hole. So cool.'

Sadiki had no clue what Bodhi was talking about and little interest, but she was on a roll.

'Anyway, the point is that Marcus would've let you slip into the next life without the benefit of all your learnings,' she continued. 'Which is pretty much robbery. 'Cos then, you'd have to start all over again, from scratch.' She nodded to herself. 'Honestly, Sadiki, it was just instinct that kicked in. I've got it in spades, just like Acharya.'

'Yep,' she said as though she was still not quite convinced. 'That was all me.'

CHAPTER THIRTY-NINE

Sadiki barely breathed. He didn't dare move a muscle, but his heart pounded.

'When you were still in hospital, Acharya and I came here to make your place nice and cosy for you when you got home,' Bodhi continued. 'I lit the fire and did heaps of cooking – you know, broths and stuff, like I've been feeding you ever since. She had your new bed delivered and burned sage. We had it all sorted.'

'Thank you,' Sadiki said softly. 'Bodhi, you are so good to me.'

'Anyway, after our community meeting about you, Acharya and I went to see him again. Marnie took you for a healing meditation at her campervan so we could talk properly. Acharya was trying to be really nice and give Marcus a second chance. She explained to him, again, why it was best for you to stay here and that he needed to drop the idea of going to Melbourne altogether. But he was all up in her face, saying she'd messed with your brain, so it wasn't a wonder you had brain cancer. Honest, the way he carried on was nuts, as though it was her fault.'

'He should have been gentler,' Sadiki said.

'No kidding,' Bodhi resumed. 'Acharya collapsed when he said he'd got things together and you were both leaving the next day. He reckoned he was taking you to stay at his sister's in Melbourne and you'd be getting treatment at Peter Mac. She literally fell in a heap she was so freaked out, but Marcus didn't seem to care one bit. He was acting like he was the only one who gave a shit what was happening to you. It was so selfish, Sadiki. I mean, I cared too. I still do.'

'I'm sorry. That wasn't fair of Marcus,' Sadiki said.

'I know, right?' Bodhi replied. 'But Marcus was like a dog with a bone. He didn't let up, even for a second. 'Cos next he starts accusing her, saying she's violated your privacy. Said he found a bug in the lampshade he'd brought from the cottage, which was how Acharya knew about your dream of owning a place like this.'

Sadiki's head was throbbing, his legs shaking as though they were part of someone else's body. But Bodhi was so lost in her own story, she didn't seem to notice.

'Well, actually, it wasn't just because of the bug that Acharya knew about your dream,' she continued smugly. 'It was 'cos I took Marcus's diary to her before that, and it was full of that stuff – well, in between his stupid love poems. She photocopied it all, you know, before she even got me to plant the bug.'

Bodhi seemed proud of this. As though she'd been entrusted with something special.

'Anyway, I'm like ... der, Marcus, Acharya uses any tools she can to watch over us. It's kind of necessary when you're running a place like Soul Haven. I mean, you gotta know who's with you and who's plotting and scheming. So I tried to explain that to him, but he wasn't paying me any attention and that pissed me off. All of it did. Marcus was disrespectful, Sadiki. And ungrateful. He shoulda been thrilled that you guys got your own place because of her. Honest, I don't know what you saw in him. I don't reckon he believed in any of our work from the start.'

'I don't think so either,' Sadiki said truthfully. 'And again, I'm sorry for your experience. Please, go on.'

'Maybe I shouldn't,' Bodhi said, and Sadiki's heart seemed to slow down to the extent that it wasn't pumping blood at all. Whatever had happened with Marcus, he knew he didn't have the whole truth. She couldn't stop now.

'I think it's important that you tell me,' he said. He thought of what Acharya had told him and decided to improvise on the idea that psychic data could be transferred. 'Whatever's happened, you can tell me and I'll take it to the next plane.'

Bodhi looked very interested in the concept.

'You mean, like, whatever I done can be forgiven? And telling you before you die will wipe the slate clean?'

'Exactly,' Sadiki bluffed. 'It seems to me that you're destined to be Acharya's second in charge, and that's because you're smart and capable. You get things done, right?'

'I do,' Bodhi agreed. 'Well, I totally got things done that day,' she said with a nervous chuckle. 'You see, Marcus was going full throttle. He started packing up your things, like really random. While he was doing it, he was raving about Soul Haven being toxic. He told Acharya she could stuff her workshops and sessions and her recording devices. He said the church she gave you was nothing but a bribe to keep you both in line with her bullshit. And that's when … look, it just happened. He was being so ungrateful, Sadiki. So bloody disloyal.'

'What did you do?' he whispered. 'Did you do something to Marcus?' He braced himself, but this betrayal was necessary. 'Whatever it was, I'm sure he deserved it.'

'Damn right he did,' Bodhi said. 'He was losing his shit, stomping all around the place and getting in Acharya's face again. And I went into action. He had his back to me. I picked up that lamp, the one I'd bugged, and I smashed him over the head with it. Honest, I didn't mean to kill him. I just wanted to knock some sense into him, is all. But there he was, bleeding onto the carpet. When I checked him, there was no pulse. He was dead. Dead as a doornail.'

Sadiki gasped and jerked forward. His heart was thumping and his arm ached. This would be his last moment, he thought. It was such an irony, such a terrible irony, that it would be of a heart attack rather than brain cancer.

And how strange that he could hear bleating. He forced his eyes open one last time, and there was Gertrude the goat, standing at the door of his bedroom.

Gertrude and … oh please, no.

Sophia.

CHAPTER FORTY

There didn't seem to be anyone in Acharya's house. The scent of sage was pungent. Her lounge room was set up with an altar, and the wax on the thirteen candles Tinker counted was still warm.

There were three felt dolls left lying on the floor. One was blank and plain. Another had a lock of hair pinned to its head, and on the chest of the third there was a photo of a teenage boy. A beanie lay beside them. Scattered around were gardening shears, a saw and various tools. Other than those, there seemed to be no clues as to who had been in here with Acharya. Or where they were now.

Tinker raced up the stairs, searching for … he didn't know. What was driving him was pure instinct. It felt almost sacrilegious to enter Acharya's bedroom – her own private space was off limits. Zanni would have been horrified, but Tinker was compelled.

It was an enormous room overlooking the grounds that were bathed in light from the starry sky, giant gum trees casting shadows on the walls. The bed was a high four-poster, and a purple canopy hung over it with a pattern of moons and stars.

Her cupboard was ajar and Tinker opened it to see nothing except caftans and shoes. This was hopeless. But ...

There was a smaller cupboard inside the large one, decorated with gold pentagons. Tentatively, he opened it. There were three shelves inside, with nine dolls neatly lined up.

He took out the one in the centre. It had charring around its head and feet, as though it had been burned. There was a name badge pinned to its torso. Linda Crossley.

Tinker imagined running. He could leave all this behind and just get out of Soul Haven. But he didn't.

Instead, he took out another doll. He recognised Lani's signature lipstick right away, the one she'd chided him for leaving behind the night of the session. It was smeared into a grotesque sneer, the corners turned down. Someone must have found her hairbrush, because it looked like Lani's hair stuck to the dolls head. And, on the doll's abdomen, in the same pink, was a cross.

Tinker grimaced as he thought about how much Lani had hated him joining Soul Haven. God, she'd been right. Acharya was no spiritual leader. She wasn't kindness and light. She was darkness itself. Pure evil in disguise.

He forced himself to keep going.

The next doll he chose represented Maya. Tinker could tell by the crucifix around its wrist.

Then there was Gino Galleta with a miniature houndstooth beret.

Oh no. The next one was dressed in a hand-knitted, pink jumpsuit Tinker remembered Marnie working on in the meeting about Sadiki's future. It was also wearing a bonnet and there was a dummy attached to a cord. It was clearly supposed to be a baby. Lani's baby? Little Valentina, who'd been born too early and could face all sorts of problems because of it?

For a moment, Tinker thought he might be sick, but he hadn't eaten for many hours and it was a dry retch.

Holy fuck, there was the sound of footsteps coming from downstairs.

'Sophia?' Acharya called. 'Darling girl, where are you?'

•

As she came into the room, Tinker stood rigid with fear behind Acharya's billowing black curtain.

'I know someone's in here,' she hissed.

Tinker could hear her opening and closing the cupboards, most likely putting the dolls back. Then he heard her knees crack and thought she was probably looking under the bed. It was lucky he hadn't hidden there. When he'd first heard her calling out for Sophia he'd been about to but changed his mind at the last moment. At least the curtains draped right down to the carpet so she couldn't see his shoes. But still, it was only a matter of time before she found him. He wished he'd grabbed a weapon.

'Is that you, Tinker?' she asked in a singsong voice. 'Come out, Tinker. I've been thinking about it and I've decided all is forgiven. Zanni is distraught and we can't have that. Darling man, we still have work to do. I will not forsake you.'

She sighed deeply as she opened the curtain on the other side from the one Tinker was behind. His rigidity had been replaced by the shakes. He was a goner. But what could Acharya do, really? Make a voodoo doll of him? He was stronger than her. He could – he would – overpower her.

The moment was coming. Tinker held his breath. He heard her shuffle sideways.

Then her phone rang.

'What is it, Bodhi?' she asked impatiently. Tinker couldn't make out what was being said, but whatever it was, Bodhi was panicking.

Within seconds, he heard Acharya descend the stairs and head out into the night.

Only then did Tinker release his breath.

CHAPTER FORTY-ONE

'Maya, this is Detective Manolo,' Mr Galleta introduced them.

It was almost 10 pm on Thursday night, and the first time Lani's dad had ever been to her house. Maya couldn't help seeing it through his eyes – the modesty of it compared to his own mansion.

'I'm not from missing persons, I'm from homicide,' Detective Manolo said after he'd shaken Connor's hand, then Luke's, then hers.

'You don't think ...' she began.

'No,' he said in a reassuring tone. 'It's just that I'm a personal friend of Gino's and he thought I might be able to help.'

She tilted her head. 'It was you who helped us when Joe Carruthers died,' she ventured.

'The less said about that, the better,' Manolo said.

'Okay,' Maya agreed, remembering how Mr Galleta had somehow magicked away the evidence of her, Lani and Tinker being at Joe's place the night he died. 'But there's just one thing I wanted to ask about that. You see, I'm starting to think that everything's connected somehow.'

Manolo nodded.

'Did you find empty Hibiki bottles at the scene?' she asked. 'I'm wondering whether they survived the fire, you know, because glass isn't flammable, right?'

Detective Manolo took a seat next to Connor, who looked distressed and bewildered.

'I'm not sure how it's relevant,' Detective Manolo said. 'But yes, there were three Hibiki bottles at the scene when the fire brigade arrived. There wasn't much else to go on, I'm afraid. The fire had destroyed pretty much everything.'

'Could anyone else, perhaps a member of the public, know about the bottles?'

Detective Manolo shook his head. 'No. In accordance with Gino's ... suggestion,' he said, looking at Mr Galleta, 'we kept that information out of the news.'

'So, nobody could have known,' Maya clarified.

'No,' he said, and scratched his head. 'Not unless they were at the scene prior to the arrival of the police.'

As she thought of what Acharya had told Lani about it she felt a sudden chill. Perhaps there was more to Joe's death than she knew, more than anyone knew. Or perhaps someone did know more.

'On the matter at hand,' Detective Manolo continued, 'is there anywhere you can think of that we should look for your daughter?'

Luke stood up. He closed his eyes and lifted his arms as though he was reaching for something. 'I get this feeling whenever Sophia's hurt or in trouble. But this time, it's worse. Way worse.'

Connor put his hand on Luke's shoulder. 'It's okay, son,' he said. 'Sophia will be all right. She's probably ...'

'Dad, Sophia's in danger. I *sense* it.'

Maya thought she saw the detective roll his eyes.

'That's enough,' Connor said. 'Luke, honey—'

'Maybe it's something to do with *Fortnite*,' Luke interrupted.

'The game?' Maya asked.

'Yes. She's been playing a lot lately. And she said something about online friends being better than real ones.'

•

'What the fuck are you doing here?' Bodhi demanded.

Sophia seemed frozen to the spot, her face as pale as Sadiki's before the make-up.

'I just followed the goat,' she said quietly, stroking Gertrude's snout, just like her mother had done at the session. 'I didn't hear anything.'

It was as good as an admission, and they all knew it. Sadiki, Bodhi and Sophia.

Bodhi looked shaken too. Like she'd stirred up a hornet's nest and now had to sit in the middle of it.

'So, what was it you didn't hear?'

'Sadiki?' Sophia said it as though she'd only just realised it was him in the bed.

'Yes, Sophia, it's me,' he said. He had to stay awake. He had to see her safely out of this predicament. But he was so weak and so very, very tired.

'What was it you didn't hear?' Bodhi demanded again.

Sophia shook her head. 'It's okay, Bodhi,' she said. 'I won't tell anyone about what happened with Marcus.' She paused and made the sign of the cross. 'I promise,' she said.

Suddenly, Acharya was there, behind Sophia. Without a word, she strode towards Bodhi and slapped her across the face, hard. But it wasn't Bodhi who screamed. It was Sophia. Instantly, Acharya clapped her hand over the girl's mouth.

'Get me some bandages from the bathroom, Bodhi,' she said. Bodhi obeyed.

The look Acharya gave Sophia, hand still clasped on her mouth, was almost tender.

'Unfortunately, we're going to have to gag you while we consider our options,' she said.

'That's not – please leave her ...' Sadiki began. But a terrible, gurgling sound came from his lips, amplified with each, struggling breath.

As Bodhi stuffed the bandages in Sophia's mouth, as he saw her terrified expression, his body convulsed.

'Tie Sophia's hands together too,' Acharya instructed Bodhi. 'You know where to take her.'

Sophia groaned as Bodhi did as she was asked. Then Bodhi pushed Sophia from the room.

Acharya sat on his bed. 'Darling, that's the death rattle,' she said softly. 'It won't be long now. And I wish this situation, could have been avoided. But what we did to Marcus, it was all for you, Sadiki,' she crooned. 'You know that, don't you, my sweet?'

'Where is he?' Sadiki managed. 'Where's his body?'

'He's here, close by,' Acharya said.

And perhaps she was going to tell him the location, but the sounds of a scuffle came from the kitchen. Sophia was fighting back.

Acharya left the room and Sadiki was alone. He'd been a fool to put all his trust in her. She wasn't who he'd thought she was.

Marcus was gone. He was dead. Sadiki understood that now. But at least he should have a proper burial. That – and seeing Sophia to safety – were the only imperatives now, before he died. He had to hang on.

He had to fight too.

•

'This is not about us, or Acharya or even Soul Haven,' Tinker said as he burst into the yurt.

Zanni turned her back on him, clearly determined to ignore him, but he grabbed her arm and spun her around to face him. She looked so different, so vulnerable with her short cropped hair that, now it had been combed, eerily mirrored Acharya's hairstyle, but she was still Zanni and he knew she was a good, caring person. He needed to make her understand … well, he didn't know what just yet, but there was something bad going on, and somehow Sophia was involved.

'Zanni, you need to trust me,' he said.

She scoffed. 'I don't, Tinker. You've led me astray.'

'Okay, I get it,' he said. 'I know you're committed to staying here and I'm not trying to convince you otherwise. But please, grant me one question.'

Zanni let out a breath, her nod almost imperceptible.

'Did you see a girl, around fourteen years old, with Acharya today?'

'Yes,' Zanni conceded. 'Acharya brought her around here. She asked me to keep her company for an hour or so. Sophia was lovely, all bright and excited about getting to visit. She seemed to have an open spirit, Tinker. She asked me what I loved about Soul Haven and what I'd learned about myself here. And she told me she wanted to join us, as soon as she was old enough.'

She paused and the implication was clear. As far as Zanni was concerned, his spirit was closed. Tinker was no longer a true believer.

'So where is she?' he asked.

Zanni shrugged. 'I had to go and pack some orders. When I left, Sophia was having a chat with Gertrude, who is, as you know, very picky about who she bonds with.'

'And when you came back?' Tinker urged.

'You said one question,' Zanni reminded him.

'Please, Zanni,' he pleaded. 'Sophia is Maya's kid.'

'Well, I guess that explains her getting along with Gertrude,' Zanni said. 'Like mother, like daughter. Just, perhaps, more open-minded.'

'Maya thinks she's missing.'

Zanni frowned. 'Maybe Sophia just didn't tell her parents about Soul Haven. You know how people are with our, with my—'

'Zanni, she's just a kid,' Tinker interrupted. 'And she's in the countryside, hours from her home, at eleven pm. Her family are beside themselves. Where do you think she went?'

Zanni shook her head, but she also grabbed her coat.

'I don't know,' she said. 'But wherever it is, I think Gertrude is with her.'

When she put on her hat, she looked like the woman he'd known and loved these past months. His Zanni.

'I'm coming with you to look for Sophia,' she said.

CHAPTER FORTY-TWO

After Gino and the detective left, Maya looked up from her phone at her husband and son.

'That was a text from Tinker,' she said. 'Sophia's at Soul Haven. At least, she's been there today. Tinker's girlfriend was with her.' She paused and the laugh that escaped her lips was guttural and unfunny to the core. 'Apparently, she was talking to my goat friend.'

The implication that they – whoever – might have given Sophia magic mushrooms wasn't lost on them. She'd never seen Connor or Luke move so fast. That was normally her – and Sophia's – way. But now she was lost in a kind of stupor. Oh, dear Lord, was that why Sophia wanted to go to Soul Haven? To experience what she had?

'Luke, I think you should stay here in case Sophia comes back,' Connor said, bringing Maya back to the urgent present.

Luke's head shake was emphatic. He raced up the stairs and returned in seconds with Sophia's laptop.

From the front door, Maya looked at her home, the beautiful, modest home that she shared with her imperfect, wonderful family. Then she made the sign of the cross. 'God bless us,' she whispered. 'Please, bless and protect us all. Especially Sophia.'

•

Maya had never known Connor to go above the speed limit, but she was glad he was now. They needed to close the gap between them and Sophia as soon as possible.

'Eureka,' Luke said from the back seat. 'Sophia's password is our birthdate, backward. I'm in.'

'Good work, Luke,' Connor encouraged. 'Maya, perhaps put in a call to Detective Manolo. Let him know where we're heading.'

As they were nearing the turn-off to Soul Haven she was set to do just that, but her phone buzzed with an incoming call.

'Listen to me, Maya,' Lani said. 'Bernadette Robinson hates us. Well, she hates Papa and me the most. He slept with her, then you did the petition to keep Stig at St Fabian's and she signed it and, well, the whole thing blew up in her face. Papa was an integral part in getting her fired.'

It was too much to process. Yes, Maya had understood that Mr Galleta was a player, but this? He must not only have slept with her but dropped her like a bag of bones and got her sacked, on top of it all. He was not a good man, but she needed him now. She needed his influence with the police.

'But what does any of this have to do with Sophia?' she asked eventually.

'I don't know, exactly,' Lani admitted. 'But Bernadette Robinson's hatred has spilled over somehow. She's dumped you and me in the same category as Papa. And, Maya, I wish I'd told you before, but I think I was in denial. I guess I thought that airing it might make it true. The thing is, Acharya put a curse on me that night, at the session.'

Maya gulped. Between the wind and the rocky, dirt road, even the Volvo was getting bumped around mercilessly. Connor had the headlights on full beam. It was so dark, though, full of unfamiliar sounds. Was that a fox's scream? She didn't believe in hexes, but if she did, this felt like a night where they might just find their power.

'What kind of curse?' she finally managed.

On the other end of the phone, Lani stifled a sob. 'She told me that the universe will conspire so that I don't pass on my father's legacy.'

'Oh, Lani, I'm so sorry. That's a wicked thing to say. I don't think I would have given it air either if I were you.'

A tree branch brushed against the side of the car and Maya started. Connor put his hand on her knee.

'Our babies – even our babies – aren't off limits to that crazy woman.'

A truck came down the other side of the road, honking its horn for them to make more space as it went to pass.

'Maya, where are you?' Lani asked.

'On the way to Soul Haven,' she said.

'Be careful, it might not be safe. Tinker called me. He was looking for Marcus against Acharya's wishes and she found out. He got booted out of the cult today.' Lani paused. 'That's a good thing, perhaps the only good thing that's happened since we were all introduced to that place. Finally, he's seeing through her bullshit. But, Maya, he thinks she might have something to do with Marcus's disappearance too.'

Maya shuddered. What were they getting themselves into?

'Regardless, we have to go to Sophia,' she said.

'Yes, I know. But can you wait for the cops?'

Maya sighed. 'We don't have any evidence that Sophia was coerced into visiting Soul Haven.'

From the back seat, Luke gasped. 'She's been talking to Acharya!'

'What?!' Maya exclaimed.

'What's going on?' Lani asked.

Maya put her phone on speaker.

'Sophia and Acharya have been messaging on *Fortnite*,' Luke said.

'I've got to go,' Maya said.

'Wait,' Lani urged. 'There's more you need to know. Tinker said he found dolls in Acharya's cupboard. And I wasn't going to tell you this, but it could be important. We were represented among them. She used what we'd left behind the night of the session. My pink lipstick and your crucifix.'

Maya doubled over.

'Tinker thinks there's a doll representing Valentina too,' Lani said.

It was surprising that Lani didn't skip a beat. Maya had almost lost sight of how strong her friend was.

And deep down, how caring.

'Papa has put security in the NICU. I'll make sure my baby's safe, but right now, the focus must be on Sophia. I'll tell Papa to call Detective Manolo. Acharya is dangerous, but voodoo isn't illegal. Is there anything, *anything* else at all, that we can use as evidence?'

'Yes,' Luke said, leaning over the back of Maya's seat. 'Sophia's in a small space … some kind of room … and she can't move or speak. Maybe she's tied up and gagged. I don't know. But there are people arguing outside her door. The closer we get to Soul Haven, the more I feel it. And I can't tell you how it works, but you've got to believe me, Lani. Do you believe me?'

'I believe you, Luke,' Lani replied. 'And I'll spin it so that Detective Manolo gets on to it straightaway.' She paused. 'I love you, Maya,' she said simply, and it hit right in the heart.

'I love you too, Lani,' Maya said, and the truth of it, the purity of it in the face of so much fear, was a balm. A single tear rolled down her cheek. 'Friendship is our religion,' she said softly.

'Let's never forget that again.'

CHAPTER FORTY-THREE

Neither Acharya nor Bodhi had bothered to close his bedroom door and Sadiki knew why. He could barely speak; he could hardly move. What help could he possibly be for Sophia?

All he could do was listen, and hope against hope that someone would come. In the meantime, if there was an opportunity, he had to let them believe he was onside with anything they were planning.

'We can't keep her in there forever,' came Acharya's voice.

'Guess not,' Bodhi said. 'Acharya, she's a … a nuisance.'

'Yes, she is – because of you.'

'Sorry,' Bodhi said. 'But it's the same situation as what happened with Marcus. You told me I did the right thing when I whacked him with the lamp. 'Cos he would've taken Sadiki with him, and you wouldn't have had the chance to do a psychic transfer before he passes on.' She paused. 'It seems like that's going to happen soon.'

Was there a scratching sound coming from out there? Sadiki strained to listen, but he wasn't sure. He wasn't sure of anything right now. Not the goodness he'd felt emanating from Acharya.

Not the beliefs he'd clung to about elevating his soul, freeing himself from the past. It had all been a lie. And when had it really started? He'd thought she'd rescued him from his sorry state in Kings Cross. But could it have been earlier than that? If she felt so at ease about 'disappearing' people, could she somehow have been involved with Joe's death too?

Marcus had been the one good thing that had come into Soul Haven. And Tinker. He shouldn't forget about how supportive Tinker had been since his diagnosis.

Tinker. Hadn't Bodhi told him he might have been booted out for his supposed betrayal of Acharya in looking for Marcus? And, if that was the case, had he gone willingly? Did he – did anyone from the outside – know that Sophia was here?

We're not us without you.

His beautiful friend would want to be with him when he passed on.

Sadiki shut his eyes and wished for Tinker to disobey Acharya's orders and come to him. For his own sake, for Marcus's, for Sophia's.

'Are you willing to make amends?' Acharya's voice was a low growl.

'Yes,' Bodhi declared. 'Acharya, you know my loyalty. I am yours. What's-her-name in there never was. She was just a tourist to Soul Haven. A sightseer. Jeez, she wouldn't even put a proper curse on those poppets. We could disappear her, just like we did with Marcus.'

'Marcus had no one looking for him,' Acharya scolded. 'Sophia has a family she's still connected with.'

'Yeah,' Bodhi conceded. 'But we know that she didn't tell no one she was coming here. So why would anyone look for her here?'

'In case they do, Bodhi,' Acharya said, 'it's your job to make sure there's no sign that Sophia's ever been here. Do you think you can do that?'

Bodhi must've nodded because Sadiki didn't hear her reply.

'I'm going to consult the ancestors about what we need to do next,' Acharya said. 'In the meantime, you make sure there's no trace of Sophia in this church. Not a speck. And when you've finished, take some water to her and ungag her just while she drinks. Do nothing else, do not touch a hair on her head, until I return with instructions.'

She paused. 'Whatever happens to Sophia, it's got to look like an accident.'

•

Tinker knew Zanni wasn't buying into his theories about Acharya. It was common decency, worry for a teenage girl's welfare, that had her looking for Sophia with him. And that was good enough, for now.

They searched the shed Zanni worked from, filled floor to ceiling with boxes of soaps, moisturisers and candles, but there was no trace of Sophia having been there.

'Let's go over this again,' he said. 'What exactly was Sophia doing with Acharya?'

'A reverse blessing ceremony,' Zanni replied. 'You know that Acharya likes to perform them with her younger clients.

The poppets resonate for them, as symbols of the power they can draw from their inner selves and release into the world. After all that's happened to Bodhi in the past, they've been a godsend.'

Tinker thought about Butch, Bodhi's stepfather, and his utter denial that he'd ever done the things Bodhi had hinted at.

'The ceremonies give younger ones a sense of personal agency, when often they have none,' Zanni reiterated.

As far as Tinker was concerned, that profile didn't fit Sophia, but it felt best not to argue over that now. Still, Zanni must have seen the doubt on his face.

'Tinker, Sophia was happy when Acharya brought her to me,' Zanni said. 'She told me she'd had a super interesting time, and there were things she didn't agree with, but she wanted to learn more.' She paused. 'This wasn't a girl in distress. Except ...'

'Except?' Tinker prompted.

'Well, she was looking forward to seeing you. Acharya had told her to keep it as a surprise, but she was busting to talk to you. I didn't have the heart to tell her you'd been kicked out. I thought it might affect her ... openness of spirit.'

It had been a so-called 'openness of spirit' that had got Tinker, and Sophia, into this situation, but still, he didn't object.

Tinker's phone buzzed in his pocket. It was an unknown number. He toyed with the idea of ignoring it, but this wasn't the time to let go of any possibilities, no matter how remote the chances were.

A woman's voice came through without preamble. 'It's Linda Crossley. I believe you've been looking for me.'

CHAPTER FORTY-FOUR

Sadiki was flying back in time. Back, back, back.

'I've made your favourite.'

He could smell the roast lamb his mum had cooked. He could almost taste it too, the anticipation of each delicious mouthful. The sponge cake with passionfruit icing was on the kitchen bench, eleven candles due to be lit after the meal.

'You're growing so fast,' his father observed. 'Marion, Stig, I was cleaning up my office today and look what I found.'

Stig had never seen a single photo of his father as a child, but this was of him at about Stig's own age. He was wearing a military jacket, clearly too big for him, with lapels and badges. His expression was sombre.

'That was my father's uniform,' he said. 'I used to dress up in it every chance I got.'

Stig took the photo and studied it. 'That could be me!'

'Yes,' his father said. 'That's exactly what I thought when I first saw it. But, if it was, you'd be wearing a smile.' He sighed deeply. 'I wasn't a happy kid like you are.'

'But why, Dad?'

'My father was a difficult man, Stig. I was forever trying

to please him, and always failing. Even when I made field marshal, like he'd done before me, he didn't seem proud. At least, he couldn't say it.' He paused. 'I hope I'm not a difficult man, a difficult father. Because, boy, I want you to stay happy.' His voice cracked. 'That's all I want for you, all I've ever wanted.'

Stig was confused. Yes, his father was a difficult man, but he couldn't say that, could he? He couldn't say that he often felt like he was a disappointment too.

But he could seize this rare opportunity.

He stood up and launched himself. For a moment, there was no response. His father's arms hung limply by his side.

The birthday candles weren't ready to be blown out yet, but Stig was going to use his silent wish in advance.

Hug me back. Hug me back. For once, just this time, on my special day, hug me back.

It was tentative at first. Stig's father was so stiff, it was like hugging a wall. But soon muscular, strong arms were wrapped around him, and he was enveloped in a firm yet tender embrace. He felt so safe and wanted and loved. Why had he forgotten that? Why were the only memories Acharya had drawn out from him during her age regression therapies always negative?

He must be hallucinating. He wasn't Stig, he was Sadiki, and he was thirty-seven years old, not eleven. He was dying and Sophia was trapped somewhere in the church he'd shared with Marcus. He had to do something.

But it was too tempting. Now in sleep or in hallucination, he couldn't be sure, but Stig returned to his father's arms.

•

'Linda, thanks for calling me,' Tinker said.

'What's this in regard to?'

'A guy called Butch spoke to you recently—'

'I'm not saying anything more about Bernadette Robinson,' Linda said. 'Lord knows how that played out last time. Let me guess – Butch told Bernadette about our chat too?'

Tinker was terrified she would hang up, but he sensed something in her voice. Linda Crossley seemed to have unfinished business. Whatever it was, Tinker needed to draw something, anything, out of her.

'I understand you had a fire at your apartment recently?'

'Yes.'

'Was there an investigation as to its cause?'

'The police are following a lead.'

The night Joe died in such a cruel manner circulated in Tinker's mind, but he had to stay on track.

'Linda, we have a … a situation here, at Soul Haven.'

There was the sound of a scoff. 'There will be all manner of *situations* wherever Bernadette's concerned,' she said. 'But they're not *my* concern anymore. I've learned the hard way to keep my nose out of her business. Now, I'm sorry but I have to go.'

'Linda, this particular one involves a fourteen-year-old girl. Her name's Sophia Donnelly and I—' He paused and beckoned Zanni over to listen, not daring to put the call on speaker in case somehow Acharya would find out who he was talking to.

Instead, he held it between them, ear to ear. 'We,' he corrected, 'are worried about her safety.'

There was a long silence and Tinker felt that she must have been weighing up the potential repercussions of speaking up again against keeping quiet.

'It's happened before,' Linda said finally. 'Bernadette ran a splinter group from Shangri-La for months before we found out there were people under eighteen in attendance. There had been a long-running course called Using Voodoo for Good. But Bernadette, shall we say, adapted it. She was teaching clients how to wreak havoc on their enemies, which was totally at odds with what we were trying to impart at a wellness centre.'

She sighed. 'I engaged the police, but no laws had been broken. They couldn't prove she'd done anything illegal, but in terms of ethics – in terms of morals – there wasn't a shadow of a doubt that she'd crossed a line.'

There was another pause.

'I'm not normally a person to flinch at my responsibilities, but I asked everyone on the board to come to the meeting in which we let her go. I didn't want to do it alone, and thankfully I followed my instinct on that one. There was something about Bernadette, something that frightened me. Because there she was, all joy and lightness in the public eye, but behind closed doors the woman was a psycho.'

Zanni was listening intently now, taking in Linda's words.

'Does Bernadette have something against this girl you mentioned?' Linda asked.

Tinker shook his head. 'I don't think so. But she has beef with her mother and one of her best friends.'

'That'll do it. Bernadette Robinson can certainly hold a grudge. And I don't believe in voodoo, not for a moment, but she's a pro at using everything in her power to exact revenge, even remotely. I'm living proof. The fire was a warning not to talk. Actually, I feel grateful that I am alive, at least. But I'm in hiding, staying with a friend until I feel safe.'

'That sounds like a good idea,' Tinker said. 'Linda, do you have any tips, any ideas about where we might look for Sophia?'

'I don't know your set-up at Soul Haven,' Linda said. 'But when she was here, Bernadette became obsessed with old churches. Since she was an atheist, I thought it strange, but she talked a lot about them. She reckoned she was going to get one and repurpose it so that it worked for her instead of for any religion. Like she thought she was a Messiah. It bothered us all that she might still be situated in and among our community, so it was a relief to hear on the grapevine just a couple of months after we sacked her that she'd inherited a large property from her aunt and was moving to Creswick. But even then, trouble followed her. Apparently, the aunt's son was contesting the will, saying it had been made under duress during a short period before she passed when Bernadette was nursing her. But, of course, those cases can drag on for years.'

'Thank you, Linda. If you're okay sending me your number, I'll let you know how all this turns out,' Tinker said before he hung up.

He turned to Zanni and was about to say it, but she got in first. 'Sophia must be in Sadiki's church.'

CHAPTER FORTY-FIVE

'Mum, Dad, you need to listen!' Luke demanded after Maya had hung up the phone after speaking to Lani. 'There are heaps of messages in the chat log on *Fortnite* between Sophia and someone who calls herself *A*. At first, they're all about the game. But they get personal.'

Even from the back seat, Luke's voice was unusually loud and clear. 'So, I'll start with this one from A,' Luke said.

'*I get the feeling that you're spending a lot of time online to avoid something,*' he read. 'There's a thumbs-up emoji on that one. A asks if there's stuff going on at school. Then Sophia says she's getting picked on about her birthmark and A does a sad-face emoji. She says she's got one on her forehead too and she understands.'

'Acharya doesn't have a birthmark,' Maya said. 'Why would she have said that?'

'Perhaps to reel her in,' Connor suggested.

'I think so too,' Luke said. 'Because then she messages: *In some cultures, birthmarks are considered lucky.* Sophia says she used to think that but not anymore. Then A writes back.

Did you know that light-coloured birthmarks, like yours and mine, are considered a connection to the divine?'

The road was getting even bumpier. A rock hit the windscreen. Connor put his hand on the small shatter to stop it spreading, but he didn't slow down.

'Sophia asks how A knows what her birthmark looks like and she replies that Sophia was using her real name in *Fortnite* and that she saw the photo in *Women's Weekly*. Then she says she was glad she didn't cover it up. Sophia puts a laughing emoji on that, then messages that she had started covering it up and that she definitely doesn't feel a connection to the divine and that she doesn't even know if she believes in God anymore.'

Connor removed his hand from the windscreen to hold Maya's.

'Then A says that's because she's smart. She says: *Try not to think of the divine as the traditional God figure. Think about it as a connection with the universe. There's a god in your heart and a spirit in your soul.* Sophia puts a question mark on that. Then A asks if she'd like to know more. After that, there's a lag of three days, then Sophia replies: *Why not? Things are getting worse. Alana has turned everyone against me.* Then A says Alana's jealous and Sophia puts another question mark on that and says that's not true because Alana has everything. Then A says: *Except a soul,* and that those girls are robots and they have nothing on her because she's smart and questioning. Sophia says: *Look how that's working out,* and A replies: *Do you want to make it work out? I have. Do you trust me?'*

Maya's stomach churned at Acharya's manipulation. Because, she was sure, despite the assertion that she had a birthmark, the messages were from her. And they were only a few minutes away from Soul Haven now.

'Sophia doesn't answer that message for two days. Then, A sends a photo with a time stamp.

'Show me?' Maya asked. Luke handed her the laptop. It was Acharya all right. Acharya with a birthmark either photoshopped or pencilled onto the right side of her forehead, a mirror image of Sophia's. Sophia had loved the image. Maya had a sudden urge to throw the laptop out of the window, but she read on.

'*I can help. Can you send me something that belongs to Alana?* Next, there's a postal address in Creswick. Sophia asks if she's going to voodoo Alana and finishes her message with a laughing emoji. There's another lag of over a week. Then Sophia writes back: *OMG. Alana was in a ski accident. Broke her leg.* She suggests it might be a coincidence, but Acharya says there are no coincidences and that she should come and find out for herself how to tap into universal powers. She says they should switch platforms. What does that mean, Luke?'

'They've probably continued their conversation on Discord or Twitch,' he said. 'There are plenty of options.'

'Detective Manolo gave me his email address,' Maya said, opening her wallet. She gave the laptop and his business card to her son.

'I'm forwarding it now,' Luke said.

Except for tapping on the keyboard, the night had turned silent. The rusted Soul Haven sign came into view.

Then Maya's phone buzzed with an incoming text from Lani.

Valentina's lungs have collapsed. Pray for us.

CHAPTER FORTY-SIX

Sadiki wasn't about to die after all. Raw, untapped energy was coursing through him. He wanted – no, he needed – to dance! It was a miracle. It didn't matter that there was no music, that he had no phone, computer or boom box to generate some. He could feel it inside. He could get up, out of bed, of course he could – why had he stopped trying?

Was that his body moving so fluidly, just the way it used to? Or was he still lying down? Either way, it didn't matter. He was swaying to the rhythm of 'Le Freak', doing the grapevine, with a flourish at each end as he clapped his hands.

Marcus! Sadiki should have thought of this before. Yes, of course he was here. His lover would always return for their favourite dance number.

'Darling, stay this time,' Sadiki entreated. 'Never leave me again.'

Marcus took Sadiki's hand and spun him around and around until he was giddy. Sadiki kept his eyes on his lover and took the chance to improvise, using every square centimetre of the sparkling tiled dance floor. It was so good to be in the moment, doing what he loved best.

My show pony. Marcus didn't say it so much as impart it.

Yes, Sadiki was a show pony and look how Marcus was eating it up. Sadiki noted his grin.

'Look at me, Marcus!'

Where else could I look? You're amazing, Stig. You could've been on Broadway.

'But this is all I want. Just you, my audience, my love.'

It was joy, pure and simple joy. But, no, hang on, why was Marcus fading?

'Where are you going?'

Stig, you know where I'll be. Look for me. I'm in everything you see and feel. Everything you eat and drink.

'Please come back.'

Marcus's outline was getting lighter and lighter. His hands were covering his ears.

Darling, I can't. I'm gone, remember? But we'll dance together again soon.

Oh god, no. Was it the noise that drove Marcus away? What the hell was going on out there? Why couldn't they be quiet?

'We can keep her in the hidey-hole until we're ready.'

Bodhi had mentioned something about a hidey-hole, hadn't she? His brain. Oh, his poor brain. Where was the energy he'd felt just minutes ago? He could feel it whooshing out of him until he was drained.

But Sadiki *would* copy it down before he too faded. There was a permanent marker on his bedside table, but there was no paper anywhere in sight.

'What are you doing up, Sadiki?' Acharya asked, coming into the room. 'Oh, my darling boy, I think we're close. I think what you're experiencing is what they call the surge before death. My darling, you don't need to know the ins and outs. Just know that I've been there to protect you – against Joe and Marcus, and against your so-called friends Lani, Maya and Tinker. Some of the things I did were crimes, in the eye of the law. I'm sad I had to act on their betrayal, but I can't regret them. My beautiful Sadiki, loyal and faithful. With the psychic transfer, you will be able to take my transgressions to the next plane and cleanse me. Isn't that beautiful? And you will gift me your good karma, as you always have.'

The disco floor was no longer there. Perhaps Sadiki was no longer here. But perhaps he was, because he was able to sip the drink she brought him.

It was in almost everything Bodhi cooked these days. In all he tasted. Okra water.

Sadiki couldn't speak, but as Acharya helped him back into bed, he pointed at the door.

'It's just me and Bodhi. We're here for you, Sadiki,' Acharya assured him.

But she'd assured him of things before. Untrue things. Oh, the evil things she had done in his name. As she stroked his forehead, Sadiki pretended to fall asleep. He had so little strength left.

But when she walked out of the room, he summoned just enough to scrawl some words on the wall behind him, covering them with pillows before he plunged back into the darkness.

•

'What caused the collapse?' Lani asked. 'I mean, Valentina was doing okay. She was stable.'

The doctor sighed. 'I wish I could tell you categorically,' she said. 'As you know, premature births carry risk factors.' She looked at the chart. 'In medical speak, what your baby experienced is called a pneumothorax. We've put a chest tube between Valentina's ribs to remove the excess air, and so far it's working. Her lungs are clearing and her vital signs are good. The rest, I'm afraid, is a waiting game.'

She put a hand out and touched Lani's shoulder. 'She's a trooper, your little one,' she said, before leaving the room.

Bridget had been so strong during the ordeal of the birth and immediate aftermath. Now, though, her wife looked as shattered as Lani felt.

'Go home, Bridget,' Lani urged. 'Get some sleep.'

'I think I have to, or I'll be no good to anyone,' Bridget conceded. 'Any news on Sophia?'

Gino's stride towards them was purposeful. 'How's our Valentina?' he asked. 'The doctor insisted she speak with you first.'

His obvious shock that such a thing could possibly happen made Lani and Bridget exchange small, exhausted smiles. They gave him the update before Bridget kissed Lani and left.

'So, Papa,' she said eventually, 'Sophia's still missing. Did you manage to dig up any dirt on—'

'Yes,' he interrupted. 'A civil lawsuit against Bernadette Robinson was filed in June of last year. Her aunt's son claimed that she'd changed her will. He alleges there was interference, that his mother was *non compos mentis*, in no condition to sign the deed to the property in Creswick over to her niece, and that she'd been under duress.'

Lani groaned. 'Those cases can take forever.'

'That's true,' her father said. 'But the lawyer put me in contact with the plaintiff, Jonathan Green. He was careful when we spoke, sticking to the facts. But the facts alone were disturbing, at the very least. His mother had a terminal illness, but she'd been in the last stages for over seven months, staying with Jonathan who was her carer. Then, Bernadette waltzed in for a weekend and encouraged him to take a break at his beach house. That was when the will was changed.' He paused. 'By Sunday afternoon, Bernadette's aunt, Jonathan's mother, was dead.'

Lani clutched her father's arm as he continued.

'That's not all. A Brisbane-based woman named Linda Crossley, a former co-worker of Bernadette Robinson, has just filed a criminal case against her, the allegation being that she hired two teenage boys to set her apartment on fire. There were two sets of recent fingerprints. The boys – juvenile delinquents – were already on the register. They've been interviewed and have both admitted complicity.'

'Oh my god,' Lani said. 'The woman is a monster.'

'Yes,' her father agreed. 'But Lani, this means that Detective Manolo has been able to get a search warrant. The police are on their way to Creswick.'

Her father smiled weakly. 'The doctors are saying I can't go into the NICU. Lani, do you think you could ask for special dispensation for me to see Valentina?'

CHAPTER FORTY-SEVEN

As Tinker banged, hard, on the door of Sadiki and Marcus's church, Zanni flinched. It was Bodhi who answered. She looked dishevelled and she tried to imitate Acharya's trademark beatific smile but couldn't quite pull it off.

'Tinker?' she said. 'Now, I was under the impression that you got booted out of Soul Haven.'

'I don't care what sort of impression you're under,' Tinker roared as he barged past her. 'Where's Sophia?'

Acharya was sitting in an armchair. She looked up, right through Tinker as he searched around for evidence that Sophia had been there and focused on Zanni. 'Sometimes, being outed from the tribe brings on, shall we say, episodes,' she said evenly. 'Zanni, I'd appreciate it if you could guide Tinker—'

'I'll take no more guidance,' Tinker spat. There was nothing to suggest Sophia had even been here. 'Not from you, not from Zanni, not from anyone. Now, where is she?'

Acharya shrugged. She put a finger to her lips. 'Shh, Tinker,' she said. 'Our friend Sadiki's time is nigh. I'm sure you'll agree this should be a peaceful, calm situation.'

For a moment, Tinker stopped to listen. From Sadiki's room there was the crackling wet sound of his friend's laboured breathing.

'It's the death rattle,' Acharya confirmed. 'Our poor darling is about to enter a new state.'

Tinker wasn't sure what to believe anymore. He desperately wanted to go to Sadiki. But in Acharya's hands, even this could be a trick, a decoy of sorts. No, he needed to stay on track. Finding Sophia was the priority.

'Where is she?' he whispered. 'Where's Sophia?'

Acharya sighed deeply. 'I think you've got things a little topsy-turvy,' she said. 'I'm sure Zanni has told you that Sophia was with me this afternoon. But, Tinker, that was hours ago. I put her on a train back to Melbourne myself.'

She stood up. 'If you need proof, as do those without faith, you can go to the station and ask for security footage from the six thirty-five pm train to Melbourne,' she said. 'Now, if you'll excuse me, I need to tend to Sadiki.'

Tender murmurings came from the room as Acharya entered. Tinker's self-doubt was palpable now. The smug look on Bodhi's face showed she recognised it too.

'It's a right shame you couldn't commit to Soul Haven, Tinker,' she said. 'Acharya reckons it's 'cos you're immature.' She turned to Zanni. 'So what's your excuse?'

Zanni crouched down so she was eye level with Bodhi. 'That was just a momentary hiccup,' she said. 'I guess I'm not as strong as you are. It's amazing, given you're still young, but you truly seem to have been blessed with the same qualities our spiritual leader possesses.'

Tinker did a double take, unsure of where Zanni was going with this flattery. But he did believe in her. Not to take instructions from, but as an equal partner and a person who would never jeopardise a young girl's safety.

'Yeah, it's weird, hey? Kind of like I'm a chosen one,' Bodhi said.

Zanni remained crouched. 'I can see that,' she said. 'I mean, it's in everything you do. You're savvy, Bodhi.'

Bodhi's smile this time was her own gap-toothed goofy one. 'You don't know the half of it, Zanni,' she said. 'Anyways, I reckon you should go now. Well, I suppose you can stay, but not him.'

'Yes, of course,' Zanni said. 'But first, can you tell me something I don't know about you? See, given that you'll be Acharya's right-hand woman soon, given that I'll be following you as well as her, I'd really like to know more.'

Bodhi leaned in close to Zanni so that Tinker had to strain to hear what she was saying.

'So much stuff has been my idea. I mean, I don't want to brag or anything, 'cos I know Acharya is the one with the true powers. But yeah, I have – what did you call it? – savvy. It was my idea to wear clothes just like Sophia's and make sure to get under the camera at the train station.'

'That,' Zanni exclaimed, finally rising again, 'is ingenious.' Her pause was loaded. 'So, you're saying that Sophia didn't go home?'

'Yeah, she did,' Bodhi said, but suddenly her smugness was gone and her expression was bemused.

A banging sound came from behind the closed door and Acharya appeared.

'Sadiki tried to get up again. He's fallen. Bodhi, get the first-aid kit from the bathroom.'

As Acharya re-entered Sadiki's room and Bodhi walked towards the bathroom, Zanni picked up a chair from the dining setting and gave Tinker a nod he understood implicitly. In seconds, she'd closed the bathroom door and placed the chair under the handle so it wouldn't open from the inside.

Tinker glanced at his phone. 'Maya's texted. The police are on their way,' he whispered.

'See to Sadiki, and try to get the truth from Acharya,' Zanni said over Bodhi's loud protests. 'I'm going back to the house to show the police where to go when they arrive.'

CHAPTER FORTY-EIGHT

It was almost 1 am and the wind was howling when the Donnellys arrived at Soul Haven. Maya shivered as she recalled walking up to the main house for the first time. The adversarial manner in which Acharya had greeted her and Lani seemed a quaint, distant memory compared to what had happened since the session. And all of it – Maya's mushroom trip, the friendship issues that ensued – paled in comparison to tonight's mission.

'This isn't the place,' Luke said, closing the car door too loudly. Lights went on in a close by campervan and a fibro shack.

'Yes, it is,' Maya insisted.

Luke put on his coat. It was bunched up at the back, and the way Connor smoothed it down, the tenderness given what their other child might be going through, seemed absurd.

'I know it's Soul Haven,' Luke persisted. 'I saw the sign on the way in. But Sophia's not here.'

'You're trespassing.' A woman Maya recognised from manning the trestle table at the session tried to block their path to the house. Maya remembered her name as Marnie. The Donnellys ignored her.

'I'm going to take a look inside,' Connor said. 'Maya, Luke, go back to the car. Check how long the police will be. Try Tinker again.'

Neither Maya nor Luke paid him heed. Calling Detective Manolo wouldn't make them arrive faster. And Tinker hadn't responded to any texts or calls for over half an hour, except for a thumbs-up when she'd texted that the police were on their way.

'I'm warning you,' Marnie hissed. 'I'm going to get help.'

The Donnellys went into the house together.

When Maya and Connor saw the altar set up in the lounge room, covered in black cloth with a single silver pentacle on it and thirteen candles positioned around, they stopped in their tracks.

It was Luke who found the dolls on the floor. And the objects – the weapons – beside them.

'This photo is of Darcy Jeffries,' he said. 'Sophia was mad with him for not sticking up for her.' He closed his eyes.

'Get out.' Marnie had returned, flanked by the ex-accountant Maya had also met at the session.

'You want us to call the cops?' Thomas added.

Maya stood tall. 'Yes,' she said. 'Go right ahead.' She turned back to Luke. 'What is it?' she asked.

'I think she's in a church,' Luke continued. 'I can feel her fear.'

For a moment, among protestations from Marnie and Thomas, none of it made sense. Until Maya recalled Tinker breaking the news that Sadiki was dying and that he was going to live out the rest of his days with Marcus.

In his church.

•

When Tinker went into Sadiki's room, Acharya was standing above him. Her hands, palms up, were moving from Sadiki's chest to her own, as though she was pulling energy from him as she chanted strange words. She put her lips to Sadiki's forehead and kissed him, but there was no response except for the jagged breathing that filled the room.

'Thank you for the gift,' she whispered to him. 'I can feel it within me now.'

She turned to Tinker. 'Put aside the pettiness,' she said. 'For this is our beloved's crossing time. You've polluted this sacred moment, but we don't blame you, Tinker. Your soul is young and unevolved.' She put a hand to her ear as Bodhi released a string of foul words from the bathroom. 'You and Bodhi have much in common.'

Tinker looked at his beautiful friend. It was clear there wasn't much time left. He wanted to lie down by Sadiki's side, to let him know he was adored, that he would be missed. And he wanted to confess the terrible thing he'd done to cause Joe's death. But god, he was torn. Sophia was out there somewhere and he should be looking for her.

'You're confused about your priorities,' Acharya said softly. 'But you're mistaken, Tinker. You should know that by now. Sophia is perfectly safe.' She looked lovingly at Sadiki again and then back at Tinker.

'Boy-man,' she said. 'Even in the shadow of your betrayal, I choose to show beneficence.' She paused. 'Clearly, Zanni has fallen prey to your delusions again. I'll see to her and Bodhi now. For Sadiki's sake, you may say goodbye in private.'

As soon as Acharya left, a small moan came from the bed. Sadiki's eyes flew open. Tinker went to his friend's side. He kissed the place on his forehead where Acharya had. And despite not having planned it, he understood it was his own small claim.

'I have to tell you what happened that night,' he said softly.

Tinker doubted that Sadiki was hearing this, but the need to go on was there regardless. He lay down in the space next to him and continued. 'After our meeting at the park, when we thought you were going to be joining the army, Lani, Maya and I went to see Joe. We wanted to get him to fess up that you two were in a relationship. We wanted him to tell the others that the "advances" you made, the ones in the video, were part of that. Then we'd go on to prove that the other jocks' accusations were false and you were innocent.'

Did Sadiki's breathing hasten? Or was Tinker imagining it?

'When we arrived at Joe's, he opened the door to his converted garage with a remote. We plied him with the Hibiki whisky Lani took from her father's bar.' The next bit, even if Sadiki wasn't listening, was harder to say. 'Maya had some valium from her mum's bathroom cabinet. It went against the grain for her but, Sadiki, she was desperate to stop you being sent away too. She crushed three up and put them in Joe's drink.'

Despite the warmth of the room, Sadiki was shaking. His nod was almost imperceptible, but Tinker took it as a sign to keep going.

'None of it was working. Joe just got so messy, so out of it, that he fell asleep on the couch without admitting a thing.' He paused. 'Sadiki, on the way out, fuelled by frustration and resentment, not just for you but for myself, I took the remote. I figured he could experience at least a taste of what I had when I crawled out the window and twisted my ankle in front of the jocks. The next morning, we found out there'd been a fire. It was ruled accidental. The cause was a curtain set alight by a bar heater.'

Tinker hadn't felt the tears coming, but his cheeks were wet.

'There's a keyhole near the top of those kinds of garage doors. If you use the right key to unlock it, you have access to the emergency release cable. Pulling on the cord would have allowed him to open the door by hand, but I suppose he didn't have time for that. I never really got why he didn't jump out the window, though. It was big enough. Perhaps he was too drunk and out of it. But, Sadiki, if the remote was where it should have been ... I'm sorry. I'm so very sorry.'

The gurgling, rattling sound upped in tempo and volume, filling the room. If Sadiki had heard Tinker's confession, it had been too much for him to take.

Then Sadiki seemed to garner one last ounce of energy. 'Not you,' he said in a croaky voice. He opened his eyes just a little, lifted his hand and pointed backward to his pillow.

Ever so gently, Tinker moved the pillow aside.

And, on the wall behind it, some words were scrawled. For a moment Tinker couldn't make out what they were. But then it became clear.

S – Hidey-hole. M – Okra.

CHAPTER FORTY-NINE

Maya had cuts and scratches on her face and hands from crawling through the bushes, but she felt no pain. The anxiety of not knowing what they were about to find seemed to block out any physical sensation.

This was Sadiki's ramshackle church.

It seemed so … irreverent to live in one and not believe. As Luke pushed open the door, Maya made the sign of the cross.

The scene inside was bizarre. Acharya was sitting in an armchair with her signature fake smile and a girl at her feet. Within a few seconds, Tinker emerged from a room off the lounge.

'It's customary to knock,' Acharya said, 'but welcome, everyone.' She turned to Maya. 'You've come at an opportune time,' she said. 'Sadiki is on his way to another life.'

At that moment, Maya couldn't find the emotional bandwidth to care about that. 'Where's my daughter?' she demanded. She turned to her friend. 'Tinker, have you found her?'

'Oh, that,' Acharya said dismissively. 'I think you're over-reacting, Maya. Sophia is most likely tucked up in bed at your house as we speak. As I'm sure you're aware by now, she did come to see me. Oh, and she's a bright thing, thirsting for knowledge and eager to expand her mind. Which is, I'll suggest if you don't mind, an anomaly in your household.'

Maya did mind. She could have slapped that smile right off Acharya's face.

Acharya put her hand on the top of the girl's head. 'We put Sophia on the train back to Melbourne hours ago, didn't we, Bodhi?'

When the girl looked up and nodded, Maya could see her eyes were filled with an uncritical, almost banal, kind of belief in her leader. 'We didn't do anything to her except give her the benefit of our learnings,' she said. 'Sophia caught the six thirty-five train, and if you want proof—'

Maya did want proof. But when Acharya put a finger to Bodhi's mouth, she doubted she was going to get it. The girl was lying. Or she knew more than she was letting on, Maya was sure of it.

'Sophia's here,' Luke said into the ensuing silence.

'I think you're right,' Tinker said. He put his hands on his hips and stared Acharya down. 'Linda Crossley reckons you have a thing for doing renovations to churches,' he said. 'So, Acharya, could there possibly be a hidey-hole here?'

Acharya looked momentarily flustered but arranged her sick smile again quickly.

'Of course not,' she said. 'Tinker – you're really suffering, and I'm so sorry for that. Your friend is dying, you no longer belong at Soul Haven and—'

She turned around mid-sentence and Maya followed her eyeline. Luke had his eyes closed again. He walked up to the wall, pressed on a panel close to the floor and, just as sirens sounded from outside, a hidden door sprung open.

•

The space was small and plain. Just four walls, a simple bench seat and a single light bulb.

Maya clutched her heart, unable to move, while Luke went to his sister.

Sophia was crouched on the floor in the corner her hands tied behind her back. Her feet were bound, her mouth gagged. There were bruises up and down her arms and legs, and her cheeks were wet with tears.

'It's okay,' Luke cooed into her terrified face. 'Sophia, you're safe now.'

Ever so gently, he undid the bandage that covered her mouth and untied the rope around her hands and feet. Then he took off his coat and wrapped it around Sophia's shoulders.

She had to bob down in the doorway to get through. Her legs looked shaky and her face was pale. There were dark rings around her eyes.

A single sob echoed through the church. Then Sophia cleared her throat.

'I've been praying, Mum,' she said. A small smile crept across her face.

'This time, it worked.'

•

'Bernadette Robinson, you're under arrest for arson,' Detective Manolo said as he handcuffed her. 'And kidnapping,' he added. 'You must be aware that you do not have to say or do anything, but that if you do, it may be used in evidence against you.'

The police officer had to wrest Sophia away from Maya to get her wrapped in a silver thermal blanket.

'The paramedics will check her out properly, but she seems okay. She's understandably in shock. Sweetheart, who locked you in there?'

Tinker could see Sophia was running on pure adrenaline.

'She did,' Sophia said, pointing at Bodhi. 'Acharya told her to. But – you need to know this. The charges shouldn't be just kidnapping and arson.'

She paused and took a sip of the hot drink the police officer gave her.

'They murdered someone,' Sophia said. 'Someone called Marcus.'

•

Soul Haven was swarming with police. Marnie was crying, while Thomas fumed and cussed as they watched Acharya being cuffed. They paid no attention when the same happened to Bodhi. But Claudine and Butch raced up to her, making an attempt to intervene that was quickly thwarted.

Tinker watched in a daze, conflicting emotions coursing through him.

'Daddy, you need to help me,' Bodhi screamed as she was guided into a police van.

'I will,' he promised. 'We both will.' Then Butch ran in the opposite direction, towards Acharya and her two police escorts.

'We've got friends in prison,' he yelled. 'And I'm going to make sure you have a lot of fun in there.'

On the church porch, Tinker noted that Maya was still clinging to Sophia.

'Mum,' she said. 'I'm going to be okay. Dad and Luke can come in the ambulance with me.' The thermal blanket squeaked as Sophia hugged Maya back. 'You need to stay. You need to see Sadiki.'

Tinker held Maya's hand as the other Donnellys piled into an ambulance.

They would get to say their final goodbyes. But first, Tinker had to show Detective Manolo where – under Acharya's instructions three months before – he'd dug the big hole in Sadiki and Marcus's vegetable garden. For okra.

CHAPTER FIFTY

'There have been several developments,' Detective Manolo told Lani, Tinker and Maya as they sat at Lani's kitchen table almost a week after Sophia's rescue. 'As you know, we found Marcus Kean's body buried in the vegetable garden behind the church at Soul Haven. There was evidence of blunt force trauma to his head, consistent with the version of events Sophia supplied. Patty Dyson has been charged with murder in the first degree. My guess is that her lawyer will plead mental incompetence, but the police psychologist deems her fit for trial.'

'She was clearly unstable,' Lani said. 'But it was Bernadette Robinson who made her more so.' She squeezed Tinker's hand, aware of how this would make him feel.

'Detective Manolo, it's not all her fault. She would have followed Acharya to the ends of the earth,' Tinker said.

'Yes, it appears so,' Detective Manolo agreed. 'She's still making declarations of allegiance to Acharya. Her parents are trying to get her permission for reprogramming but she's resisting.'

'The course of Bodhi's life has changed forever because of Acharya,' Tinker said.

Lani wished he'd use their real names, but she was reluctant to say it aloud. The way she understood it, the course of *all* their lives had changed forever because of that woman. Valentina was doing so well that the doctors had suggested she might be able to come home earlier than the four months they'd originally thought she'd need in the NICU. But, until that time, Lani, Bridget, Bridget's mum, Dawn, Papa and Mama were tag-teaming to be by her side, along with the security guards her father had hired indefinitely. Even with Acharya in remand awaiting trial and relatively powerless, Lani knew that the curse would never entirely leave her consciousness.

Tinker and Zanni had moved into an apartment in St Kilda together, but their relationship seemed fraught because Zanni teetered between rejection of the cult they'd been part of and desire to seek out a similar experience. She still believed that Acharya was, in many ways, a chosen one who had ultimately taken a wrong turn and that there were others out there who would use their powers the right way.

Lani oscillated between thinking Zanni was lovely and hoping she and Tinker would break up.

'And Bernadette?' she asked.

Detective Manolo rubbed the stubble on his chin. 'Jonathan Green, her cousin, has filed a civil law suit against her for coercing his mother to bequeath the farm to her. He has also attempted to file a criminal law suit, calling the manner of his mother's death into question. But, since other members of her family aren't willing to exhume her body, that case will probably be tossed out. Bernadette Robinson will go on trial for aiding and abetting a murder, kidnapping, arson and a string of more minor offences. Her lawyer has applied to the Supreme Court for bail.'

'What other offences has she been accused of?' Lani prodded. She was desperate to get back to the hospital. Every minute away from Valentina was a minute too long.

'It seems that, in league with Thomas Bonier, an experienced accountant, the pair had acquired several properties,' Detective Manolo said. 'There's an investigation happening around the legality, since they were all purchased under a dummy company that's hard to trace back to Soul Haven Inc. In the meantime, until the results come through, all of the assets we suspect may have come from it have been seized.'

Lani turned to Tinker. 'Weren't you under the impression that Thomas sold his house to contribute to Soul Haven?' she asked.

Tinker nodded.

'That's definitely not the case,' Detective Manolo said. 'At one stage, Thomas Bonier did have a large estate, and a healthy amount of savings. He gambled it away months before he went to Soul Haven. There were four lawsuits filed against him and the ATO was after him for tax fraud. Our understanding is that he figured the association with Bernadette Robinson was his best chance of clawing back his wealth. But, Lani, one of their holdings is in Gino and Yvette's Street, just two doors down.'

'Oh fuck,' Lani said. 'So much for Acharya's declarations about wealth and privilege. But why would she choose a place near my parents? Is she still obsessed with Papa?'

'It appears so. We were able to attain a search warrant. The settlement was three weeks ago and, since then, they've been moving items into the house. They'd installed cameras at an angle that caught Gino's yard and parts of the living area at the back of their house. He paused. 'There were several felt dolls found in a cupboard in the living area that have been taken as evidence.'

Lani gulped. Surely, given she was in custody, there was nothing more Bernadette Robinson could do to her family. And yet ...

Detective Manolo stood. 'Maya, how's Sophia recovering?' he asked.

Maya shrugged. 'Connor and I worry about her,' she said. 'But she seems to be doing okay. As is Luke.' She paused. 'They're closer than ever now,' she said, looking at Lani.

Lani smiled at her friend. Strangely, the twins seemed to have blossomed since the ordeal. Luke's confidence had grown. He looked people in the eye when he spoke and his voice rarely wavered like it used to. Sophia had shown amazing resilience. She was back at school. From her own telling, she'd been embraced as a bit of a hero after so much reporting of what had happened. And, in typical Sophia fashion, she was lapping up the attention.

Lani still wished that Valentina would grow up to be like her goddaughter.

'There's one more thing,' Detective Manolo said. 'It's the reason I've brought you all together today.'

The three waited for him to continue.

'During the interrogation, Bernadette Robinson admitted to another crime.'

Detective Manolo swallowed. 'She says that, after you left on the night Joe Carruthers died, she went to the converted garage he lived in, behind his parents' house to confront him about owning up to his relationship with Stig Johannsen. As we established in our initial investigation, the cause of the fire was accidental. It appeared that Joe Carruthers had fallen asleep and his blanket touched the bar of a radiator. What we didn't know then was that he'd been trying to escape through the window.'

Detective Manolo sighed deeply before continuing. 'Bernadette Robinson claims she arrived at the scene intending to speak with Joe. She said that she spotted Hibiki bottles in among the debris and took it as a sign that you, Lani, and possibly Maya had been there.' He paused. 'Of course, that claim was a moot point since I'd removed them from evidence at Gino's request.'

Lani reached out for Maya's hand and squeezed.

'Bernadette Robinson stated that what she did was on impulse, but my view is that she wanted to lead us to believe you were implicated in Joe Carruthers' death. Besides, her account doesn't seem consistent with the facts,' Detective Manolo continued.

'What are the facts?' Tinker asked.

'There was a large metal trolley in the shed behind Joe's bungalow, filled with heavy tools. Apparently, she wheeled it in front of the window and put on the brakes. When Miss Robinson saw Joe Carruthers was already on fire inside, when she saw there was no hope for him, she put it back in the shed.' He paused. 'It wasn't damaged, which is why it was never considered in evidence.'

'So, it wasn't us,' Tinker said simply. 'All these years we thought ...'

'All these years,' Maya echoed.

'Bernadette Robinson won't be getting bail. She'll be going away for a very long time,' Detective Manolo said.

EPILOGUE

'When he was born, Carl and I called him our bundle of joy,' Stig's mum said from the pulpit. 'And it was true. Sometimes I wonder if we didn't show our love enough. We weren't demonstrative parents. It wasn't what we learned from our own. But we privately marvelled at our small miracle – time and time again.'

Pictures of Stig played across the screen behind her.

The cheeky toddler, blowing out birthday candles.

The five-year-old with an awkward bowl cut, attempting to ride a bike, his father giving him a push.

Then came the dancing shots. There he was, around ten, in a top hat, cane, bow tie and tap shoes, pointing proudly to a trophy on the mantelpiece behind him.

A little older, in a spangly blazer and tights.

In the next, he was wearing the lion costume he'd adored so much. In each image there was that gorgeous grin.

'Maybe a funeral isn't the time for airing regrets, but I have them,' Stig's mum continued, wiping a tear. 'I regret never acknowledging his sexuality, because it meant I was locked out of a big part of his life.' She paused and took a deep breath.

'I'm so sorry that, when Stig finally found love, it was ripped away from him. I wish I could have saved him from that.'

Her gulp sounded through the microphone.

'But one thing Stig managed for himself was to find true friendship,' she continued. 'I'm grateful for that. I'm grateful that Maya and Tinker were there for him at the end, and that Lani was there in spirit.'

The three friends sat together, all crying now.

The timing of the next photo was perfect. Lani, Maya and Tinker at fourteen, sitting on a park bench in their school uniforms. Stig lay across all three of their laps. Lani was making bunny ears over his head. Maya was rolling her eyes. And Tinker looked to be surreptitiously tying Stig's shoelaces together.

'When he was a teenager, before the terrible things started to happen, Stig informed me that friendship was his religion.' She stopped and smiled weakly. 'I told him not to tell his father that.'

There were giggles now, from all three of them. They seemed to ripple through the smallish congregation. Even the previously solemn priest cracked a smile.

Maya turned around to look at her daughter in the row behind. Sophia was sneaking a look at her phone. She suspected, from the look on her face, that it was a romantic message from Darcy Jeffries. Which was both worrying and satisfying. But Sophia had been so strong – both twins were – Maya could see that now. She'd let Sophia navigate her own way through love – with a little guidance.

'It's an open casket,' Stig's mum said. 'You're invited to ...'

It was clear she couldn't continue.

Maya got up and walked to the pulpit where she delivered the first prayer.

•

After the service, when everyone else had gone outside into the sunshine, Lani, Tinker and Maya stayed behind. The make-up was too heavy, but Stig looked serene. Like he was finally at peace.

Lani put her hand on his first, then Tinker, then Maya.

And the same sentence, the one coined by Tinker but owned by all of them, ran through each friend's mind.

We're not us without you.

ACKNOWLEDGEMENTS

This novel was something completely other when I started it two years ago. Gab Williams, to whom it's dedicated, suggested a writing partnership. We only managed one session before she was cruelly taken from all those who loved her. But she was an inspiration and remains so.

I shared early drafts with generous and talented writing friends. Hilary Rogers, Jacinta Halloran, Thalia Kalkipsakis, Melissa Thurgood and Wendy Phillips provided invaluable feedback. Meredith Badger was particularly instrumental in shaping this novel. I feel so lucky to whirl around your orbits.

Embarking on the editing process was daunting. But, despite feeling overwhelmed at times by my writing foibles and failures, I always felt I was in the best hands. So, I knuckled down. I'm taking credit for that.

So much praise and thanks and love (pun intended) go to Brigid Mullane, Dianne Blacklock, Adolfo Aranjuez, Alisa Ahmed and everyone else at Ultimo Press. What a crew! This book was a beautiful mess before your constructive feedback and eagle eyes. I still can't believe I get to work with people of your calibre.

To my mum and dad, Frank and Mavis Keighery, for passing on an obsession with books and reading. What a gift. It has sustained me in my darkest hours and continues to do so.

Lastly, and most importantly, thanks to my beautiful family. My husband, Marty, who continues to support me in every way, and our divine adult children, Jack, Billie and Hugo. I'm guessing (or may have been told) it's not easy to coexist with someone who lives in multiple worlds. But you do it beautifully.

BOOK CLUB QUESTIONS

1. Who was your favourite character and why?

2. Did that change throughout the novel?

3. If you were to fashion your own cult, what techniques would you employ?

4. What do you see as the similarities and differences between religions and cults?

5. What do you make of the connection between the twins, Sophia and Luke, as opposed to the magical element of Acharya's sphere?

6. Tinker is referred to as the 'sweet, malleable one'. Do you agree with that depiction?

7. If you were asked to cast the four main characters in a TV series, which actors would you choose?

8. Acharya uses workshops and sessions to help clients recover memories. What are your thoughts about 'false memory syndrome'?

9. Do you know people who have been part of a group you considered to be a cult?
   If they've retracted from it, have their perspectives changed?

10. Lani asserts that friendship is a kind of religion. Do you agree?

Christine Keighery (who also writes as Chrissie Perry) is the author of more than thirty-five novels for children and young adults. Christine wrote thirteen books in the hugely successful *Go Girl!* Series. Her YA title, *Whisper*, won a White Raven Award and an IBBY award and was shortlisted for the CBCA and the WA Premier's Awards. Her work has been published in ten countries, including the US, UK, Spain, Brazil, Slovenia and Korea. Her first novel for adults, *The Half Brother*, won the 2024 Davitt Award for Best Debut Crime Book. *We're Not Us Without You* is her second novel. Christine divides her time between coastal Fairhaven and Southbank, Victoria.